**Watch for the next Thorn & Thistle romance
from Jennie Davids,
coming Spring 2020**

To my mom. Thank you for always supporting me and
believing in this dream. Your unwavering optimism
might not be something I always share,
but I sure do appreciate it, and you.

NEW INK ON LIFE

JENNIE DAVIDS

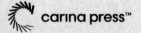

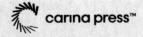

carina press™

ISBN-13: 978-1-335-21579-6

New Ink on Life

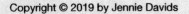

This is a work of fiction. Names, characters, places and incidents are either the product of the author's imagination or are used fictitiously, and any resemblance to actual persons, living or dead, business establishments, events or locales is entirely coincidental.

This edition published by arrangement with Harlequin Books S.A.

® and TM are trademarks of the publisher. Trademarks indicated with ® are registered in the United States Patent and Trademark Office, the Canadian Intellectual Property Office and in other countries.

www.CarinaPress.com

Printed in U.S.A.

NEW INK ON LIFE

Chapter One

MJ

One glance at the girl looking around with big eyes and I knew she'd want a butterfly or worse, a Chinese symbol she'd Googled.

I groaned, not bothering to lower the volume. I didn't give a shit if it wasn't polite. It wasn't polite to expect me to do inferior garbage like that.

Heading to the front of the shop, I stretched my arm behind my back until my shoulder cracked. The girl was studying the designs hung on the wall, all drawn by me and the other employees.

She turned and smiled at me. "Hi. I'm…"

Bending, I snatched a design folder and tossed it on the receptionist's counter. Not that I actually had one of those. Receptionists cost money, money I didn't have. "Here. See if there's anything you like."

While she looked, I propped my elbows on the counter. Close up I could see I'd been wrong. She was a woman not a girl. The pixie haircut and delicate features had tricked me from the distance. Might've got the age wrong, but I wasn't wrong on the type of tattoo.

This pale woman wore a sweater. An honest to god sweater with little pearl buttons.

Ugh. Why couldn't Maya be here? She didn't mind doing the newbies. Hell, she seemed to get a kick out of it. But nope it was just me. The rest of the staff wouldn't be here for another hour when the shop officially opened. Until then I was here trying to squeeze in some more work. Every dollar and minute counted and I didn't have enough of either.

"See anything you like?"

She set down the binder and went to the wall, tilting her head back. "Everything. I've been an admirer for a long time. Your shading technique is like no other."

I drew my gaze from the blue vein running up her neck to the picture of a lion I'd done. I had to give her some points on taste. That was one I showcased in my bio for magazine articles.

"Something like that is a special commission. It takes a while. Plus, something that big is gonna hurt."

Her lips twisted in a weird kind of smile. "I can handle pain." She turned away from the wall and faced me. "But that's not why I'm here."

"To get a custom piece?"

"To get a tattoo."

I pushed away from the counter. "As much fun as it's been chatting, I don't have time for this shit. I got things I could be doing for clients. You know, paying ones."

"No, please wait. I'm sorry. I'm not explaining this well. I'm here because of Zan."

I did an about face, the name of my mentor guaranteed to get my attention. "What about her?"

"I was her apprentice."

Holy shit. This woman who could barely make eye

contact, not only wielded a tattoo gun but had worked with Zan—a fucking trailblazer and one of the best artists ever.

She took my stunned silence as some kind of invitation, stepping closer. "She always talked about you with so much pride."

I jerked my chin at her to cover my flinch. "How long were you with her?"

"Four years."

Well shit. In that time I'd only talked to Zan a few times on the phone and maybe stopped into her shop here in Portland once. That's all I had for the woman who'd made me who I was.

"I'm Cassie Whiteaker by the way."

"MJ Flores." I took the hand she held out, not tempering my grip just because her wrist bones looked like they could bust through her skin. "So what do you want with me?"

"Oh. Um." Her gaze darted around the shop again before grazing me. "When Zan got sick and things started to look bad, I promised her I'd come to you to be my mentor."

"No." I took a giant step back.

Apprenticeships were a time suck. You shared all your skills and knowledge in return for some grunt work. As soon as they were done, they could go and open a shop next to you, take the clients that were yours, not theirs. No thank you. The field was crowded enough.

If I ever did decide to strap myself with an apprentice it wouldn't be this woman, Zan's apprentice or not. I could tell we wouldn't mesh well. She looked like she'd piss herself the first time I smashed something.

"Do you even have any tattoos?" burst from my

mouth. Yeah, I believe the words I was looking for were "Get out."

"I do." The woman—Cassie—reached up and unbuttoned the first button of her sweater and then moved on to the next one. There was nothing sexy about her movements and yet I stared at each inch of skin revealed. A light gray T-shirt was underneath, lines of a tattoo peeking out of the scoop collar.

For a short woman with generous hips, I would have expected her to have more on top. She pulled one arm free and it actually took me a few seconds to focus on the tattoo on her forearm, not the pale skin.

Stepping closer, I drew her arm to me. "Better a diamond with a flaw than a pebble without." The lettering was exceptional and there was a small diamond at the top corner of the words that looked so real it practically shined.

Cassie wiggled her other arm from the sweater, revealing a bird flying free from a cage. Not exactly groundbreaking, but the work was impeccable. Dark purple surrounded the cage, fading into black and grays. I reached out and traced the bird that was stark in comparison to the cage it had just sprung from.

"Nice," I conceded and let go of her arm.

Now that her sweater was off and I was this close, I got a good whiff of something sweet. Not like a bouquet of flowers sweet. This was like cinnamon and sugar. It reminded me of the buñuelos my mom used to make.

Not saying anything, she pulled her shirt to the side, exposing a small phoenix on her neck. I bent to get a closer look and inhaled deeply, that sweet fragrance even stronger, like the heat of her body had warmed it and given it additional spice. The lines and color of another tattoo farther down snagged my interest. I went to move her shirt to the side, but she stepped back and righted her clothing.

"As you can see I have tattoos."

Well, I'd seen some of them and what I'd seen had been good. That didn't mean jack shit when it came to actually tattooing. Except Zan, damn it. That meant a hell of a lot. "So you've got your license?"

"Yes." She bent down. When she stood up again she held out a folder.

I grabbed it but didn't open it. Fact remained I didn't want or need an apprentice.

As I continued to stare at her, she wrapped her arms around her stomach, shifting her weight from foot to foot. "This is a really nice shop."

For fuck's sake. If she started on the weather, I really would kick her ass out.

"So you're giving tattoos?"

She shook her head, blond wisps of hair falling over her forehead. "Not to customers. I've given them to other employees at the shop and Zan."

And there went the hope she might not be any good at tattoos. Even though Zan had been a damn pioneer, her skin hadn't been covered. Every single tattoo had a meaning behind it. The day I'd been allowed to add to her collection was one of my proudest. Pressing that needle against Zan's skin had made everything shake all the way to my toes.

"I've never been so honored in my life," Cassie said in a hushed tone expected in church.

I got it. I'd never had so much trust placed in me and I'd wanted to live up to it. Still did today. "Yeah, never had such a fucking rush."

We shared a smile that I quickly flattened on my end. Still didn't need an apprentice.

"Was yours the cat o' nine tails?" she asked.

"Yup."

Her smile widened, showing off straight white teeth that only came from braces. Mine were fairly straight, only my bottom front ones crooked. With four kids to feed that was close enough for my parents.

"I thought that looked like your work."

"Good eye." I pushed her book back toward her. "Still not interested in an apprentice. I've got new hires and the shop to run."

Her face sobered. "Yes. I've heard about your... changes. I think that was one of the reasons Zan made me promise to come to you."

Nice to know my "changes" were making the rounds. Some called them changes. I went with straight up betrayal.

"I could help, take some of the burden off your shoulders. Ordering, front desk help, cleaning."

Usually I had wannabes coming in the door who thought because they were good at art and had watched some show on TV they could become a tattooer. Pissed me the fuck up. Now I had someone begging to be a receptionist or an assistant, not a tattooer. That was either the stupidest pitch or brilliant. It was all the shit I hated doing. Same with my other employees who never failed to bitch when I had them do it.

"I need to finish my apprenticeship and Zan insisted it be you."

Zan. My one fucking weakness.

This woman obviously knew it and was playing it hard.

"Damn it." I flipped open the folder.

Whoa. I whistled at the cherry blossom, its limbs shriveled and the pink petals scattered at the base. A melting stopwatch filled the next page, its numbers sliding from the face. What was supposed to have been a courtesy glance to honor Zan became me poring over every page. How had stuff this dark come out of someone looking so sweet? I spent even longer on the pictures of actual tattoos on skin. I studied the line work, shading and placement.

I glanced up at Cassie who was twisting her hands in front of her. "You're good. Good enough to be on your own."

I flipped to the last page. My stomach jackknifed. I recognized that skin. That wrinkled, rough skin had guarded one of the softest hearts there was. The skin also sported a lighthouse that hadn't been there the last time I'd seen her.

"Well?" I demanded. "Why aren't you?"

"I'm not ready yet. I won't be ready to be a full-time tattooer until May."

Uh, did this little pixie really not know the way things worked? Zan couldn't have been that lax. Apprenticeships didn't have a particular end date. When your mentor thought you were ready, you were ready. Judging from her portfolio, she was ready.

So why the hell wasn't she tattooing? Maybe she choked when it was time to work on clients or freaked them out with her nervousness. There was no way in hell I'd get ink from someone if their smile had the desperate edge hers did. But it wouldn't take long to teach her to get it together. Not four months.

In total Zan had spent five years with me. She'd had a shit load of stuff to work on. The tattooing I'd gotten

down. It was the keeping my lips zipped and not starting shit that had taken so long. But Zan had kept with
it. She'd stuck by me.

Now this Cassie didn't have that. She'd been tossed
out on her own without the best fucking mentor on the
planet. I'd been there, left without the person I revered.
My dad hadn't died, but to him I might as well have.

Shit. I brought my hand up and caught myself before
I put my fingers in my hair. I was using a new gel for
my pompadour. I was going to test every minute of the
fourteen-hour hold it claimed.

"Ten tomorrow. Be here." I pointed my finger at her.
"Not a second late or it's a no. Got it?"

"I'll be here." She'd almost made it to the door before she came back and grabbed her portfolio, cheeks
bright pink. "You won't regret this."

Cassie

"You're proud of this?"

I dropped my gaze from MJ's brown eyes drilling
into me to my drawing. I'd thought it was good, one of
my best. But if she had to ask, it must mean it wasn't.

"Well?"

And now she was impatient with me. The churning in my gut intensified. In the three days I'd been
at Thorn & Thistle she'd had two moods with me—
impatient and angry. The worst, by far, were the times
I'd caught her looking at me with her lip curled.

"This is the best you can do?" She shook my sketch
in front of my face.

What could I have done to make her like it? Was it

the colors? The line work? If I admitted that yes, that was my best, how much angrier would she get?

"I... I... I don't think you should do newspaper ads anymore."

Her expression questioned my sanity. "What?"

Yes—what? Had I thought blurting out my opinion would impress her? Not working. Definitely not working. A drop of sweat trailed down my back to gather with the others. Nothing I did impressed her. Not cleaning the bathrooms. Not reorganizing the front desk.

I needed something. Anything. With each hour I could practically see her regret growing for taking me on.

I licked my lips and tried to find my voice, which now, when I wanted it, had gone hiding. "I overheard you talk about revenue and I don't think you should do another newspaper ad. It isn't helping."

Slowly, so very slowly, she lowered my sketch. Her eyes never left me, not even a split-second reprieve from her severe stare. "Are you listening in to my conversations now?"

Oh god. What had I done? I was not going to admit that yes, I listened every opportunity I got. It was all part of my quest to win her over. Something she said might give me insight on how to do that.

There were few benefits to being quiet, but one was how often people forgot I even existed and talked around me.

"I want to help," I said, hoping we could gloss over the fact that I'd been eavesdropping, since it was to her benefit. Beneficial eavesdropping, I'd make it a thing. "I've asked each new client what's brought them in and only one person told me the ad. Three days, one person.

The ad was three hundred dollars, but the person's tattoo was only one hundred and twenty. You lost money."

MJ folded her arms over her chest. "Are you a tattooer or a secretary?"

"I don't believe in labels. I'm a lot of things."

Her eyes widened and then her lips started to curve upward.

I'd done it. I'd gotten her to smile. What a smile it was. She didn't go all out. But the curving of what I now realized where surprisingly full lips was enough to soften the edges, to draw my eye to the lines at the side of her mouth instead of the deep grooves in her forehead when she frowned at me.

"Is that right?" She shook her head, her smile disappearing as fast as it'd come. "Three hundred fucking dollars."

Relief pushed out the tension. If she liked that one, I had plenty more. I reached for the little notebook I always kept with me. Before it could even clear my pocket, MJ was lifting my sketch and waving it in my face.

"We were talking about this piece of shit. You were telling me if this was…"

"Hey, I need to talk to you," Jamie, the most senior artist, said, coming to stand by me.

She was already my favorite because she showed me the least hostility. With her perfect timing now, she cemented she'd be getting the best berries from the fruit tray I brought tomorrow.

"What?" MJ snapped.

"We got four more reviews this week."

I took a step back even though MJ's murderous expression wasn't directed at me. If it had I was pretty sure I'd need a defibrillator.

MJ snatched Jamie's phone.

"Don't break it."

"It's not your phone I want to break." MJ glared at the screen. "'Got a tattoo there that looks like my kindergartner's drawing. No wait, he's better.'"

As MJ continued to scroll down and read, I got out my phone and tried to find the site MJ was reading from.

Shop has really gone downhill.

Heard under new management. They suck.

Think all the good artists are gone.

I was so uncomfortable in there I left.

Wow. The one stars had exploded since the last time I'd checked. Once Zan told me that she thought MJ should be my mentor, I'd researched the shop. The truth was that I'd been keeping tabs on MJ's career before that. I'd always been in awe of her talent, while at the same time, it was women like her who had kept me from tattooing. I saw how tough and commanding they were and knew I didn't belong in that club. Until Zan showed me different. From Zan I'd learned that tattoo artists could be anyone. There was room for everyone.

I clicked on the reviews for the two newest team members. They had less experience and their work showed it. But most of the bad reviews, if they listed a specific artist, focused on MJ, Jamie and Vivian, the other senior team member. It made no sense. Their work was unparalleled.

None of these reviewers had left a picture of the tattoos that were supposedly so bad. Nor did any of them have a picture or any identifying information. In fact, for most of them the review of the shop was their only one.

"You guys are being targeted."

Jamie nodded at me before looking back at MJ. "Yeah, we are."

It didn't take a genius to know who was doing the targeting. Months ago MJ's business partner, Heidi, had left the shop, taking half the staff with her. Rumors were there'd been no notice and it'd been far from amicable.

"Fuck them." MJ glared at the screen and then carefully handed Jamie's phone back like she didn't trust herself not to throw it after all. She blew out a breath and tilted her neck from one side to the other until it cracked. "Ugh. Anything else?"

Wait. Else? They needed to focus on this.

I clasped my hands together and swallowed, trying to lubricate my mouth as much as possible. "Ha...have you reported it?"

MJ's head twisted in my direction. Her eyes narrowed in warning. Warning that I was trying her patience? That it was none of my business? That she hadn't given me permission to speak? That look could be used for so many things.

All of them made me want to throw my hands up and promise to never speak again.

"Yeah, and I got nowhere." She spit the words out like they were acid burning her from the inside. "Forget it, they'll give up eventually."

"Except they haven't," Jamie said.

MJ's snap trap focus, eager for a misstep, shifted to Jamie and I took some deep breaths.

"What the fuck do you want me to do? Go on the site and comment, whining how they're not real customers. You ever read when other businesses do that? They look pathetic and desperate. Once people come and see for themselves, they know how good we are."

Jamie's body remained relaxed in spite of the rapid-fire words coming her way. "If people read these then they're not going to give us a chance to prove how awesome we are."

"Then we need to find another way to get people in here," MJ said.

She didn't seem to understand how influential review sites were. Action needed to be taken. Plans needed to be made. Preferably with bullet points.

"Maybe you could sue them to make them stop," I said.

MJ angled herself so she faced me directly and I automatically took a step back. Her shoulders weren't actually much wider than mine, but she seemed so much larger. Her attitude, her dark hair, dark eyes, and the black pants and steel-toed boots she favored all added to that impression. Pretty much everything about her made her seem big and scary.

"Yeah, I'll get right on that. Got my lawyer on speed dial. Think he'll take payment in ink?"

I squeezed my hand tighter around my notebook, the pages curling. "There's some lawyers that take on cases and only expect payment if they win."

"My cousin used one of those," Kayla, the artist two stations over, broke in. "He's still in jail."

MJ nodded as if to say point was made.

No. It wasn't made. They had to do something. "You…"

"Enough." She crumpled my design in her hand. "This is what you need to be worrying about." She held

the ball of paper up to my face. "Don't give me something unless you know it's your best."

She walked past me, her shoulder barely clearing
mine.

I stared at my drawing still clutched in her fist. I
wanted to ask for it back so I could refer to it, which was
probably why she'd kept it. There was nothing about that
she liked. Behind me someone snickered. Stress sweat
drying on my skin, I could feel the stares. After pretending I was invisible for days, these people were all
too happy to witness me being put in my place. Kayla,
the newest artist, enjoyed it the most I was sure. She'd
taken one look at me and treated me like a threat. I
couldn't figure out why she'd be threatened by anything
about me. She was outgoing, gorgeous and accepted by
the other artists.

MJ made it seem so easy. To be strong. To speak
up. Well, I'd spoken up and now all I wished is that
I hadn't. Instead of making headway, I'd taken a step
back. I didn't know how many more of those I could
take before I was out the door.

God, I missed Zan. I missed knowing what was expected of me. Most of all I missed being liked.

Chapter Two

MJ

"Be right there," I yelled out as the door to the shop opened.

My client, who'd needed an early appointment and made me drag my ass out of bed at eight, lifted her hand in acknowledgement and took a seat.

Cassie'd already been here when I arrived. Like a good little apprentice, she had a cup of coffee for me and something that smelled disgustingly like tea for herself.

I went back to reviewing Cassie's latest sketch. It should've been so easy.

I picked it up and held it in front of her until her pretty eyes crossed. "Did you forget the part I said about happy?"

"Teddy bears are happy."

"Uh, yeah, usually. He's got stitching from where his arm's been put back on."

No response, not that I expected one. My new apprentice didn't do much talking. Not something I'd normally be complaining about. I hated chitchat. But even more than chitchat I hated fakeness. You couldn't trust fake people. They could be gearing up to betray you while complimenting you to your face. It was a wonder my new apprentice didn't overdose on all of her fake. If I asked her a question, I wouldn't get the truth. It'd be all about what she thought I wanted to hear.

For shit's sake she'd not only smiled when Kayla told her that not everyone could pull off a pixie and it was brave of her to do it anyway, she also thanked her. There was no way Cassie had missed the bitchy comment for what it was. She'd fingered her hair the rest of the day. Instead of thanking her and fake smiling, she should've told her she was sorry Kayla had to hide behind her hair.

I smacked the page down on the desk. "After we're done with this one, you're doing a unicorn with a goddamn rainbow. Even you can't make a depressed rainbow."

With a quick nod, she scurried out to the lobby. Funny, I didn't remember saying we were done. I followed after her, catching up in time to watch the show. Five feet from the desk she became all smiles and perky voice as she greeted my client.

The woman looked to be in her mid-thirties and dressed like she'd just finished running errands in a pink polo shirt, jeans and sneakers. At least she wanted something custom. That perked me up more than the caffeine.

"Hi. You must be Lauren. I'm MJ."

"Thank you so much for doing this all in one day for me," she said, shaking my hand. "I know it's your day off. I really appreciate this."

She seemed to think I was doing it out of the kindness of my heart or some crap. It was all about the green. She had it and I wanted it, so here my tired ass was. "No problem." I inclined my head toward Cassie. "This is my apprentice, Ca…"

"Cassie. Yes, I know." Lauren turned and held out her hand. "You're actually the reason I'm here."

"Me?" Eyes wide, Cassie took a step back.

"Yes. Candace told me about you in group. As soon as I heard, I knew you were the one to do my tattoo. When I called to make my appointment, they explained you worked under MJ."

Group? Whatever this group was, it made my apprentice look even more panicked.

"Oh. I don't tattoo clients yet. I'm licensed but I'm only in the designing stage of my apprenticeship right now. I'm sorry…"

I put my hand on the small of Cassie's back. Jesus, was that dampness? "All right, breathe before you pass out."

Once I was assured Cassie was at least doing that, I looked to the client. "As you can see she's not ready for the big leagues. If you want to hold off, it won't be long before she'll be able to ink. Or I can do it."

"No, I know. I don't want to wait. Not now that I've decided to get one." She turned to Cassie. "But you'll be here and can help me?"

"Of course." Cassie stepped forward and patted the woman's arm. "I'll help any way I can."

And she was back. Jesus, as if one apprentice wasn't bad enough, it was like I had two of them.

I looked between Cassie and Lauren. "So are we doing this?"

Lauren nodded. "We're doing this."

I motioned for her to follow me. "All right. Time

to talk about what you want. Hopefully you brought some pictures."

"I did." Her pace slowed. "But I don't want it exactly like the pictures."

"That's good," Cassie said. "They're just a way for us to get an idea of what you're thinking and then we can go from there to personalize it to what you want."

I rubbed my hands together. "Okay, show us what you got." Please, let it be something good. Please let it be…

"I want a sun and a moon, separate but connecting in the middle." Lauren reached into her purse and pulled out some printouts, obviously from a Google search, as well as a torn-out page from a magazine. "Shh, don't tell my doctor, but his magazine had one of the best."

"Hey, no judgement here." I spread the pages out, making room for Cassie to come stand next to me in the tight space.

"The thing is," Lauren said on my other side, "in all of these the moon is peaceful and sweet. I don't want happy. I want fierce. Protective."

I slowly turned to look at Cassie and found her doing the same. Our eyes held. Her lips turned up in the barest of smiles and mine twitched, wanting to join in on the action.

"That's not going to be a problem," Cassie said.

"You've come to the right place. Happy is not our thing."

I rearranged Lauren's examples so the magazine picture alternated with the printouts. "You point out what you do like."

For the next twenty minutes, we brainstormed ideas and then moved on to placement and size. This was going to be a breast tattoo, which got me even more excited. It'd been a while since I'd done one and anything that broke the routine was welcome.

"Okay, I think we've got what we need here." I shot Cassie a questioning look and received a nod. "So if you'll give us an hour I'll draw up a sketch. Cassie will too, and you can see if they're what you're wanting."

"Great."

My oh-so-helpful apprentice added, "If you're hungry there is a deli two stores down that is pretty decent and also a coffee shop on the next block. Most of the other shops in the neighborhood will be closed this early. Or you're welcome to stay here."

"It's okay if I watch you? I'm fascinated by this whole process."

Cassie stiffened. She hated having someone watch while she sketched. Which was why I did it as much as possible.

"Sure," she said, giving a big fake-ass smile.

Lauren didn't seem to notice, smiling right back.

We headed toward the drafting table, Cassie's feet dragging. It wasn't just being watched that she hated. "All right, time to see who's got the goods."

"It's you," she said, setting up her supplies.

No shit, but she should at least want to try to make a better sketch than me. Competition was good…

Cassie's sweater and shirt had ridden up. Like me, she drew standing up, hunched over the raised table. On the other side of the color spectrum of me, she had pale, almost translucent skin. Yesterday I'd spotted a red mark at her back, like her skin was so sensitive it'd been bothered by a tag.

My gaze dropped to her ass. She might look like a

grandmother with the sweaters, but the jeans she wore cupped the high and tight curve of her ass.

"Everything okay?"

I jerked at her voice. "Yeah. Giving you a head start."

There was the slightest lift to her eyebrow before it smoothed out and she bent back to her work.

That was enough of that. No more looking at her. No more searching her eyebrows for signs of a backbone. I went to work and got it done. Cassie finished a few minutes later. Already she was getting faster, spending less time second-guessing herself and erasing things.

"You guys are amazing. I can't believe how quickly you were able to do that," Lauren said, smiling.

"Tell us what you think." I laid my sketch on top of the supply cabinet and motioned for Cassie to do the same. "Which one do you like?"

Lauren turned to Cassie, her face twisting. "I'm sorry, I think I like hers better."

Cassie's laughter echoed in the shop. It was real and rich and what a laugh should sound like, not that high thing she usually used with the clients.

"It's okay," Cassie said. "That's why MJ's one of the best. I don't blame you. It's amazing and it's going to look perfect."

"Both are amazing." Lauren picked up the two sketches. "I really like what you did with the sun's rays the way they curve, but her moon is exactly what I was thinking. Oh, I wish I could mesh them."

I stepped closer, staring down at the sketches. "It's your tattoo." I grabbed the pages from her and put them together until the different parts overlapped. "I think we could do this."

While Lauren made a high, excited sound, Cassie's head snapped up and she stared at me with wide eyes.

"What, you don't want yours with mine?"

Her eyes got even wider, a mix of green and brown that'd be hard to replicate with ink. "No, I do. I just didn't think you'd be okay with it."

Yeah, me either. I didn't collaborate, and I sure as hell never thought if I did it'd be with a mousy apprentice, but as I stared at our overlapping designs, excitement amped me up.

"Well, I am." I motioned her closer and started to redraw my part. My pencil floated across the paper in a way it hadn't in a long time.

I handed over my pencil to Cassie. I stared down at the paper and then to the back of her neck and the short blond hairs growing there. They weren't even noticeable unless you were close like this. Little strands that looked so soft.

"Excuse me," she said, trying to angle her arm, but unable to with me crowding so close.

Right. I stepped back and watched with Lauren as Cassie worked on our shared tattoo. It was turning out dope.

Cassie thought so too, going by her slow, real smile. I knew it was real because it wasn't as big as her one for the customers and it lingered, not like the others that she could drop immediately.

"Yes," Lauren said. "That's exactly what I want."

In a short time we were ready.

"All right." I said, holding up the freshly created stencil. "You can put your shirt and bra over there and then climb on up."

Lauren's face paled and her eyes widened as if now

that the time had come, she was realizing what she was getting into.

Damn it. That's the thing about virgins. They're all happy and great until it came time to assume the position.

"You scared of needles?" I asked, trying to leash my impatience. Tattoos hurt, people. Get over it.

To my surprise, Lauren snorted. "No. Not anymore." She eyed Cassie. "Um, would it be okay if she helped me get ready and then you came back in?"

I hesitated. Which was stupid. I had an apprentice. She could do the handholding crap. "Yeah, sure."

Up front, I stood by the windows that looked out on the street. Cassie was right. This time of the morning it was dead. A hard thing to achieve in Portland. In the reflection, I watched Lauren put her hands on the hem of her shirt. She paused, our gazes meeting in the glass.

Cassie's reflection joined Lauren's. "Don't worry. We've got privacy curtains." The fabric rustled as Cassie pulled them closed.

I plopped my ass down on the bench to wait.

Was Lauren hesitant to take her shirt off in front of me because I was a big lesbo? Not like it was a secret. I was damn proud to be the owner of a queer shop. The rainbow flag hanging outside proclaimed as much.

Then again, she hadn't come to this shop for me. It'd been for Cassie. Cassie who I wasn't sure was gay. Unlike mine, Zan's shop hadn't been strictly queer. Zan herself had been, but she could have chosen to mentor a straight artist.

Even with all Thorn & Thistle's artists being queer, my shop's clientele wasn't always. Yeah, the vast majority were women. A lot of women just really appreciated and felt more comfortable having a female artist. But we didn't refuse men. They were welcome.

"Those are beautiful."

My head snapped up, my phone forgotten in my hand. That might've answered the question of Cassie's sexuality right there. She was viewing another woman's chest and complimenting it.

"Yeah, he did nice work. I'm really pleased how they turned out."

I tried to picture Lauren in my mind. Her rack hadn't really made an impression on me so the work must have been subtle. She didn't need to be shy about them with me. Yeah, I liked tits, loved 'em in fact, but not here. Skin was skin. I was focused on getting my lines right and making a wicked piece when I was working, not getting worked up by some nakedness.

"They truly are some of the best I've seen."

Damn how many had Cassie seen? I stood and frowned at the chuckles coming from behind the curtain.

"I'm really glad you're here," Lauren said. My tattoo chair creaked as she obviously climbed on it.

"So am I. I'm really glad I can be a part of this with you," Cassie responded with a hell of a lot of warmth in her voice. Even without being able to see, I knew she was smiling.

"You guys ready in there?" I walked up to the curtain, stopping myself from yanking it aside.

There was a long pause and then Cassie's head peeked out from between the gray fabric. "Ready."

I walked in, my attention immediately going to my client.

So that was the type of breast that drew Cassie. Per-

fect, round, bouncy breasts. The exact opposite of my
barely-there A's.

And my breasts had nipples.

I paused as I lowered myself to my stool. My gaze
fixated to the pale flesh where a nipple should have
been.

Both women tensed and Cassie took a step closer
to Lauren, putting herself between me and my client.
I shook myself and finished sitting down, rolling my
seat closer. These kinds of things didn't bother me. I'd
done plenty of tattoos over scars and done a couple of
realistic nipples before. That's not what had thrown me.

No, it was Lauren seeking out Cassie. The connection they obviously had. The way Cassie's shirts always
billowed around her and she always wore a sweater
even when I cranked up the heat, like she was hiding
something.

It was the fact that Zan had died from breast cancer.

Chapter Three

Cassie

MJ was staring at me again. I ignored her and blotted the extra ink off Lauren's skin. All the while MJ transformed Lauren's breast.

Discreetly as I could, I took a tissue and dotted at Lauren's eyes and received a watery smile in return. I understood. These tears weren't from pain. They were from Lauren taking a piece of herself back.

If MJ noticed that things were getting emotional, she didn't acknowledge it. She continued working, her face set in fierce lines of concentration. For as impatient and no-nonsense as MJ was, it was remarkable what a light touch she had as an artist. It was beautiful the way the needle went through the skin and deposited the ink.

Unlike Zan, she didn't keep up a constant stream of conversation with her clients. MJ didn't waste time making someone like her or feel comfortable. All of her attention went to doing an amazing tattoo.

Well, all of her attention, except when she was cleaning out her needles. Then MJ's gaze was directed at my chest. Seeing as she'd never had any interest in it before, she didn't need to be looking now.

I turned my upper body away.

Of course she didn't lower her lashes or flush in embarrassment at being caught. No, she continued to stare, so much speculation in those dark eyes.

"How you hanging in there?" I asked, leaning over Lauren so she could see me.

"Good. It's not that bad."

"Can I get you anything?"

Sometimes their clients needed a break—a chance to stretch or get something to drink. Not everyone could go straight through and we'd already been at it for four hours, not including the time it took us to design.

"No, I'm good."

I looked MJ's way and there wasn't even a dark look for suggesting they take a break. A dull ache radiated in my chest, not unlike when I first came to after my mastectomy surgery.

From this point on, I'd be treated differently. I was more than the abnormal cells that had invaded my body, yet once people heard about them, that was what I consisted of. This had to be the one time MJ was like everyone else.

Through the rest of the tattoo and the aftercare instructions, my stomach clenched tighter and tighter, the faint tremor in my hands spreading. At the door, I accepted a hug from Lauren.

"I'll be back when you're doing it on your own."

"Thank you." I smiled and then locked the door behind her. Usually once I flipped that deadbolt, it was a signal to my brain that I was done and a wave of relief would lower my shoulders. Not so today.

I took a deep breath and turned back toward MJ's station.

She was waiting for me. "So that's why Zan took you on."

Smile. Nod in agreement. That's all I had to do. I did it all the time whether I really believed it. My lips refused to rise. "I like to think it's because she saw potential in me."

MJ popped up the trashcan lid and tossed her gloves in. "No doubt, but I knew there was more. Plenty of people have potential and she didn't mentor them. That was the connection."

Right. Because as MJ made it so abundantly clear my skills weren't reason enough. Only a deadly disease could be responsible for linking Zan and me.

"So?" MJ prompted.

All my life there'd been a censor that analyzed every word before I spoke, making sure nothing I said would give a person reason to dislike me, or could be misconstrued or used against me. In the face of MJ's smug expression, the censor failed. "So we connected over art, over our love of Chinese food—except the egg dishes— and yes, having breast cancer."

"Did you have the same kind as her?"

"No. She had invasive ductal. I have triple negative."

MJ froze, still feet from where I remained in the lobby area. "Have?"

I shrugged. "I did chemo and radiation as well as had a mastectomy and hysterectomy. My last scans came back negative, but it won't be until May that I hit the five-year mark and can call myself cancer free."

"May," she repeated. "Is that why you won't start tattooing until then?"

"Yes." My muscles twitched. I walked forward, intending to clean up and release some of this pent-up energy. "Then I'll know it's behind me and I can officially start my new life."

MJ's hand curled around my bicep, pulling me to a stop. "After that you're free?"

The warmth of MJ's hand penetrated my sweater. Why did she have to touch me now? For eight days I'd been waiting, hoping for a reassuring pat on my arm, back, or heck I would've taken my head. And she did it now. I didn't want a pity touch.

"Then I have a much better outlook. Triple negative is a really aggressive cancer, but I took really aggressive steps that hopefully rid me of it. Still there's always the risk. Once you have it, you're more likely to have it or another cancer."

Her grip tightened. "Like it did for Zan."

"Yes."

"If it does, you'll fight it."

It was a command. "I will."

Crazy as it sounded, in some ways my life was easier when I was fighting. All I could focus on was survival. There was no desperation to get people's approval, no worrying about what people thought of me, no wondering what more I could do.

"So I have four months to make you a badass tattoo artist."

I nodded, apprehension building at how she was going to go about making me "badass."

"I have the perfect spot when you're ready."

I had no idea what she was talking about until she lifted her tank top, exposing the warm brown skin of her hip. I stared at the jut of her hipbone over the waistband of her pants. My fingers twitched. That was one of my favorite parts on a woman's body.

Okay, this was my boss and a woman I wasn't at all certain I even liked, but I couldn't be anything other than grateful for that tug of awareness.

A few months ago, it'd been such a relief when I'd been in the grocery store and felt attracted to a woman in the checkout line. All the drugs and procedures had killed my interest in pursuing anything sexual. But it was starting to come back. I'd even begun to masturbate again. There was so much triumph in having wetness coat my fingers and being able to climax.

I could add the pleasure I received from looking at MJ's skin to signs my body was coming back online.

"This one was from Zan." MJ pulled her shirt up even further, exposing most of her ribcage, stopping at the thick black edge of a sports bra. A female samurai in a fighter stance covered her side.

"You've got to come closer to see all of it." She crooked her finger.

I stepped closer, trying not to breathe too deep. MJ's woodsy scent lingered in my nostrils long after I left the shop each night, and this close it was sure to torment me even longer. Except now every time I smelled it, would it bring memories of her bare skin, not her curt words? I didn't know which was worse.

Below the samurai, wrapping over her stomach, was a depiction of the shop logo. My hand reached out, but I pulled myself up in time.

"Go ahead," MJ said, nodding.

I trailed my fingers over the exquisite rendition of roses wrapped with thistle, their thorns entwined. Goosebumps rose under my touch on MJ's skin. How I wanted to curl my fingers around her hip, draw her closer to me and…and what? She was still the woman who, two nights before, had said in front of everyone that when I talk she hears squeaks.

Sufficiently cooled, I lifted my hand and focused on the tattoo. "This isn't Zan's work."

"No." She looked down as if her gaze was a laser and she could etch it out of her skin. "Heidi. My ex-business partner did this."

From one of the thorns, a drop of blood hung suspended. Someone who had caused MJ so much pain shouldn't be able to produce such a beautiful piece.

From snatches of gossip I'd overheard from Maya, a newer artist, I didn't think MJ and Heidi had been strictly business partners. Which had to make the betrayal all the more painful.

"Suddenly, I don't like it as much," I said.

MJ's lips twisted. She let go of her shirt and it slid down, covering all that distracting skin. I should be happier about that. "Yeah, me either."

"Are you going to have it removed?"

"Nope. It stays." MJ notched her chin up. "It's a reminder I want to see every day."

How different we were. I'd never want to look at it again.

"Your turn." MJ grabbed my arm and tugged at the sleeve of my sweater.

By the time I sucked in a gasp she was already working on the other arm. Then she was tossing my sweater on the desk.

I crossed my arms over my stomach, not so much from the chill air, but to protect against how exposed I felt.

MJ wrapped her long fingers around my wrist and slowly lifted my arm away. Her dark eyes didn't exactly ask for permission, but the slowness with which she did it gave the impression that she'd stop if I asked.

My mouth remained closed.

Her fingers traced the quote on my forearm. It was as if her fingertip had a straight connection to deep inside me, spreading warmth.

"Did you have any tattoos before or did they all come after?"

My body snapped taunt. "After," I bit out, twisting my arm free.

After.

I hated that word. That was my life now. Before cancer and after cancer.

MJ moved her inspection to my other arm, focusing on the bird flying free. The fingers that I watched for hours each day, studied each day, were now touching me.

Putting a finger under my chin, MJ tilted my head to the side. She trailed her finger down and stopped at the puckered skin of my port scar.

I stiffened, ready to pull away. MJ's hand was there, stroking, soothing me until the fight left me, and I had to lock my knees to keep from swaying into her.

"This one," MJ said, tapping my forearm. "This is the first one Zan did."

"Yes. I saw it on a poster at my doctor's office." I tilted my head so I could see it. I smiled even as that wisp of sadness hit me with the thought of my first mentor. "I was admiring a tattoo another patient had and she told me about Zan. How Zan had also been a cancer patient and I knew that I had to have her do a tattoo. I could tell Zan wasn't that impressed with my choice of design, but she did it."

MJ's fingers flattened against my skin. "This is safe. Someone else's words, not yours." Her gaze roamed over me, as potent as her touch.

Reminded that I stood in front of her in my plain

camisole, which was meant to be hidden under my sweaters, I fought not to squirm.

"This one. This one was next." She moved to my bicep. "I can see more of you, more of her. She liked this one better."

I nodded, an all over shiver claiming my body. Did she even know her finger was swiping back and forth against my skin? The callus on the side of her middle finger drew my blood up closer to the surface.

"Then this one." MJ's breath skated across my neck. "This one you gave her more freedom. Let her do some designing, but she kept it true to you."

"Yes," I said, my voice barely audible. "I didn't bring a picture for that one."

MJ circled my port scar, her touch sure, not more careful there than the other places she'd touched me. "This one was a challenge for her. You can see it, feel it."

"We designed it together."

She framed it between both of her hands, encircling it. "I can see her on you."

My heart kicked in my chest.

MJ's mouth hitched back up, her gaze ensnaring mine, her pupils so large her eyes looked black. "I want to see more."

Her hand went to the strap of my camisole.

MJ

Cassie stiffened. I kept the strap of her shirt in my fingers. It was soft and warm but missing that charge I got when touching her skin.

"I don't let anyone see them." Cassie took a step back and the fabric stretched taut between us.

"I'm not just anyone."

"No, you're not. You're my boss."

Fuck. I released the strap and shoved my hands in my pockets. What the hell was I even thinking? I would never get involved with anyone connected to my business. Not even a toilet paper supplier, a delivery driver. No one. I'd already done that once and I was still paying the price.

"Pull the plug on your freak-out. I'm not trying to look at anything but your ink." After everything that'd gone down all I needed was some harassment shit.

I turned while she grabbed her sweater. I didn't need any part in her dressing, didn't matter whether it was putting on or taking off. I stretched my arms over my head, groaning. This starting and finishing a project all in one day was hella hard on the back.

"Do you want me to get the front lights?"

She could've turned them off by the time she asked me and waited for me to tell her to, but I kept my mouth shut and nodded. I hit the lights on the main part of the shop and held back until we headed toward the break-room.

I waited while Cassie grabbed her bike helmet and put on her coat. One glance out the window showed the rain that'd been holding off had decided to let her rip. She'd be soaked in minutes.

"I'll give you a ride. There's plenty of room for your bike in my Jeep."

Cassie spun toward me.

I held my hands up. "Whoa. I offered you a ride. You know, something nice."

"No thank you." The words were polite, but her tone was all fuck you.

A spark almost as strong as when I'd been touching her skin raced through me.

I pointed out the window. "It's really coming down. You're going to get drenched."

"Yes, I know. One of the hazards of biking."

"I don't mind taking you. I've got nothing better to do." Yeah, the beers in the fridge were calling to me, but they could wait.

"Thank you, but no."

"It's going to be dark soon."

She stopped and carefully leaned her bike against the wall before slowly turning to face me. Gone was the woman who curled her arms around herself and kept her eyes glued to the floor. Now she not only stared me in the eye, she damn near scorched me with her gaze.

"You know it's no secret that I ride my bike to work."

"True. Kind of hard not to notice the bike taking up half the wall of the breakroom." It actually wasn't that bad. Not much more space than the skateboard Viv insisted on keeping there. The real estate hogs were the helmet and pads because she was shit at skateboarding and needed all the protection she could get.

Cassie crossed her arms and I couldn't help but look to her chest, wondering what was hidden under all her clothes.

"It's been raining before. It's dark every night I leave, yet this is the first time you've offered to drive me home." Frost coated her every word.

"Uh-huh. Your point?"

Her jaw tightened and it didn't look right with her pixie-like features. "So you just happened to pick this night?"

"No. I…" Faced with the hurt, the real hurt she was

letting me see, I did something I almost never did. I shut up.

Cassie dragged her bike to the door, leaving a black mark on the floor she cleaned yesterday. "I'm still the same person riding out of here as I was when I came in this morning. Nothing has changed."

Hadn't it? It felt like every damn thing had changed. I'd learned she'd had cancer. I'd learned she was in danger of getting it again. I'd learned her skin was the softest I'd ever touched. "You're wrong."

She flinched. "I'm not some weak thing that can't ride her bike home. I don't need your aid."

"It's just a drive home."

"No." The word held so much power, my back snapped straight. "This is another instance of you thinking me weak."

I wrapped my hands around the metal bars of her bike, pulling her to a stop. "You're not weak. You're a warrior."

"Surviving cancer doesn't make me a warrior. Just as Zan not surviving doesn't make her less of a warrior. She fought."

"I'm not saying it does. Zan was as hardcore as they came."

"Aren't you? Aren't you saying exactly that?" Her lips twisted in a sad excuse for a smile. "Before today you've given every indication that the only people you see as strong are those with muscles or people who are loud. I fit neither of those requirements."

I couldn't deny it. Before today if asked to describe Cassie, "strong" would never have made it to my list. Eager. Fake. A follower. Strangely sexy. But no, not strong.

I cleared my throat and slid my fingers over her white-knuckled ones. "I see your strength now."

"No." She jerked back, taking her bike with her and pushing the door open. "I don't want you to treat me differently," she said, having to speak up to be heard over the pounding rain. "I don't want to be strong because I had to kill off abnormal cells in my body. If I'm strong, I want it to be for my actions, my beliefs, for being me."

Her back a rigid line of "fuck you," she jabbed her feet on the pedals, rocketing forward until there was nothing but the faint blinking red light on the back of her bike.

Holy shit. Why would someone who had that much fire in them work so hard to contain it?

Chapter Four

MJ

I rolled my seat to the corner of my station while Cassie rang out my last client. Side eyeing the stack of bills she'd dropped off earlier, I snatched up the first one. Fuck. That would be coming out of my personal account. I needed to get more foot traffic in here rapido.

I scanned the shop, mentally tallying who had clients and how much money I was losing by people sitting around. My gaze halted on my client who was taking off the protective wrap I'd just put on her.

That's all I needed was another bad review because this person couldn't follow simple instructions. Healing, people. It was an important part of the process.

"Thank you so much," Cassie was saying. "We love to showcase new ink on our website and on Instagram."

Our website? I tried to think of the last time I'd even updated it. God, months ago when I'd hired Kayla and put her info up. On the long list of shit I had to do each day, the website wasn't even a blip. I was also pretty damn sure I didn't have an Instagram account.

My client smiled. "No problem. It's awesome. People should see it."

Posting pictures was smart. Those were what people should be seeing, not the shit on some review site. Now they would, thanks to my apprentice. Had the idea come from that little notebook she carried around?

Client gone, she turned and faltered upon spotting me.

I uncrossed my arms and motioned for her to follow. "I want to talk to you in my office."

Her throat bobbed. "I hope you're okay with me taking pictures. I think it would be a great way to promote. I made sure the date was on them so people can see the shop is still creating great work and..."

"Jesus, breathe. We'll talk in my office." For the rest of the walk, if I listened hard enough I was pretty sure I'd hear the desperate thoughts in her head. If that frantic energy made me want to tear my skin off, what the hell was it like living that way?

Leaning back, I plopped my feet on top of my desk. There was just enough room for them between the pile of invoices and the stack of client release forms.

Cassie sat on the edge of the chair, her legs pressed together, hands folded on her lap. The woman couldn't even relax into a seat.

"What did you do before you got into tattooing?"

"I was an executive assistant."

"And that means?"

She squirmed. "It means I was as close to a robot as a human could be."

I barked out a startled laugh. "What?"

"It was my job to make sure everything was perfect. I did the scheduling, training, prepared for meetings, research, pretty much anything."

"So you made sure things got done and looked good."

"Yes."

I could totally see that. What I still couldn't see—even after her being here three weeks—was her with a needle in her gun, inking a client. "So how did you go from that to tattooing?"

"I've always loved art and I loved the self-expression aspect of tattooing. You are changing someone forever." As she spoke, her words got more natural, less like she was trying out every word before she said it. "Once I went to Zan for my first one I knew it was time to stop secretly dreaming of what it would be like if I could do it. No more talking myself out of it. I was going to do it. Zan helped me make the change."

That was a better answer than my "because they're badass."

"So you quit your job and went for tattooing." Who'd have thought I'd have something in common with her? Not that I'd had as much to lose as head of the lumber department at a hardware store.

"Well, first I took classes after work and did most of my apprenticeship with Zan in the evenings and weekends before quitting."

Ah, that was more like it. Cassie wasn't the leaping type. She seemed more like straddle and keep both feet planted until they couldn't spread any further. I pointed the tip of my boot toward her. "You still keep in contact with your old job, don't you?"

"I do."

I folded my hands behind my neck, studying this apprentice I'd saddled myself with. "So you planning to keep running the front desk and being everyone's bitch when you're a full time artist?"

Her body jerked like my words had walked across

the room and smacked her. The silence in my office became what people would probably call heavy, but it didn't bother me and no way in hell was I going to fill it with an apology. Thin skin and tattooing didn't go together. Actually, thin skin and being around me didn't go together either.

She licked her bottom lip with its perfect little dip right in the middle. "Um…"

"Yeah, you don't even have to answer that. I saw you bring Maya gloves on Saturday because she can't remember to put in her order for the damn things. You're my apprentice, not hers."

"It was on my lunch. It didn't take away any time that I work for you."

"That makes it even worse. So you're going to spend your time doing shit they should do?"

For a split second, her eyes narrowed and her nostrils flared before her expression smoothed and yeah, I could kind of see the resemblance to a robot.

But I'd almost had her.

"I'm going to spend my time building a good working relationship with them."

I rolled my eyes. She could leave her executive assistant talk outside. "Doing their shit isn't going to get them to like you, it's going to get them using you."

"That's better than the way they glare and make snide comments now."

"Who cares what they think?"

Mouth dropping open, she gave me a glimpse of all the pink inside. "I… I do."

"Yeah, you should stop. You're just screwing yourself."

"I don't agree."

"No? Why are you working so hard to get people to like someone who isn't even real?"

She quit twisting the edge of her sweater. "I'm real."

"Somewhere in there. But not the woman who comes in with a smile and a compliment for people who don't give a shit about her and doing everything for everyone even if that means she doesn't get to eat."

The tightness of her jaw emphasized her cheekbones. "That's called being an apprentice."

"Yeah, the 'getting shit done' part. Everything else is all you. Or not you. Who are you? Who's the real you?"

"I don't know what you mean."

"No?" I smirked. "I bet you'd like to tell me to shove it about now, but here you sit perfectly straight with that mask." I said "mask" like it was one of my favorite four letter words.

Her eyes flared with life, with fire, and then I watched in real time as she reined it in, leaving behind someone a lot less interesting.

No, damn it.

"Last night you said you want to be seen as a fighter. No one is going to see you like that unless you act like it."

"That does seem to be the way it works."

"Like there, you just accept it instead of asking what you can do. That's not a fighter."

Cassie sighed, her shoulders rounding.

"I can help you with that," I said in my most helpful voice. I tried an innocent look. Without a mirror, I wasn't sure I was capable of pulling it off. I'd never had much success with it as a kid and I'd had chubbier cheeks working for me then.

She cocked her head. "Like you'll mentor me on that too?"

"Kind of." It's what Zan would've done. Hell, the most important things Zan taught me weren't about tattooing, but life. "Didn't Zan teach you things beyond tattooing?"

"Yes. We'd got to the point that I realized it was okay to quit my corporate job and do what makes me happy."

It'd taken her four years to get to that point? Holy hell, I had a lot of work ahead of me.

"I happen to be an expert on not giving a fuck what others think."

Her cheeks went all pink. If I pressed my fingers to her skin, would I be able to feel it? "That was one of the first things I noticed about you."

Instead of wondering how far down the pink went below Cassie's sweater, I needed to be thinking about all I had to do to get people to remember her after first meeting her. "I'd be willing to help you find your backbone."

She nodded eagerly, inching even further out of her seat until I was pretty sure she was defying gravity. "I would appre..."

"It'll cost you."

Her shoulders slumped. "I don't have any money."

That made two of us. I waved my hand. "Not gonna cost you money."

Her teeth scraped against that little point in the middle of her bottom lip. "What's the price?"

"As you've already pointed out I need some help with my business. Now that I know you're a whiz at those things, I'd like you to come up with ideas and give me pointers on how I can bring in some money."

"Oh." She perked right back up, a bright smile on her face. "I would do that for nothing."

"Yeah, don't be telling people that. You come across too desperate."

She nodded and holy shit, yup, she pulled out her notebook and wrote it down.

Watching her, the weight that always seemed to be pressing down on my shoulders didn't get heavier. Yeah, this would be more work for me, but this might be the kind of work I could like. Getting someone to loosen up and let go was a hell of a lot better than invoices.

I put my feet down and leaned forward, stretching my hand out to her. "Then we've got ourselves a deal."

She put her hand in mine and gave it a weak-ass, limp-as-hell shake. I curled my fingers around her wrist, not letting go.

"Try again. Like you mean it."

Her fingers wrapped around my hand and then she shook. It wasn't what I'd call strong and nowhere near Jamie's bone grinder, but it would do.

Cassie stared down at our hands, her lips slightly parted, a confused little line in the middle of her eyebrows. I followed her gaze. It wasn't just our hands she was looking at it. Specifically, it was my little finger that was stroking hers.

I slowly lifted my finger. What could I say? She had damn soft skin.

I grinned. "This is going to be fun."

She smiled with a lot less enthusiasm. It was almost like she knew what I had in store for her.

I jerked my head toward the door. "I've got payroll to do. Head out front. First lesson: if the girls ask you to do something for them, tell 'em no."

She swallowed, and it was hard to tell but she might have gotten even paler.

I made a shooing gesture with my fingers. "Go on now."

She slowly rose and headed for the door, no longer the eager puppy ready to do my bidding.

"Hey," I called out just before she opened it.

When she turned to look at me over her shoulder I said, "You'll be tattooing tomorrow."

Those lines on her forehead deepened. "There's nothing on the books."

"That's 'cause it's not a client getting tattooed. It'll be just you and me here."

She reached out and held on to the doorframe.

She didn't look so robotic now. I'd done that. And she'd done the impossible and had me looking forward to coming in on my day off.

Cassie

I unstrapped my helmet and waited for MJ to arrive. All my extra nerves had me keeping up with the guys in spandex shorts in the bike lane. Understandable. I was going to tattoo my mentor today. I couldn't even talk to her without shaking and now I was going to have a needle to her skin with permanent ink. Maybe the more logical progression would be for her to give me some lessons and have me more comfortable before taking this step.

Twenty-five minutes later, MJ's red Jeep pulled into the alley. Nearly simultaneously with the engine turning off, she jumped out. My nerves surged.

MJ opened the back door of the shop, holding it while I wheeled my bike in.

"No coffee this morning?" she asked.

I hadn't wanted her on the caffeine. Her being any more alert or keyed up while I worked on her would not be a good thing.

"No, but I brought you something else."

MJ's eyebrows shot up. "Yeah?"

I dug into my bag and pulled out a manila envelope, handing it to her. "I know you didn't want to go the lawyer route, but this was free. My previous job has a legal department and they liked me."

She stared at the envelope like it was a trap.

"It's a cease and desist letter. It might be enough to scare Mutiny Rose into stopping."

She tapped the letter against her palm. "This is very kiss ass-y of you."

My body sagged. All of the bus transfers it'd taken to get that.

"Not that it's a surprise," she said. "That's how you get people to like you, right? It'll be interesting to see how long that lasts with my...help."

I looked at her sharply, running my hand through my hair to get rid of helmet-do. "Your 'help' is starting today?"

MJ smiled. "Yup."

As MJ disappeared into the interior of the shop, I took the opportunity to take a few more deep breaths and visualize a calm, serene space in my mind.

I set my supplies down and waited for MJ who stood by the front counter, staring up at the sketches and pictures on the wall.

I joined her. Nothing had changed. They were the

same pictures that had been there since I arrived. "Everything okay?"

"Hey." MJ turned to face me. "I'm wanting to get a tattoo."

"Ummm…"

"So are you the one to help me?"

I recoiled. Not roleplaying. I was still haunted by memories of the last corporate team-building exercises I'd been forced to participate in.

This had been a bad idea. I needed to be eased into this. I already went to a cancer survivor's support group, but that's what we did—we supported each other. We didn't push each other or point out flaws. So maybe I needed to see someone who would be gentle and caring like a therapist. Yes, I could go the therapist route. That would involve me sitting in a comfortable chair and talking one on one. Except I couldn't afford a therapist and I'd probably spend the time trying to convince her I was fine.

There was no convincing MJ. She'd already seen the truth—I was a fraud.

She wanted me to be the real me. I didn't even know who that was. I'd been this…this creature who cared what everyone thought and just wanted people to like me for so long. At first it'd started in school, so I could ensure I'd be a daughter my father would be proud of and hopefully remember when he started a new family. I'd stifled myself and made perfection my goal, all the while being in awe of women who went about their lives and did what they wanted, not waiting for anyone's approval. With MJ's help maybe instead of just admiring strong women, I could become one. It wasn't going to happen with me sitting down, standing back and watching.

I stepped closer. "Um, welcome. I can help you, if you want, with a tattoo."

Okay, that hadn't come out as confident as I'd planned. I swallowed and tried to calm my heart. I did not want a stress test unless it was under medical supervision, not with my unsympathetic boss.

The only two positives I could find in this upcoming humiliation was MJ might not treat me so carefully after the cancer revelation and the other artists weren't here to watch this.

"Oh, cool." MJ's eyes swept over me in the assessing way someone would check out their potential tattoo artist.

I pushed up the sleeves of my sweater, letting her get a good look at my ink. "So did you have a particular tattoo in mind?"

"Yeah. I want a butterfly."

"A butterfly?"

"Uh-huh. One busting out of its cocoon."

"Okay." Ideas immediately swirled to life, but I didn't let any of them fully form yet. I needed more details. "Did you bring pictures of what you have in mind?"

"Nope," MJ answered in an entirely too happy voice.

Of course she'd play a difficult customer. "No problem. Why don't you come back and we'll try to narrow it down and create something you'll love."

An hour later and MJ and I were just agreeing on the size and style of the butterfly.

I did a quick sketch of my latest idea on the back of one of my earlier attempts. "Okay, how about something like this?"

"Yes, like that. Except the butterfly needs to look scared and determined. Right now it only looks determined."

Scared? I wouldn't have thought MJ would want anything on her body that could be considered weak. She was swords and warrior women.

Didn't matter. She was finally being agreeable and giving me something concrete to work on. I'd take it.

I made some adjustments and then held it up for her.

"Looks good."

Oh, thank god.

"Okay. I'll make the stencil." I jumped up and headed toward the printer set up outside the breakroom before she could make any other changes.

"Uh…"

I turned back to MJ. If she changed this design, so help me I would…

"Do you want me to wait here or, like, how long is this going to take?"

"Really?" The only thing keeping my hands from curling into fists was I didn't want to damage the sketch and prolong this. "I get that you have to test me and know that I can handle myself in all areas, but you know I'm good with clients. In fact, I'm better with them than you."

MJ laughed. Full out, fill-the-shop-with-joy laughed.

I'd done that. Me. Without even trying, I'd got my angry, tough mentor to…not be those things.

Still chuckling, she smacked her hand on her thigh. "An hour and eleven minutes before you cracked. Holy shit, you've got fake down to an art. Now retract your claws and go make your stencil."

I would, but first I was going to finish soaking up

how warm her voice sounded as she teased me. I knew I'd need this memory in the hours to come. Nice MJ wouldn't last.

Once I'd finished the stencil, I made my way back to her station to find her sitting on the bench. Oh god. I was going to be tattooing her. I'd be touching her for hours. Could I really do this?

MJ's dark eyes met mine, her eyebrows rose and the right side of her mouth quirked up the slightest bit. It was enough. There was no mistaking the challenge.

I squared my shoulders and patted the tattoo chair. "I'm ready. Take your pants off and hop on up."

Chapter Five

MJ

I actually had to fight off a shiver at Cassie's words. The urge was strong to drop trou and do what she said. "No can do."

Cassie's eyes narrowed, her look downright suspicious.

As well it should.

I shook my head and tsked. "I've only seen pictures of your tattoos and never watched you do one. You can't seriously think I'd let you ink me. That's got to be earned."

Red rushed to Cassie's cheeks. Man, that color looked good on her.

She opened her mouth and then snapped it shut. Closing her eyes, she drew in a noisy breath and kind of just held it until she opened her eyes again.

"I can't believe you pulled this. I barely got any sleep thinking about today. And that game." She stomped her foot. "That stupid game you made me participate in."

Well, well, well.

Hello, Cassie, it's good to meet you.

I leaned against the partition and crossed my feet at

the ankles, almost brushing her leg. Not that she seemed to notice. She was too busy mean mugging me.

"Now, now. You've never been more real than you are right now. Look at you, mad at me and letting it show." I pointed to her still tapping foot.

"Of course I'm mad. You tricked me into thinking I'd be tattooing you. You wasted all of this time." Cassie lifted the paper, obviously prepared to trash it.

I caught her hand. "I wouldn't do that if I were you. You're going to need it."

Cassie thrust her cute little jaw toward me. "Why? You know someone who needs a scared but determined butterfly?"

"In fact I do and I wouldn't want you having to make a new sketch. Think of all the time that would waste."

The frustrated look she sent my way had my muscles zinging.

"So I'm tattooing today?"

"Of course. I told you you were."

She turned and looked over her shoulder at the still-empty reception area. Her eyes when they returned to mine were very, very accusing. "Are you trying to drive me crazy?"

"Trying? No. Now drop your pants."

"What?"

"That's not my tattoo. It's yours."

"You're going to tattoo me?" Her gaze dropped to my hands and she licked her lips.

I'd noticed that when I took off my gloves she always watched. I'd thought it was because she was a clean freak but now... I flexed my fingers. Cassie's eyes followed the action.

"No," I answered her. "You'll be tattooing yourself. I'm gonna watch."

Well hell, I hadn't meant that to sound so porno worthy.

Cassie's mouth dropped in a perfect, beautiful O. Not helping me get rid of the porno vibe going on in my head.

"This is for me?"

"Yup."

Her eyes narrowed and she searched my face. "You want me to put this butterfly on myself."

"Uh-huh." Why wasn't my "yes ma'am" apprentice moving? "You do realize I'm your mentor and you're supposed to be impressing me."

She pulled in her bottom lip and chewed on it. "You're also mentoring me on not caring what others think. So this might be a test for me to stand up and tell you that I don't care if I impress you by putting any tattoo on my body."

"Hold up. This isn't just any tattoo. It's one I designed especially for you."

Cassie studied the butterfly. "I do like it."

"Of course you do. I know my design."

"Since I'm the one who drew it, I think you meant to say *I* know design."

I boosted myself up to sit on the countertop, my legs swinging against the steel doors. "I'm the one who came up with it."

Cassie popped me some attitude with the tilt of her head. "So you're telling me you let all the clients take credit for the tattoos that go out of here? Because I call bullshit on that."

"Say it again," I demanded.

"What?" She blinked, the fierceness fading from

her expression, uncomfortableness taking its place like she'd realized that for a whole second she'd stopped censoring herself.

"Go ahead, curse at me again. It was cute."

She covered her face with her hands, a half groan, half growl coming from behind them.

I laughed, my feet kicking faster. I could feel the smile still on my face, pulling on muscles that didn't get much of a workout. Unless I was around Cassie. That was all kinds of wrong.

"Now get those pants off and get to work."

"All right, let me get my supplies."

She bent down to her bag and I blew out a breath. This was going to take forever, I just knew it. Dear god her inks were arranged from darkest to lightest. Her closet was probably sorted by color too.

"Just use mine."

She shook her head, pulling out more colors. "No. These are organic."

"Are you fucking serious?"

"Yes. All the ingredients are listed and safe. I want to know what's going in my skin."

There went any more insults about her ink choice. "You think it makes a difference? That the other could somehow cause it to come back?"

She didn't take her attention away from getting everything exactly where she wanted it. "I don't want to take any chances."

"You gonna use those on your clients too?"

"I'm going to offer them."

I grunted. That kind of stuff had always seemed overpriced and unnecessary, but maybe not. Organic and all natural were the rage now. I could appeal to different clients if the shop offered that.

Cassie looked at me under her lashes and then rose. "Okay, I'm ready."

I sucked in a breath, thoughts of business forgotten. My fingers twitched at my side. She held my gaze for three—nope, make that five heartbeats with the way mine raced—and then unbuttoned the top of her jeans. She slid the zipper down, the sound of those metal teeth lowering giving me goosebumps.

So much creamy skin. She pulled her left leg free from her jeans. I didn't know where to look first as she climbed onto my chair. My eyes settled on her thigh. She picked up one of the shop towels. Quicker. I needed to look quicker. Her upper thigh. Her ankle. The towel descended, covering everything but the curve of her hip and her stomach. Damn it. I hadn't looked at her knee. I loved a woman's knee, especially the dimples around the side. Could I ask her to do it again? Slower this time.

What the hell was I even doing? I didn't need to be looking at Cassie's skin, no matter how nice it was. If it was one of the other girls or a client in that chair, I wouldn't have noticed the blue vein traveling over their thigh.

"May I put it where I want or do you decide that too?" She held the stencil over her hip, waiting, a pop to her chin.

Deciding meant inspecting her skin, maybe touching it. "No. Wherever you want."

From a safe distance, and sitting on my hands, I watched her shave and disinfect the area before transferring the stencil. Then she pressed the gun against her skin, took a deep breath and began.

The gun moved over her skin in an even, precise rhythm. I could practically feel the needle piercing my skin. Why had I made her do herself? I could be the one lying down, feeling her hands on me, the glide of the needle. I bit back a moan and looked to Cassie's face.

Unlike me, she didn't seem to be getting any satisfaction out of it. Her teeth were gritted, her eyes narrowed and focused. So quiet and contained.

Is that what her face had looked like when she'd been getting chemo treatments? I didn't want this moment somehow reminding her of that time.

I had clients cry, moan, shriek and I watched it all straight-faced, waiting for them to shut the hell up so I could continue on. It was part of the process, and there was no way around it unless I was working on one of the few who actually got blissed out on the pain.

Yet the fact that Cassie wasn't even making a sound and bearing it in silence made me desperate to do something.

"So last night you said that ca—" No, I didn't even like the word. "After you were diagnosed you decided to do tattooing, to be okay with it."

She moved to the lower part of the cocoon and then answered, "Yes. I was good at my job and I got satisfaction from that, but it wasn't making me really happy. Cancer made me realize how important that is. I wanted to be happy, you know?"

I nodded, though I wouldn't be any help to her in that area. What the hell did I know about being happy?

"After my treatments ended, I knew it was time to make some changes. I'd been given a chance and I wasn't going to waste it."

It was working. In her distraction talking to me, she

was relaxing. The tattoo gun moved like an extension of her instead of something she was attempting to manage.

"Besides tattooing, what else are you changing? What else did you do different?"

She didn't answer for a minute, finishing up the outline of the tip of the wing. Lifting the gun, she looked at me. "I came out."

"Yeah?"

Another sound, this one more of a sigh. "I was twenty-five when I had my first relationship and even then I was still in the closet. Was for most of that relationship. It's only recently that I've accepted that part of myself."

Hell, with the way she worried about what me, the other girls, and customers thought of her, I was actually surprised she came out at all. I'd never met someone so concerned about blending in to the norm.

I shrugged. "There's no rules when you got to do it."

"No? I can't imagine you living in the closet, denying part of yourself so people wouldn't look at you differently."

"People have been looking at me differently way before sixth grade when Kelly grew breasts and me and all the boys in the class couldn't stop staring. I've never had much of a filter."

Her mouth twitched up at that.

"I used to go and help my dad at his construction sites." I ignored the pang in my chest. "Loved all the tools and the machines and the dirt and noise. Man, I lived for that."

She winced, tattooing now directly over the bone. Her chest lifted with a deep breath, which she let out slowly. "How old were you when you came out?"

"Fifteen."

"That must have been so hard."

I shrugged and watched her hand. Now that she was at the most painful part, she had slowed. For a lot of artists working on themselves this was when they sped up to try to get it over with as fast as possible, and sometimes their work suffered for it. Not so for Cassie.

She shot me a glance and I realized she was expecting more from me. "It wasn't fun. I'm from Arizona and our town wasn't exactly gay friendly, but I did okay."

"It must have been a relief to come here."

"I don't know if it was so much a relief as a shock. I'd never been somewhere so damn accepting. I'd never been around a large group of people like me. It was why I moved here."

"Yeah? Good for you."

Her praise didn't sit right. Or at least what she thought she was praising me for. "It wasn't actually for me. The girl I was with in my hometown had had enough of being harassed and looking over her shoulder. So we moved out here."

"What happened?"

I wanted to jump down and pace back and forth, but it'd probably make her nervous, which would get her all tense. That would just make it hurt more. I popped my knuckles, one by one. "Turns out once we got here and she was safe, she didn't need my ass anymore. I wasn't the only option. There were plenty of other women."

The buzz of the gun shut off. When it didn't start back up, I stopped messing with my hands and looked at her.

"I can't imagine anyone settling for you," she said.

I stared into those eyes that could never seem to decide if they were green or brown. Heat fanned out on my neck. How the hell had I started talking about myself? I'd only meant to distract her. I pulled out my phone, going through my messages.

Thankfully the buzz of the machine started up. "I still need to fulfill my part of the bargain. A business plan for the shop."

I shoved my phone aside. Yes, anything but me spilling my damn guts. "You want to do it now?"

"No. I thought we could set up a time for a meeting."

"A meeting?"

"Oh yes." Her eyes held a gleam that I didn't like. "With graphs and charts."

Fuck me. Cassie's version of revenge sucked.

Cassie

Once I was sure the coast was clear and no one else was using the back alley for an impromptu break, I pulled out my phone and opened my contacts. Most of them were from my previous job and should be deleted. But I couldn't. Scrolling through the long list made me feel like I had people in my life. Without them, my phone would hold four numbers: my mom, my doctor, my ex, and my dad.

I didn't even end up hitting one of the contacts, instead dialing the number.

My mom answered on the second ring. "Hey, you."

Hearing her voice gave me the same relief as getting home at night and locking myself inside. Except with her I wasn't alone. "Hi, Mom. Sorry I didn't call you back last night. I was working."

"Wasn't it supposed to be your day off? Are you back to not even taking them anymore?"

Now I'd gone and set her off. The exact opposite of what I'd been hoping for with this call. I'd wanted Supportive Mom, not Down-with-Capitalism Mom. It was her firm belief that companies sucked the life out of their employees. My decision to become an executive assistant on salary, expected to be available all the time, had prompted her to check the birthmark at my hairline to make sure I really was the baby she gave birth to.

"It was my day off. Well, I came in for a few hours, but it wasn't exactly work. I'll show it to you when I see you." She'd like this one. Probably the only complaint she'd have is that I never wore anything where anyone would see it. "I was working on a project at home."

"An art project?"

"No. A project for my boss."

I could hear the excitement in my voice, could feel it in my bloodstream. There was something about going through a trough of information and deciding what was important. I'd missed it. I'd missed knowing exactly what I needed and finding the facts and statistics to make my case.

"I thought you were going to focus on your art."

Ah yes, my other love. While MJ'd been busy in her office between clients, I'd worked on the happy unicorn she'd challenged me to draw. Two hours had gone by without me even noticing. I'd been lost in my creative world, giving life to what I saw in my head. Researching was concrete while drawing was abstract and subjective. Both called to me, and last night and today I got to do both. "I am focusing on my art. This is something extra."

"Extra. Why would she need you to do anything extra? You are already working for her for free."

"Mom." I matched her exasperated tone. "It's not like that. She's going to help me in return and not as a mentor."

"How?"

I couldn't even blame her suspicion. She knew me, possibly the only person who really did, and we both knew that if my boss—heck, anyone—asked me to do something, I was going to do it whether I got something in return or not. It just so happened this time it was reciprocal.

"I'm going to give her some marketing advice in exchange for some life help."

There was a squeak in the background, which meant she'd sat on one of the barstools that she'd had since I was in fourth grade. She refused to get rid of them because they were her present to herself when her divorce was finalized with my dad. "Oh, Cassie. This is sounding worse and worse. What kind of life help?"

I looked around to make sure all the windows that faced the alley were closed. Even though they were, still I lowered my voice when I said, "With not craving everyone's approval so much."

Silence stretched instead of the cries of joy I'd been expecting. Happy claps wouldn't be unheard of with her. This was what she wanted. This was what she was always "gently" prodding for.

"That's good," she finally said. "I've looked at her pictures on the website. She looks like someone who can finally get you to make some changes."

The tension that'd gone lax talking to her snapped back, pulling me taut. "I've made changes. Quitting my job, selling my house, going to school, becoming an apprentice." Was any of that ringing any bells? Just listing them had my head spinning with all the changes I'd made.

"No, I know and I was really proud of you."

Was. The word stuck in my brain, stabbing me repeatedly. I couldn't win with anyone. Going after my dream of tattooing had made my mom ecstatic and we'd become closer than ever. My father on the other hand had been "deeply disappointed." He'd thought it foolhardy to leave my successful career, one I'd only got involved in to try to make him proud. Our weekly calls had trickled down to once a month, and I'm sure in no time would be spread out to Christmas and birthdays. I'd lost his respect and for a brief time gained my mother's, but now I was losing hers as well.

"I'm trying."

"I know. I just want my girl back. God, you used to be so fun loving. You sang so loud in the apartment that the neighbors complained and the manager had to warn me. As if I'd ever stop my girl from singing." She sighed. "Every once in a while, when you forget someone could be watching or—god forbid—judging you, I see my girl. I miss her."

That girl sounded wonderful. When I'd quit my job, it wasn't only a new profession I'd been hoping for. I'd wanted to be more outspoken, less fearful of messing up, less cautious. I told myself to speak up, to not worry what others thought. Still I couldn't stop. Would MJ be able to succeed where I'd so utterly failed?

"Cassie."

My mom broke into my thoughts, but this time her voice didn't lessen the pressure pushing down on me.

"I love you. I just worry about you."

My heart squeezed. "I know."

I didn't want her worrying about me. There'd been enough of that.

During my chemo, it'd been my mom there with me. She'd hovered over me, asking me how I was, taking my temperature, forcing me to drink water. She'd been unshakeable even when all I'd wanted was to be alone. If I was alone, I didn't have to wear my fighter face and promise I was going to make it. I would forever be grateful for her help and support, but there were times her worry had been another burden to carry.

Now that those times were past us, the worrying should be over for her. That she worried I was the greatest threat to living a fulfilling life was so much worse.

The back door of the shop opened and I jumped.

"Hey, you ready?" MJ called out.

"Yeah, I'll be right there."

I waited until she was back inside before I spoke to my mom again, not wanting MJ to know who I was talking to. It seemed too pathetic to be speaking to your mother before a presentation. Though really, MJ had made no secret that she already saw me that way. What was a little more fodder?

"Mom, I need to go. I've got to get back to work."

"Okay, I love you." That was one thing I never doubted.

"Love you too."

I turned to face the shop. Time to present all of my printouts and research. They were my chance to show MJ that I excelled at something and hopefully I would finally impress her. I wouldn't exactly be impressing her if I wasted her time when it came to my end of our deal. Even my mother, my biggest supporter, doubted my ability to change.

Chapter Six

Cassie

"All right. Hit me with them," MJ said from behind her desk.

Some of my earlier excitement returned. I had the chance to make things better for her. Ideally I would have had an easel to display my chart. But I didn't and I wasn't going to let it fluster me. All the printouts I had to share with her were in a folder for her perusal. The fact that it'd already become lost in the stacks on her desk—I also wasn't going to let bother me.

"My first suggestion is to hire a piercer."

MJ's dark brows drew together and she shook her head. "We're a tattoo shop. Always have been."

I licked my top lip. Not exactly the start I had practiced in my living room this morning. "Maybe it's time to change that. Piercing can expand the customer base."

"It also takes someone who's specialized and more permits and inspections."

"Fifty-one percent of adolescents are likely to get a piercing."

Her hard stare didn't waver, triggering my someone's-not-happy alarm. The words "say whatever she wants to hear" wailed in my head. But I was right.

After opening my copy of the printouts, I put it on MJ's desk and pushed my index finger down on the paper. "This week I answered one hundred and twenty phone calls. Of the new customer calls, twenty-five percent of them were inquiries to see if we did piercing."

MJ's glance flicked to the printout, then quickly away.

Too late. I'd piqued her interest.

"These are the statistics on how many people have piercings." I leaned forward and flipped to the next page. "As you can see…"

MJ flinched and leaned back in her chair.

Stopping, I looked from the picture I'd included of someone getting their tongue pierced back to MJ, who was pointedly staring at the wall behind me.

Was the big, bad tattooer scared of piercing?

I stood back up to my full height and smiled.

"I don't like the idea of a piercer," MJ said.

"I bet you don't."

She frowned at me and yeah, my mind urged me to be quiet and beg forgiveness, but my hip still stung because of a tattoo that she'd led me to believe she'd be wearing. "As I was saying, seventy-two percent of women and twelve percent of men have piercings. Ears being the most common. Second is belly. Have you seen the needle they use for that? It's this big." I held up my fingers two inches apart. "The demand for genital piercing has sky rocketed. That entails…"

MJ slapped the folder closed and pushed it back toward me. "We stick with tattooing."

"You haven't seen the best part yet. That's on the next page."

She crossed her arms over her chest, leaning back in her seat. "I'm not looking."

"An additional twenty percent is revenue. That's what you could easily make in a year with a good piercer."

MJ's eyes flared, probably thinking about how many bills she could pay with that kind of money flowing in.

"What else do you got?"

Stubborn. So stubborn. As I worked to make myself more like her, I'd omit the stubbornness, especially when it went against my best interests. "We'll come back to this."

Her eyebrows rose. "Will we?"

My flare of rebellion sputtered out.

I took a deep breath and went to solution number two.

"Next up is the time you spend on tattooing."

Her eyes narrowed.

"Even though you spend the most hours at the shop of anyone, you spend the least amount of time tattooing."

"Yeah, you know I'm kind of busy running the shop."

"I know. Trust me I get that. But the thing is you're the main draw to the shop. It's your name that has the recognition. It's you that's been featured in magazines. It's you who has such a distinct style."

Seeing that MJ was going to open her mouth again, I hurriedly added, "I think you should promote Jamie to assistant manager. Then she'd be doing some of the things that keep you in your office and you can be out front more."

"No."

One word. All of that work. This is what I did. What I was good at. And she wasn't even giving me a chance.

"You won't get different results if you don't do anything different," I said.

"Give me something I can use and then we'll see."

"You can use these. I get that this is new and uncomfortable. I'm trusting you and following your guidance to push myself. I need you to do the same for me."

She plopped her steel-toed boots on the floor so hard her chair rocked. "There's a big difference in asking me to hand over control of part of my business and teaching you not to be so uptight about what other people think."

I stared at her face and a white haze descended over me, blanketing everything except the woman sitting in front of me. How dare she?

"I get to you this is no big deal. That every day you say what you're thinking and do whatever you want. It is a big deal for me." My voice wavered and I hoped like hell she understood it was anger. But since her anger was all about loud, I'm sure it was just another weakness in her eyes. "If your idea of helping is to cut me down and humiliate me, I do that enough on my own and don't need any help."

Panting, I stood there, slowly taking in the room.

My head swam. Had I just practically yelled at MJ? Oh god, I had.

I collapsed into one of the chairs in front of her desk and clutched the arms. Breathing shouldn't be this hard.

"You okay there?"

I nodded.

She came to stand in front of me, her hands stuffed in her pockets. "This is hard for you and I need to respect that."

Hard? Just because I was about to pass out from

giving her a piece of my mind. Nah, not hard at all. "Thank you."

She dropped down so our faces were level, her knees cracking with the movement. "It doesn't mean I'm going to go easy on you. I'm going to push you."

My body couldn't even produce the appropriate surge of panic. It was like I had used everything to speak up to her and now I was too exhausted.

I met her gaze squarely. "What about you? Are you even going to listen to what I have to say about your business?"

She stared at me, not as an unwanted burden or a cancer patient, but as an equal.

Doing things for her and being nice hadn't done it. All it'd taken was me speaking my mind and sticking up for myself. Mindboggling.

She cracked her knuckles one by one before answering, "I'm going to listen. That's all I can promise. I'm not going to give anyone else control over my business. That's not happening. But I'll listen to other suggestions."

"Anything I suggest is with the intention of helping your business."

MJ put her hand on my thigh and pushed to her feet. "Yeah, I'm actually starting to believe that."

I stared down at my thigh. There should be a lasting impression, a handprint left behind, but my pants looked the same, as if that touch hadn't happened.

Her words fed the part of me that'd been empty for weeks, desperate for praise. The very part that I was trying to get rid of. What then? How would I feel necessary? Nothing I did produced that feeling of being important. It required other people.

Standing, I gathered my printouts. "I need to do some more research. Give me a few days and then I can give you another presentation."

"Yeah, okay." She flicked the glossy cover of the printouts. "Though you don't have to do all of this."

But then all my research wouldn't be displayed for maximum effect and…

"Yeah, never mind," she said. "You're obviously one of those crazy people that likes doing it. Have at it."

"I will. Though I might put it in a neon folder so it doesn't get lost in all of this." I gestured to her desk.

MJ laughed. "You do that."

Her laugh echoed in my mind. The husky timbre filled me. Oh no. MJ would not be my new source of that feeling. She couldn't be.

MJ

"Hurry the fuck up or you're not getting one," I yelled.

Taking their sweet-ass time, the girls finally filed into the breakroom.

"How is it?" Viv asked, snatching a magazine off the pile I held in my hands.

"I don't know. I was waiting for your slow asses."

Kayla took hers, hurrying over to the table. "I hope they used a good picture of me."

I hoped they used a good picture of the shop.

Thankfully Jamie and Maya didn't feel the need to give any commentary and just took their magazines and sat down.

Pulling up the rear was my apprentice.

Since I knew she wouldn't ask—*yet*, because hell yeah I was going to keep working on her—I handed her a magazine. "Here. About a month ago, before the holidays we had a reporter from *Three Layered Ink* spend the day with us to do a piece about the shop. It came out today."

She smiled. "That'll be nice promotion."

"Better than a newspaper ad?"

"Much."

Squeals and chattering surrounded us, but it was Cassie's smile that held my attention. So sweet. No wonder my clients seemed to like her more than me.

"Look," one of the girls cried.

That got me to stop staring at Cassie's pink lips and back to the magazine.

I flipped through the pages, going faster and faster, waiting for something I recognized. Jesus, had they put it all the way at the back? I glanced over. Cassie skimmed the first page. Who even looked at a table of contents in a magazine? Cassie, that's who.

I turned the page and my breath got stuck behind my ribs. Holy shit. My shop. Yeah, I'd been in trade magazines before, showcasing my tats, but this was Thorn & Thistle. My throat got tight and I didn't want to swallow because I knew the girls would hear it and know why, but damn. That was mine. I did that. Everyone could see it.

Maybe I'd send a copy to my dad. I might not be worthy of helping him around his job sites anymore, but it'd be a nice way to show him that a woman could get shit done even if a penis hadn't penetrated her vagina. Gold Star Lesbians for the win.

Someone gasped. Based on the volume it was Maya, but I didn't look at her. I was too busy taking in all the pictures. There was one of me leaning against the front door, arms crossed over my chest. No smile, of course. Another picture was taken from the lobby, trying to get the whole shop. It looked good, but now that Cassie'd been working on it, I knew the glossy black trim around each station could be fingerprint free and the concrete floors could shine like brand new. They'd taken a picture of Maya working on a client, the blue streaks in her hair gleaming, and then the final picture was all of us standing in front of the wall of designs.

The noise died down, thank god. I wasn't so hot at reading with distractions on a good day, and with their yammering and my Thunderdome heart, it'd be impossible. The first part of the article focused on how I'd started the shop. It mentioned that me and my former partner had not agreed on how the business should run, so we parted ways. Not even a mention of Heidi's name. Good. Next it went on about me and how I'd started tattooing and built a name for myself. Then the writer went on to talk about the day she visited.

I'd always heard a tattoo shop was like a family. Well, if Thorn & Thistle is a family, it's a highly dysfunctional one.

I clenched my hands, crushing the magazine. "What the fuck?"

The rush in my head was so damn loud that I had to read out loud to try to understand the words. "'The environment seemed hostile. After only being there a day, I was tense and uncomfortable. I can't imagine how the workers feel. No one looked to be having fun or enjoying what they were doing. It all seemed a cold transaction.'"

I stopped, popping my jaw before I could continue reading. "'The tattoos I saw ranged from extraordinary to mediocre. The skill level of the staff varied, and you would be best advised to check the work of any artist before setting an appointment or dropping in. Of the clients I spoke with, they were split evenly between long term patrons of Thorn & Thistle and those visiting for the first time.'"

The article went on to describe what the typical day at the shop was like. I slammed the magazine shut. I'd seen enough.

Jesus. How many other people were seeing this shit? Were Heidi and the other girls even now reading it? Laughing?

It hurt to breathe my chest was so tight, everything squeezing.

I hurled the magazine into the trash. Where it fucking belonged. Where every fucking copy belonged.

"One thing," I roared. "I needed one thing from you. One fucking thing. I needed you to get your shit together and act like a team."

Five pairs of eyes blinked at me.

I grabbed the trash can and threw it. It didn't help. Their winces as I slammed it into the lockers didn't help. The anger was still there wanting, *needing*, to come out.

"Do you not fucking get it? This was supposed to help us. Get us back on our feet. Instead it dragged us through the gutter."

Of course they didn't get it. It wasn't them with a second mortgage on their house. It wasn't them with maxed out credit cards. It wasn't them who stood to lose everything.

Exhaustion slammed into me. No, this was more than exhaustion. I was exhausted every single day. This went deeper. This made me question it all. Why? Why keep going? What was I even fighting for anymore?

Fuck it all. I could start over somewhere new. Somewhere where all I had to do was tattoo. I'd lose my house. Pain stabbed my chest, and I grabbed at it. My house. The day I'd signed the papers for my bungalow had been one of the proudest of my life. But I wouldn't have to put up with this shit. I could find an apartment that would take me and my cat.

"It's real nice to know you guys have my back. You're all a bunch of…"

Cassie planted herself in my way. "I need to talk to you."

Glaring, I shook my head and went to slide sideways. "Not now."

"It's important."

"Yeah, so's this." I glared over Cassie's head at the rest of the girls who kept sitting there, not saying anything. Not even a fucking useless sorry. "If you want to…" I broke off as Cassie wrapped her hand around my arm in a surprisingly strong grip.

"Now," she said, pulling.

I stumbled and then righted myself, trying to shake free of her. "Kind of busy here. Apparently my staff are…"

"La,la,la," Cassie repeated over and over. Loudly.

I stared in shock as that godawful sound continued to come from her mouth. "What the hell?"

Had I finally managed to break my apprentice?

Her continued "la, la, la, la" all the way to the back door and once we were outside, led me to believe yes, I had.

Chapter Seven

Cassie

MJ rounded on me as soon as we stepped out the door. "What the hell do you think you're doing?"

I linked my arm through hers and walked. "Helping you out." She started to jerk away and I tightened my grip. "Keep going."

MJ craned her head toward the shop.

"Come on, one foot in front of the other. We're going for a little walk."

Her feet finally fell in line, but her upper half remained twisted toward the shop. "I still need to deal with those ungrateful bitches. Think they can throw me under the bus."

"Trust me, they know what you think of them. Now we have to keep you from saying something that can't be taken back."

MJ whirled toward me. "What the hell was with the singing?"

Oh god. I didn't want to think about that. "It wasn't singing per se. It was more a distraction from whatever ill-advised thing you were going to say." I smacked her forearm. "That was completely your fault."

MJ looked at me, incredulous. "I can't believe you hit me."

Uh, now that she pointed it out, neither could I. Was this the kind of thing I'd done as a little girl that my mother was reminiscing about? I'd sung. I'd danced. And now I hit my boss. No wonder I'd stopped—it was terrifying.

And yes, a little exhilarating.

"It was hardly a hit and I needed to get your attention."

She sent me her sharky smile. "You've got it."

Sweat gathered at the middle of my back. The urge to roll over and show my belly was strong. But that would ensure she wouldn't listen to a word I had to say. "This isn't all their fault. If you're a dick about it, it's only going to make things worse."

Mj stopped. "Did you just call me a dick?"

"I did."

She threw her head back and laughed. She drew some glances, not that she seemed to notice. Like with everything else she did what she wanted and didn't worry about what anyone else thought about it.

If only that was something taking notes could teach me.

When she was done, MJ looked a lot less likely to do something that would get her in handcuffs.

"That's the best insult you could come up with? Almost a month of me ragging on you and dick is all you got?"

"I thought it fit," I said primly.

"You're too much, you know that?" She pulled her arm free from mine and when I squawked in protest, she said, "I'm not bailing. Switch sides with me."

I let myself be maneuvered so I was closer to the buildings and MJ to the street.

"So how far do I have to walk?" Her boots pounded against the concrete.

"Until it works its magic." I wrinkled my nose. "With you I'm guessing it's going to take miles."

The crazy woman smiled, obviously taking my words as a compliment. "Did you say magic?"

"Yes."

MJ sent me a sidelong look. "I wouldn't have thought my fun-challenged apprentice would believe in frou-frou stuff."

"Not like magic wands and spells, more like the magic of relaxation and clarity." I swear she looked disappointed. "Are you into magic?"

She shrugged. Already her body was loosening up with each storefront we passed. "I like Harry Potter."

"Books or movies?"

"Both." She pointed a finger at me. "Don't look so surprised. I do read."

"I have a hard time picturing you sitting still long enough to read a book."

MJ kept her smug look as we slowed for some people leaving the gastropub and then she scrunched her face. "It took me like ten years to get through them."

"You're a fantasy fan. I never would've guessed."

"I think every artist has to be. At least a little bit."

I smiled and turned the corner, taking us away from the busy street. Now I wouldn't have to yell to be heard. I'd drawn enough attention to myself today, thank you very much. "And a philosopher. I'm learning so much about you."

MJ glowered at me.

My heart didn't even palpitate.

Slowing my pace, I tilted my head up to the sky and enjoyed the sun on my face. I couldn't be out here too much longer because I hadn't reapplied my sunscreen, but for now I'd enjoy my vitamin D intake.

"Are you coming? You're the one who insisted on this stupid walk and now you're just standing there."

"Maybe you should try it."

"If you don't get your ass moving, I'm going back."

"If you go back, you're going to say or do something you'll regret and only end up hurting yourself in the end. You don't need more tension with the others."

"Fine. Can we at least keep moving? I'm not into your weird sun ritual."

MJ positioned herself almost like she was blocking me from the few passersby. To protect me or to hide me? Since she wasn't exactly the type to get embarrassed easily, I had a feeling it was the former.

There was a flutter in my chest.

I'm sure her protection was from violence or a thief. It wasn't those things I worried about. I wanted protection from stares and disapproval. People right now were staring at us, drawing conclusions from how close we were standing, the way MJ's body was angled toward me. They could think we were a couple. They were probably judging me, having an opinion on my sexuality, maybe not accepting it, not accepting me. But staring at MJ with the hero worship I couldn't seem to tame—I was okay with that. In fact I liked the thought of someone seeing us together and thinking MJ would ever be interested in me.

I was out in public. I was *out* and I was okay. No

panic. No jumping back and putting "appropriate" space between us.

I was making progress, minuscule progress, but it gave me hope. Hope that I could build on this and get to the point where it wasn't someone else's opinion of me that was the most important, but mine. The hope, combined with experiencing attraction after so long, made a healthy sex life not seem the impossibility it had a few short months ago.

So far sex had amounted to a lot of worry for me. Was I being loud enough? How loud could I get before it sounded fake? How much moisture was normal? Had I shaved? How red was my face? I was getting uptight thinking about it. Maybe if I followed MJ enough, I could progress to the point that I learned to shut all of that off and enjoy sex like others seemed to. Sex with other people, not MJ. I could never see myself being relaxed enough with her. But oh, it'd be nice to touch someone and be touched, to forge that connection and enjoy it.

"Okay," I said, agreeing to keep going. Movement would be good. In all things in my life.

We walked side by side and she continued to relax, her march easing into a stride.

We'd just turned another corner when she broke the silence. "Okay this fresh air, walking thing might not be totally crazy. I don't feel like stabbing everyone's eyes out so they can't read that fucking article as much."

"Always good." I took another deep breath of air, the midwinter cold of it shocking to my lungs and making me want to cough. "I do this every day."

"What, take me off the ledge?"

"That too."

"Where were you when I was a teenager? Could have saved me from a lot of trouble."

"I don't doubt it." Anyone who had the mouth and attitude of MJ was not afraid of run-ins. "Actually, I couldn't have helped you back then. I was in the library."

MJ snorted. "We'd never have seen each other. Only the geeks hung out there."

"Calculator carrying member."

MJ's arm brushed against mine. I couldn't feel her skin through my sweater, but I could imagine it and that was almost worse. Because in my imagination it went farther and her hand wrapped around mine and our fingers entwined. Not her hand, but someone's. And it would feel nice to walk down the street holding hands.

"I was busy ditching class, smoking and tagging empty buildings."

I had no trouble picturing a young MJ trying to prove to the world her toughness in all of the tried-and-true teenager ways. "So long as they weren't anarchist symbols." MJ stared out at the street and cleared her throat. "You did," I said. "You actually did. You would have been too corny even for a geek like me."

MJ's gaze returned to me. The dark liner surrounding her eyes made them that much more intense and mesmerizing. "Oh, you would've secretly been crushing on me hard. I can see it now, your eyes wide, peeking over your book to watch me."

"I think I would have been too scared of you to crush on you," I told her truthfully, figuring she would take the words to mean that it was her I would have been scared of instead of the feelings she would have induced.

"Ah, a sweet thing like you wouldn't have had anything to be scared of. I only would've corrupted you a little. You would've loved every second of it." She winked at me, her eyes doing that deep, penetrating thing that always had me wanting to reach for an inhaler I didn't even own.

"Don't start." My words were strong and commanding, a complete contrast to the pleading in my head. I couldn't handle flirting from her. My body didn't understand that flirting was just flirting for a lot of people. Not the soul barring admission it was for me.

As we turned and went down an even quieter street, getting closer to residential areas, MJ let out her breath in a big whoosh. Me, I went with a controlled three count.

"So you do this every day?"

Grateful that we veered off the sexually charged talk, I answered, "I do. I also try to meditate."

"The organic ink should've clued me into your new age-yness." MJ reached out and flicked my shirt, her finger brushing against me. "Where's your tie-dye?"

I swallowed and ignored the way my skin tingled. If I had nipples, I had no doubt they would be stiffening. "Please, that was hippies. Now we are into responsibly grown bamboo."

"Right. Duh." A woman passing next to MJ moved her hands to clutch the strap of her purse. "So why do you walk and meditate so much? To relax?"

"Partially. Mostly to think and purge any negative thoughts with activity." I smiled wryly, hearing how "new age-y" that sounded. "I started when I was getting my treatments."

MJ stopped and turned to face me completely, that

hawkish expression coming over her face like it did every time I mentioned my cancer. I knew the reaction wasn't all about me. Cancer had taken Zan, her mentor and friend.

Still I appreciated that reaction so much more than the worried one I received from my mom, or the awkward way it was avoided by former coworkers and friends. MJ's "I'll kick its ass" look gave me strength instead of feeding my own worries.

MJ didn't say anything and didn't keep on walking so I took that to mean that she wanted more. "It gave me some normalcy and allowed me to get out of the house since I couldn't work. No matter how sick I was I made myself go for a walk. Some days it was only a block, but then there'd be the days I could go a mile."

"You shouldn't have been walking in the rain or the cold." She stretched her neck from side to side. "I see why you like it though. I do feel better."

I smiled. "Good. My job is done."

"So how long does this good feeling last?"

"Varies. Sometimes a few minutes, sometimes the rest of the day."

"A few minutes?" MJ whirled around and started walking back the way we'd come. "Oh hell no. We've already wasted thirty minutes."

"They weren't a waste. I really enjoyed it." I flushed and wanted to throw myself into oncoming traffic, except of course we hadn't made it back to the busy section yet, so I'd only wind up standing in the middle of the street. "I meant the exercise."

A lie. I'd enjoyed every second of this time with her.

MJ's gaze snapped to mine, looking almost…soft. It had to be a trick of the sunlight. "Yeah, me too. If you can do it with walking, what else can you make me like?"

"Delegating and printouts."

"Uh, yeah, no." She shook her head and smiled. "I still can't believe you dragged my ass out of there." She nudged my shoulder. "By singing."

I groaned and covered my face with my hands. "Don't remind me."

"Oh, but I am. Every chance I get. Bet I won't be the only one either."

"I'll have to consider it a learning experience in not caring what they think."

"There you go." She flung her arm over my shoulder. "Soon you won't need me at all."

Distantly it registered that she was talking about a time when she wouldn't be helping me. We'd just gotten started. I'd have to probe that later when I could focus on something other than MJ's arm around me. Warm. Heavy. Welcome. So welcome. I wanted to lean in closer. I could picture myself wrapping my arm around her waist.

No.

I couldn't long for those things. Not from her. Not from anyone. Not until my scans in May.

Chapter Eight

Cassie

I found myself in MJ's Jeep, giving her directions to my apartment. I'm not quite certain how I got here. Well, I'd climbed in on my own, but somehow in the rush of finishing the day without MJ confronting anyone and her telling me to come along, here I was.

"Take a right at the light."

MJ turned without using her blinker. In the few minutes I'd been in the car she hadn't used her turn signal once, but she sure seemed fond of the gas pedal.

"It'll be on the left."

MJ ducked her head and stared at the apartment complexes lining my street. I pointed to the turn-in and watched the lines on her forehead furrow deeper. As we passed the carports, she tilted her head as if to ask which one.

"Um, there's visitor parking up ahead."

"You don't get a carport?"

"I do, but my neighbors are using it since I don't have a car."

I swore she knew when I said "using" I actually

meant they'd taken it over and I wasn't willing to start anything by bringing it up.

As soon as MJ parked, I jumped out and headed toward the back of the Jeep where my bike was.

"So, um, thanks for the ride."

MJ looked around us and then hit the alarm button on her keys. "I'm walking you to your door."

"Oh that's…"

"I wasn't asking."

Of course she wasn't.

I nodded, not that she was waiting for my agreement. We walked shoulder to shoulder toward my apartment. Her eyes scanned all around us.

Pretty much she was the complete opposite of me. When I came home, I kept my head down and made my way to the door as fast as I could. It was kind of nice not to have to do that with MJ by my side.

Not that my neighborhood was that bad. It was comprised of hard-working people like me or those trying to get by on their social security checks. For the most part everyone ignored each other and kids played in the parking lot and sidewalks.

MJ and I trudged our way up the stairs, me carrying my bike. I unlocked my door and turned to face her. "Thank you for walking me…"

"Yeah, still not done." MJ passed me and walked into my apartment.

My pulse tapped a warning at my wrist. I wasn't sure MJ in my space was a good idea. Actually, I was pretty sure it wasn't.

MJ let out a low whistle as she trailed her fingers over the rainbow chevron throw I had draped over the couch. "Aren't you full of surprises."

I was full of surprises, but most people never took the time to discover them.

She wandered over to my melted crayon art, and then looked at me over her shoulder. "I thought you might be allergic to color."

Hard to miss the way her gaze swept down my clothes. That's it, I was adding at least one bright sweater into the rotation.

MJ went around my apartment, touching everything, leaving an impression behind, visible or not. Last she went into the kitchen. She stopped at my pink "Nope, Not Today" towel. She lifted it up questioningly.

"I took up cross stitching during chemo," I said.

She dropped it and jammed her hands in her pockets. Tour completed, she headed back to the living room and I invited her to sit. "So this isn't the kind of place I'd expect you to live," she said.

Taking a seat next to her on the loveseat that acted as my couch, I shrugged. "It checked off all of my requirements—cheap, cheap and cheap."

She surveyed my apartment again, this time seeming to see past the bright colors and the scarves I had pinned to the wall, to the patch jobs underneath. Along with the cracked linoleum, the scratched floors and of course, the peeling counters. "Can't say it has anything else going for it."

"True." That's why I'd added as much color and texture as I could.

I leaned closer to her, which didn't take all that much, considering how small my loveseat was, and lowered my voice to a mock whisper when I said, "I'll tell you a secret. Apprenticeships are unpaid. Not only that, but you're supposed to be on call all the time."

"You don't say."

My field of vision was filled with her and it was so much better than my depressing apartment.

"Executive assistant sounds so fancy. I would've thought you'd have been raking it in." Her lips quirked up. "I can picture you with some spreadsheet keeping track of how much you have down to the last penny."

I didn't know if it was the little smile or the teasing tone, but one of those had my heart pounding so loud I couldn't hear my words to review them before I spoke. "I don't detect the proper amount of respect for my spreadsheet skills. You're right that I did make a good salary, even had a nice retirement savings." *Had* being the operative word. "Even with insurance, cancer is expensive. And now I'm going on two years with no income."

"Yeah, that sucks." MJ shook her head and put a foot on my coffee table. "Hell, I'm impressed your savings lasted that long. I'd last about oh, a week."

Wanting a repeat of the closeness I'd felt this afternoon when I'd been honest and shared, I said, "My spreadsheets now consist of bus fare and my weekly cup of tea."

MJ put her fist out and after staring at it for a second, her intention clicked and I bumped my fist against hers.

"I hear ya," she said. "First time in six years I'm not going to Musicfest."

I'd never thought I'd be bonding with someone over money problems. Not when my father had instilled in me that money, your house, your car, were all measures of your success. While I wouldn't meet anyone's definition of successful, especially my dad's, I couldn't say the same about MJ. She was a sought-out artist whose shading was unparalleled.

MJ flexed her feet, the heel of her boot digging into the teal I'd painted my old wood table. "Damn what a day." She stretched her arms above her head, displaying her neck.

The skin on the deepest part inside of her neck was free of ink. I couldn't look away. That part held my attention more than the bright art surrounding it. It felt like I was being allowed to glimpse something special that not many people got to see.

She lowered her arms but didn't straighten her tank, which left the black strap of her bra visible.

I forced my gaze away, past her boot on the table, and to my darkened TV.

What a day indeed. It'd reminded me why I lived here and sold my car. Today I hadn't let my fear stop me and I'd taken control. I'd gotten MJ out of the situation. I'd been the one to take action. Why, I'd almost been a superhero. My body was still humming hours later. I'd be lucky if I could sleep tonight without the help of some chamomile tea.

That'd never been a problem as an executive assistant.

Oh, I'd come home still thinking about work. What I wanted to prioritize for the next day. Checking emails. Yes, somedays I'd come home with the satisfaction of knowing some piece of information I'd provided had been integral for an important meeting, but it couldn't compare with this. I'd helped MJ today. I'd kept her from making a big mistake.

She yawned, which spurred one in me, and then stretched her feet out, a second boot landing on my table.

"Everything okay?"

"Mm hm."

"You sure?" She knocked her feet together.

Those were heavy boots and the paint I'd used had been cheap and I'd only applied two coats. I...

She burst out laughing.

Seeing the glint in her eyes, I didn't think. I smacked her thigh. Hard. My palm tingled and the sound of the smack lingered in the room.

MJ clutched her side. "Man I thought your eyes were going to bug out when I put my other foot up."

"Ugh. That was mean."

She beamed.

"That was not a compliment."

MJ laughed some more.

I couldn't help but join in, it was so infectious. I didn't know what we were even laughing at. Maybe her teasing me? It didn't matter. It felt good. It felt completely different than when I laughed by myself on this sofa after watching something funny.

A smile lingering on her lips, MJ shook her head. "Man, I did not think I'd be able to do that after that hit job of an article."

I smiled back, pleased.

Her gaze roamed over my face, down my neck, to my chest, over my sweater. It was like an electrical current ran beneath my skin wherever she looked. "I sure as hell didn't think it'd be someone like you that could get me to do it."

Someone like me.

I slouched back into the cushions. Of course it was only on my side that sharing a smile meant we'd made some deep connection. She wouldn't with someone like me. I trailed my finger down a small snag in my jeans.

"How's the tattoo doing?" MJ asked.

I flicked at the imperfection. "Good."

"Yeah? You better be taking care of it. It's got my name on it."

My eyes met hers.

She wouldn't have been surprised to find herself laughing with someone who was more forward, confident. More like I'd been earlier today. More like I wanted to be every day. I straightened my shoulders.

"Do you want to see it?"

MJ

Did I want to see it? Hell yes. This was about ink. I didn't let anything stop me from seeing ink. Except she was my employee and we were sitting in her tiny apartment and this didn't feel like any normal show-and-tell of a tattoo.

"Do you want to show me?"

She bit her bottom lip and then released it, nodding. A slight indentation remained from her teeth and I couldn't look away until it was completely gone.

"I do."

"All right then." I scooted back to give her room.

Her hands went to her zipper. The sound of it lowering was loud in her apartment, louder than my quickening breathing. She pushed the waistband of her jeans apart as far as it could go, exposing a pair of black briefs. Oh, baby Jesus.

Holding the side of her sweater behind her, she lowered the edge of her underwear. There it was. The beautiful, pale skin that looked like it belonged on some fairytale princess.

"See?" Her voice was so soft that the sound of her

neighbors' TV coming through the walls was louder. But I heard her, especially the shakiness of her voice.

"I do." This is what I did, put ink on people, but seeing my concept on her smooth skin like a brand, my brand, flipped some prehistoric dyke switch in me.

My hand hovered over the butterfly. "Can I?"

She nodded, a blush covering her cheeks. Jesus, how could that be sexy? I liked strong women, but this shyness got me fucking wet.

I traced around the healing skin. Damn but that felt good. Goosebumps rose on her skin. From under her lids she watched my finger move on her skin. I could see the longing there. Reclining against the cushions, she canted her hips toward me, pressing up into my touch.

I stared at the contrast of my finger against her. No wonder she couldn't look away. I circled around the cocoon and butterfly two more times, her skin getting warmer after each pass. I pulled my hand back. I had to before it was too late. Already I wanted to put it right back, to keep feeling her.

A half moan that was quickly cut off had me looking at her. She stared right back, little pants of air coming from her lips. Her eyes were desperate.

"What?"

Her hips bucked toward me.

I licked at my top lip, tasting the sweat caused by forcing myself to stop doing what I wanted.

Her eyes followed the movement of my tongue, another little moan coming from her. She didn't cut it off this time. I felt a matching rumble in my gut.

"You want something from me?"

She nodded, biting her bottom lip again. I wanted to

suck on that lip, bite down where she'd held it between her teeth, but harder so she'd feel it later.

"A kiss? Is that what you want?"

"Yes."

She sprang forward until our mouths touched.

Soft. Her lips were like a fucking cloud. I flicked my tongue out and licked at the middle of her bottom lip, right over the spot that drove me crazy. Yes. Needing more, I slid my hand to the back of her neck, pulling her tighter against me.

Her mouth opened and then her tongue was there, tasting me. These were not the tentative, polite flicks I'd been expecting. Her tongue stroked and twirled with mine as if she was discovering every bump and ridge. I did the same, not wanting to miss anything. I pushed my knee deeper into the cushions, so I could get closer to her, feel her pressed against me.

Needing air, damn it, I pulled back. Each inhale of her scent reminded me of the best dessert and made me even hungrier for her.

Holy hell. She was small, but she packed a punch.

"Of course, you would taste sweet too," I groaned.

Her pupils blown, no green visible, she licked the wetness from her lips. So that's what she looked like when she let her brain turn off and passion take over.

"You taste dark," she said. "Like coffee and back rooms."

A shudder went through my whole body. Killing me. She was killing me.

I wanted to grab her and lose myself in her. I wanted to think about nothing but how damn good she would taste, and smell, and feel. Was she even now soaking that black cotton? Instead of thinking about how many

Chapter Nine

Cassie

I stood next to MJ at the reception desk wondering how silence could be so complicated that I could write a thesis paper on it. Silence while we were waiting for a client shouldn't be such a big deal. Should I say something? Was MJ feeling uncomfortable too? She didn't seem it. So were we going to act like nothing happened? If so, shouldn't we be talking? Or did we usually keep quiet and I hadn't noticed? I couldn't remember.

The door to the shop opened. I jumped forward ready to greet the person, get them coffee, anything to break the silence.

MJ grabbed my arm. Before I could even fully register her touch it was gone. "I've got her."

MJ greeted the woman with a lot less smiles and small talk than I would have.

"Come on back," she said, motioning for her client to follow.

I smiled as they went by, turning to fall in line.

MJ looked at me over her shoulder, shaking her head. "You stay up here. I'm good."

people had seen that magazine article, I wanted the numbers in my head to be counting the orgasms we gave each other.

This white girl fairy look-alike was dangerous.

I pushed away from her. "I need to stop this."

She blinked at me slowly, like she'd gone somewhere else and wasn't ready to come back.

I groaned. "I can't do this. Fuck, we work together. I can't go there. Nothing can happen."

Some of the flush left her cheeks and she leaned back from me, smoothing her hands down her thighs. "I'm not interested in any kind of relationship right now." Great. That was settled, except why was she still staring at me that way? Like she wanted to latch right back on my mouth? Did that mean she was interested in something outside of a relationship? Something like me taking off her pants, spreading her legs and burying my face in her.

It didn't matter. She worked for me. Jesus, didn't I fucking learn? The last time I'd hooked up with someone at work, I'd been left with half of my staff gone and no fucking clue how to run my business on my own.

I rubbed at my chest. What the fuck? I wasn't bummed that nothing could happen between us. We agreed. That was a good thing.

So why did I want to grab her wrist and stop her from buttoning her jeans? Why did I want to stay here in this crappy-ass apartment, rather than go back to my place? It shouldn't even need an explanation. Cassie was attractive. What couldn't be explained is why she made the part of me that didn't allow anyone close want to curl up like a pussycat.

I jumped up and headed toward the door. "I've got to go."

"Oh, okay." I blinked stupidly after them, my stomach churning. I knew *that* silence wasn't normal.

Unmoored, I hung out in the lobby but no one entered. Most of our clientele was appointments, not walk-ins. The desk was clean. There was nothing for me to do, because what I was supposed to be doing was helping MJ. I started to go check with the other artists to see if they needed help and then stopped. MJ said I did that too much. Was this some kind of test? Ugh. I liked the kind of tests where you knew the material and could study for them.

I opted to stay at the front desk. I could at least answer the phone and find refuge in sketching. The idea of a female grim reaper had been floating in my mind for the last few days.

The door opened and I eased back from the floaty space that creating put me in. My eyes widened, taking in the tall, dark-haired woman in front of me. "Marissa."

"Hello, love."

I rushed around the desk and wrapped my arms around her. Marissa grunted as I made impact with her. "I'm so glad to see you."

"So I gather."

My cheeks went hot. Okay so my greeting might have been enthusiastic, but it was so nice seeing a friendly face.

She patted my back and pulled away, giving me a thorough examination. "Can you take a lunch break? I brought C'est Fresh." A take-out bag hung from her arm.

I glanced at the clock over the door. I'd been sketching close to two hours. MJ had blocked out three hours for her appointment. She wouldn't need me for another hour, if she wanted me at all.

"Perfect timing. We can have it in the breakroom."

Marissa nodded, regarding the main waiting area. The shop was a far cry from the conference rooms she usually presided over, but somehow she surveyed it like she belonged. I was here every day and still bumped into the receptionist desk as I turned to lead the way.

MJ watched us from her station, frowning.

My steps slowed, my heart rate spiking before I remembered I hadn't done anything wrong. She had no cause to be unhappy with me. I was surprised to find myself wanting to frown back. Instead I settled for a nod and continued on into the breakroom.

"So this is it."

"It's fine." Marissa waved a hand, the large diamond ring on her finger sparkling. She'd gifted it to herself because "she didn't need anyone to buy her anything." Every time she achieved a major goal she added another diamond. The piece had to be nearing five carats now.

While I unpacked the bag, she slipped out of her black suit jacket. I swept my gaze down Marissa's curvy figure, pausing on the darker outline of her nipples visible beneath the sheer lace.

Every once in a while I missed lingerie like that. But then again, even before the cancer I'd never filled them out like she did.

"This was really nice of you." I took my seat and opened the first carton, the steam hitting my face and bringing with it the scent of basil and oregano.

Marissa shrugged. "It's been a while since we've gotten together. I wanted to see you at your new place." She looked around the breakroom which consisted of a metal table, plastic chairs and painted dark blue metal lockers.

Her gaze returned to me. "You look good."

I swallowed my bite of noodles tossed with feta and herbs and held back my moan. I couldn't remember the last time I had C'est Fresh. Even their lunch specials were more than I could afford. "Thank you."

"Everything's still…good?"

I understood her tentativeness. It was as if saying it could somehow jinx it and my body would start spreading the cancer cells again. Maybe it already was. I wouldn't know until my scans. Even if they came back clean I doubted I'd ever truly trust them. I now knew the truth. You could feel good and healthy and in the background, your body could be betraying you.

"Yes. I haven't had any new scans since the last time I saw you, but I feel good. Things are going good."

Marissa let out a breath, her eyes closing briefly. "Good."

Now that we'd worn out that word, I had another bite of my delicious pasta.

We ate in silence, Marissa's stare starting to make me squirm. "You look different," she said suddenly.

My hand jerked and a piece of tomato fell back into the container. "I'm sure."

I ran my palms over my jeans. The metal stud at the pocket caught on the sleeve of my green sweater. That wouldn't have happened in any of the pant suits I used to wear when Marisa and I did lunch.

"No, not that. Something on the inside." She cocked her head, still surveying me. "You're holding yourself taller. You look more confident."

"Really?"

"Yes, that's what it is." Seeming satisfied that she'd solved the mystery, she started to really eat.

I pulled my shoulders back even further. Were they straighter? "I've discovered that it wasn't only my job that needed overhauling. I do too."

"Overhauling how?"

"I'm never going to be happy if I spend all my time worrying about what other people think of me."

"Wow. I have to say I never thought I'd hear you say that." She nudged me with the toe of her black heel. "For too long you've let others dim your sparkle."

I laughed. Yes, I had. Nowhere was it more obvious than being around Marissa. "You sound like MJ except with a lot less cursing."

"I've done some research on her. I'm not sure that's a compliment."

Oh please. Marissa respected formidable women, surrounded herself with them, and there was no one more formidable than MJ. That's why it'd always been such a wonder that Marissa spent any time with me and I'd always been extremely grateful when she did.

"Trust me, it's a compliment. She's actually the one helping me with…that."

"Is she now? How is that working?"

Since I couldn't even verbalize, obviously not too well. "We're in the beginning stages."

"Ah. I'm sure it'll come in time."

Was the goal at some point not to feel this needy desperation to do or say whatever would take away that disappointed look on her face? Or was it for me not to care that it was there in the first place? Either way, I was far from that point. Because I did care and it was a struggle, a real one, not to rush to give excuses or list all of my accomplishments. It would be a very small list.

I scooped up more of my pasta. It no longer tasted like heaven.

She ate a few bites of her salad and then said, "You can always go back. I know Bill would rehire you in a second."

I knew it too. On the days when it'd been especially trying dealing with MJ and the other employees the reminder hounded me. But I wished Marissa had faith that I wouldn't need a fallback.

She must have taken my silence as encouragement. "Rumor is he doesn't like your replacement."

"So I've heard. It doesn't matter." I stared into her eyes. "This is what I'm doing now."

To my surprise she relaxed back in her seat. "Okay, then."

"Okay."

"So tell me how is Momma Whiteaker doing?"

I eagerly latched onto the change of subject. "Good. She's on the search for a kiln. She took a glass-fusing class and wants to do it more often. Soon she'll be firing things at thousands of degrees."

"Just like old times," Marissa said. "My favorite was when she got into soap making. I still have some of those bars left. Do you think they ever expire?"

"Probably not. It's mostly glycerin. Be glad you missed her short-lived earring phase. She didn't make any money for those two months."

MJ rounded the corner. Her gaze didn't linger overly long on my friend's body. At the shop MJ was always professional. I'd never caught her staring at someone in a sexual manner, no matter what was exposed, or how beautiful the woman doing the exposing.

Marissa pressed her napkin to her lips and then rose and held out her hand. "Hello, I'm Marissa."

MJ stared at her for a long second. Her lip lifted in a sneer. "Didn't realize we were running a country club here."

She turned on her heel and headed to her office.

I covered my face with my hands, my cheeks warm. "I'm sorry. She's actually like that with everyone. Including her paying clients sometimes."

Marissa flicked her hand. "Do I look bothered? Enough about her. On to something more exciting. I'm thinking it's time I got a tattoo."

"You?" She'd never shown any interest in them before. Upon seeing mine for the first time she'd said they were "nice."

"Yes. I better get one before you're too famous and don't have time for your old friends."

I smiled. I liked the idea of Marissa wearing my ink. She'd left such a big impression on me, and now I'd get to leave one on her. "Where would you want it?"

She twisted in her seat, her breasts almost spilling out of the neck of her camisole. "Maybe my hip or here on my side."

"Both would look really good."

"Something small."

Because when I thought of Marissa I thought of small. "What is this dainty tattoo going to be of."

She tapped her polished fingernail against her lip. "I don't know. Something that represents me. What do you think?"

Marissa was strong but not in the samurai soldier way of MJ. "A peacock."

"A peacock?" She sat back in her chair but then her frown faded. "A peacock. Hm."

"You are a peacock. Always preening and showing off." I gestured to her with my hands. She was sitting in the chair in what basically amounted to her bra. Pretty and frilly, but still undergarments.

"Then a peacock it is. So you'll make one up for me and then I'll set up a time to come in and get it?"

"You don't want to have more input into it? The style, the colors…"

She waved her hand, her diamond glittering even in the terrible lighting of the breakroom. "No, I trust you."

Marissa who refused to leave the house without her lipstick and heels, who had a standing appointments at the salon for her and nails and waxing, was going to be okay with whatever I designed being on her body forever.

My stomach dipped. This wasn't about trusting me. It was guilt.

Chapter Ten

MJ

Another loud laugh drifted out from the breakroom, a softer one joining in. It was the quieter one my ears focused on.

"Jesus. What are they doing?" Maya asked, twisting her neck in that direction, looking bummed that she might be missing out on something. "It sounds like a party up in there."

"Um, it's Cassie back there," Viv piped in, bent over her client. "How much fun can they be having?"

I grunted and looked at my client while I switched out inks. "How you hanging in there? You need a break?"

Head burrowed in her arms, she shook her head. "No. Just finish it."

Oh sure, now I had someone who wanted to sit straight through. Usually a gold star client, but now she was preventing me from going to see why my breakroom had turned into a comedy club. Which I shouldn't even want to do. After last night we needed some space. Cassie in the breakroom was more space than her sitting up front. This was a good thing. I should be thanking her friend.

I got back to work, maybe going faster than I normally would, but nothing that would jack up the tattoo.

Cassie's and her friend's voices came up behind me. I turned to look at them over my shoulder and scrambled to catch my tattoo gun. Yeah, I'd already seen my apprentice, but it still came as a shock to see her in something other than a gray sweater. She hadn't gone crazy or anything. Still a sweater. A green one. The effect was fucking intense. Her skin somehow had more color and she looked even more like my Tinkerbell.

Well, not my Tinkerbell. Everyone's Tinkerbell. I'm sure other people looked at her and thought the same thing.

She walked by, still talking to her friend and ignoring me.

I hurried through the aftercare instructions and wrapping up the fresh ink in order to get up front. Cassie and her friend—something with an M—were still hanging up front, their heads bent close together talking. Even after my client had gone, they were still there.

That was enough of this love fest. I had a business to run and they were blocking it. I smacked my hand against the counter.

They both jumped and turned my way. I met their stares with a frown.

"I've taken up enough of your time." Marissa—yes, I remembered her stupid name—reached out and patted Cassie's cheek. "It was really good to see you."

Cassie smiled. "You too. Thank you. This was exactly what I needed today."

I bit my tongue with the need to remind her that it was me who'd had her gasping on the couch last night. And people said I didn't have any impulse control.

Marissa did one of those fake kiss things to Cassie's cheek. A nod in my direction and then she walked out the door, her heels clicking.

"What no air kisses for me? I think I'm hurt."

Cassie didn't react to my words, which was no fun and probably her intention. My apprentice, the fun stealer.

"Do you want me to go prep for your next client?" she asked.

"In a minute." I jerked my chin to where her friend had just exited and waved my hand at the cloud of florally perfume that continued to stink up the lobby. "You guys friends from your last job?"

"No. We're friends, but we didn't work…well, I met her through work. She's the financial control officer for a company that liaisons with mine. We would cross paths and hit it off."

Hit it off. I'd never known there were so many ways those words could be taken. But my mind was coming up with lots. "Cross paths, huh? Is that some office lingo for hooking up?"

Cassie's cheeks flamed.

"Ah." I perched my hip on the desk. "Do tell."

"Like I said. We met and hit it off. We dated."

"How long ago was this?"

Cassie started packing up her sketching supplies from earlier, obviously not liking the direction this conversation was going. I couldn't say I was too fond of it either, but I wasn't going to drop it. The next time she snuck a peek at me, I made sure my look told her that.

She sighed. "A while. We hadn't been together all that long when I got diagnosed and…"

I stared at her, trying to put together the little pieces

of information she'd given me. I was missing a hell of a lot of the pieces, but... I launched up from the desk. "Wait, are you saying she dumped you because you got cancer?"

Cassie's gaze flickered but held mine. "Not right away. It's a lot. There's treatments and I felt sick all of the time and I didn't have the energy to go out. Most of the time we spent together I'd end up falling asleep. Marissa has a stressful job already. Like I said, it's a lot."

I knew I didn't like that woman. It was damn good to have a reason now. "I can't believe you're defending her."

"Some married couples can't handle the pressure. It makes sense our relationship couldn't."

That was pure shit. "How long were you together? Days, weeks, a couple of months?"

This time Cassie's gaze dropped. "A year and a half."

"A year and a half!" Holy shit what was this craziness? "Why the hell are you still friends with her?"

Cassie flinched, because yeah, I might have gotten a little loud. But Jesus.

"She was my first. She was with me when I came out. It might not have worked out romantically, but we'll always have that connection."

Shaking my head, I walked right up into her space. "Let me tell you something about friends. Friends stand by your side and are there no matter what. She is a shitty friend. Sorry your cancer crimped her life."

Cassie didn't look nearly pissed enough. Come on, she had to see it.

"I don't hold it against her."

"Why the fuck not? You should. You're acting like she's doing you some favor by remaining friends. That's got to change." I crossed my arms over my chest. "We're going to get you to the point that you won't accept anything less than someone there through it all. Someone who won't ditch you when you need them."

Cassie reared her head back, her eyes narrowing. "We are still talking about me, right?"

I grimaced. Score one for Cassie. She was right. What the hell did I know about that? Zilch. Not like I'd ever experienced dedication like that from anyone.

Cassie covered her mouth with her hand and reached the other one out to me.

I waved her off. "Don't punk out now. You look good with a backbone."

She drew herself up. "Um, thank you. Marissa isn't bad. In fact she gave me some ideas to help out with the shop."

I went rigid. "What?"

"We brainstormed on some things that…"

I made a slashing motion across my throat. "Hold up. I never gave you permission to talk about my shop with anyone. Never."

"I thought she could be useful."

As if it wasn't enough that people in the industry knew my fucking dirty laundry, I'd had it showcased in a damn magazine. Now Cassie was spreading it to outsiders. "I don't need anyone else up in my business."

I'd allowed her in. Cassie. I decided to take the risk that someone who seemed to have a life-long pattern of helping everyone wasn't setting me up to screw me over. I hadn't made that decision with anyone else.

Cassie licked her lips. "Okay, I get that. But she's an expert. You didn't like my ideas so…"

"So you thought you'd push your end of the deal on to her?"

"No. I explained our bargain to her. How you were helping me and what I would be doing for you in return." She spaced each word slowly and evenly, playing some "the louder and angrier you get, the calmer I'm going to stay" game. That was some straight up passive aggressive tone usage.

Damned if it didn't work. "You told her I was helping you?"

"Mm hm. She said she noticed a little difference."

"A little, huh?"

"Yes. She had some really great ideas…"

I held up my hand. "I don't want to hear them. If I wanted her advice, I'd hire her."

Cassie nodded and bit her lip, right smack dab in the middle where I'd been kissing it the night before. She kindly didn't point out there was no way my broke ass could afford to hire anyone, especially her friend. I'd seen the rock on her finger.

"I really am sorry. I won't ask anyone else again."

I took a deep breath, trying to do the "holding it in" thing she did. She hadn't been trying to pull one over on me. She'd been trying to help me. I blew out my breath. "Yeah, yeah. You tried to do your part. Now it's my turn."

She cocked her head, her eyes wary. "Your turn?"

"Uh-huh. I wouldn't want your friend thinking I wasn't upholding my end of the bargain."

"Oh, I don't think…"

"Go to all the artists and tell them one thing you like about working with them."

Her expression eased and she started to relax.

"And one thing you will no longer be doing for them. Tell them they need to do their own shit."

Her eyes got huge. Yup, the sweater really brought out the green. "In those exact words?"

"Yup."

"Are you crazy? They're going to hate me."

"Probably. But what do you care?" I shooed her with my hand. "Go along."

Unsurprisingly, she didn't move.

I leaned closer and flicked the edge of her sweater. "Unless you want to call off our deal? I don't have to help you."

"No. No. I don't want to call it off." She stared over my shoulder to the shop and all the girls working. "I just…" Her gaze shot back to mine and finding no quarter there, she headed toward Jamie first.

I followed right behind. No way was I missing this, plus I was blocking her path if she tried chickening out.

She looked at me like I was leaving her behind with some long-lost relatives that thought being queer was a choice and then tiptoed closer to Jamie, watching over the artist's shoulder.

If up to her, she'd probably stand there until Jamie was done, which was why I cleared my throat. Loudly.

Jamie turned toward us.

"Um, I wanted to let you know that I really think it's great what a calm influence you have over everyone," Cassie said.

"Thanks," she said, bending back over her client.

Cassie shot me a desperate look. I buffed my fingernails against my shirt.

"But you're going to have to do your own shit. I

can't run things over to your parents' house for you anymore."

Jamie whipped back around. Her gaze raked over Cassie from top to bottom, and then she went back to her work without a word.

Ouch. And Jamie was the nicest and most laid-back of the girls. I motioned for Cassie to keep it moving.

Next she went to Vivian whose bright smile when Cassie complimented how inclusive and welcoming she was to our clients turned to a frown damn quick. Guess she didn't like that Cassie wouldn't be completing transferring her massive digital music collection to a new system. I could even hear the word "bitch" from where I stood.

As she moved on to Maya, she didn't even send me a begging glance. She slunk over there, her shoulders slumped, not making eye contact. Damn it. There was no satisfaction in this.

Hell, nothing went as planned with her.

She praised how enthusiastically Maya defended the shop before dropping the ax on running any errands for her.

Sighing, I walked up and grabbed Cassie's wrist, pulling her to a stop before she could hit up Kayla. Kayla already hated her, seeing Cassie for the real deal she was—which Kayla had no chance of matching— and there was no need to level up to homicidal.

"All right, come on. You're done."

Holy hell, her face was sweaty and splotchy. Her trembles were making their way up to me through where I still held onto her arm.

Jesus.

"Come on, you can help me in the office. There's a shit load of stuff that needs to be filed. You can do that."

Her eyes lit up. She'd been itching to clean up my desk since the first day. Now she got her chance, all because I'd become a sucker. A sucker who couldn't stand being responsible for upsetting my apprentice. That was my job—to push her, to make her strong, to have her prove how much she wanted this. But I didn't want to break her.

"Can I devise a new system for you. It'll…"

I knocked my shoulder into hers. "Don't push it."

Cassie

"Tapping out?"

MJ's voice snagged my attention. "What?"

"You haven't drawn anything in minutes. You stuck?"

One glance at my paper showed she was right. I was still in the outline stages. Hers was already filled in. MJ needed mine at the same time because she was going to present our sketches together. The client would pick which she liked better without knowing who had designed it. Whoever had drawn the sketch she chose would be the one who tattooed. It was March and in all that time, the clients who had agreed to go by design instead of artist had complimented me, but no one had picked mine.

Thank god.

Probably not the reaction I should have. That was the point of apprenticing—to tattoo clients. I knew it was time that I take this next step. I would have by now under Zan. It was time for me to do the same under

MJ. She needed to be able to assess my skills and critique my work. But if I started doing clients I was taking another step toward this new life, a life I wanted so bad without knowing if I was going to get to enjoy it. I wouldn't know for another two months.

MJ's knuckles rapped on the table. "Well?"

"No, not stuck. Thinking."

"Huh. Didn't know that a tropical beach was such a stumper."

"Well, there's determining the time of day and what the tide would be."

MJ squinted at me. "I can't tell if you're kidding."

"I don't know if that's an insult to my sense of humor or yours."

"Yours. Did you want me to explain to the client that it'll be longer because you need to go clear your head and meditate or something?"

"No need."

She might knock it, but I could only imagine the benefits meditation would do for MJ. Tonight I'd do some research so I could show her some statistics. Except instead of focusing on the numbers for reducing stress, I'd focus on how much it could boost productivity or save money. Money was what motivated MJ.

MJ grunted and then continued to hover. That wasn't helping me finish. I was the person who could get immersed in a book in a crowded room, or create a power point with the TV blasting. By only standing behind me, MJ shattered my concentration. She'd always intimidated me, but now there was a new layer, an awareness of her and that those lips that were pressed in such a thin line had kissed me. A month had passed, but the memory hadn't faded. I was reminded of it every time I looked at her.

"Finally," MJ groused as I laid aside my pencil.

Roxy, our client, and the friend she'd brought along, stood as we approached. The friend gave MJ a once-over—at this point it was more like a tenth-over.

MJ remained focused on the client. "You ready?" she asked.

Roxy smiled, no signs of hesitation or nervousness on her face. "Yeah. I've been looking forward to this for weeks."

"All right then." MJ motioned for her to follow us back to her station.

"Is it okay if I come?" the friend—I think she'd introduced herself as Sabrina—called out.

MJ looked over her shoulder, her gaze doing its own thorough scan. "Please do."

As soon as we entered MJ's space, Sabrina took off her jacket. Beneath she wore a tight pink tank top with itty bitty straps. At least she wouldn't get cold. MJ kept the shop warm, much warmer than I would expect from someone pinching pennies.

Once Sabrina was settled, MJ snatched my sketch out of my hands. "Here it is."

Frowning, I stepped forward. "Wait. Where's yours? Aren't you…?"

MJ ignored me. "What do you think?" she asked Roxy.

Roxy stepped closer, a slow smile coming over her face. "It's amazing."

"Yeah, it is."

I again tried to get MJ's attention. This isn't how it was supposed to go. She was supposed to put her design down too, and then the client would choose which one they wanted. Instead this lady was going to get mine.

MJ patted my shoulder. "Have fun."

Fun? Hoping my eyes weren't too wild, I looked to Roxy. "Are you sure? I don't have much experience. It's MJ that's famous."

Roxy's smile didn't dim. "No, I get that. But this sketch." She fingered the edge of the paper. "I feel it."

I ducked my head. "Thank you. I just want to make sure you understand I'm still an apprentice. I don't have the same skills. In fact, um, I'm thinking it isn't fair for you to pay the full price. Maybe...."

MJ's hand clapped down on the back of my neck, squeezing until I stopped talking. "What she means to say is hop up onto the chair and get comfortable while she gets this ready."

Um, no, I was trying to control expectations here.

MJ motioned to the bench. "I'll be right over here."

The words sounded more like a threat then the supportive words of a mentor ready to be there as backup.

Sabrina, the helpful friend, patted the space on the sitting bench next to her.

I turned away. My first client was the only thing I needed to focus on. I set up my gun, my hands shaking in a way that wouldn't inspire confidence in someone that was going to have to pay full price for my work.

Now that she was a paying customer, the middle-aged friendly woman had become much more intimidating. I pulled out my inks, nearly knocking the tray I'd already set up. "I carry both regular or organic ink. Which would you prefer?"

"Organic."

I aimed a "see" look at MJ, but her and Sabrina's

heads were turned close as they stared at a phone screen. The contrast between MJ's harsh dark buzzed pompadour and Sabrina's feminine long blond hair was beautiful. This time it was harder to pull my gaze away.

"Good choice," I said to Roxy, snapping on my gloves. Already my hands were down to a faint tremble. Hardly noticeable. "I'm ready to start when you are."

My client, *my client*, pulled off her shirt and then lay on her side. I tucked up the thick band of her bra to keep it out the way for this rib piece. Once the stencil placement was perfect it was time to start.

Luckily while my mind took great pleasure in reminding me how many things I could do wrong and ways I could ruin this, my body knew what to do. I'd traced an outline so many times it was second nature. Once my body started going, I was able to get my mind to follow suit and I got into the rhythm.

Occasionally I'd catch the timbre of MJ's voice, soon followed by higher pitched giggles from Sabrina, but I was able to banish them and keep working. I was almost prouder of that feat than not having messed up on my first customer.

When it was time to switch colors, I patted Roxy's hip. Unlike many customers, she hadn't brought headphones to distract her from the pain. That probably was supposed to be Sabrina's job.

"Doing okay? Need a break?"

"No. I'm good."

I smiled. "I lucked out with you. No squirming and not even one moan."

Roxy smiled back at me. The lines around her eyes and mouth hinted that smiling was something she did often. "I think we're mutually lucky."

Oh god. Was she flirting? Was I supposed to respond? Or maybe she wasn't flirting and she was complimenting my skills. How could I tell? I didn't know the difference. What...

"So, I couldn't help noticing your scar."

I jerked my hand back and pressed my shirt tight to my skin to make sure it hadn't draped open. Following her stare, my heart rate slowed. It wasn't my breast area she stared at, but instead my upper chest. Compared to my others, I hardly even counted that one anymore.

"It's a port scar?"

"Mm hm." I'd never snap that I didn't want to talk about it, could never be that rude, but oh, how I wanted to. Whenever anyone discovered my scars it was the beginning of them treating me differently.

Roxy sucked in a breath through her teeth as I got back to work on her tattoo. "My mom had cancer."

My brain latched onto *had*. Had as in cured, or had as in past tense and she hadn't made it? "I'm sorry. Cancer sucks."

"It does. The whole thing sucks. I've never seen her so sick and I couldn't do anything to help her."

I glanced up, not at all surprised to find MJ staring at me. She seemed to have super hearing when it came to the C word.

I dabbed Roxy's skin and then met her gaze. This was too important to not be looking in her eyes. "Knowing you cared and were there for her helped her. It makes a difference. I know."

This time Roxy's smile did not produce any laugh lines on her face.

"Did she make it?" I had to know. The question would haunt me. It didn't matter if it was someone I'd never met. There was a tally in my head of those people that had survived and those that hadn't.

"Yeah. She beat the breast cancer." Her mouth twisted. "Four years later she wasn't feeling well so they did another scan. This time it was in the lungs."

I squeezed Roxy's hip. Even without the sadness tinging her eyes, she wouldn't have had to say anything else. Lung cancer had one of the worst survival rates. I swallowed the burn of acid in the back of my throat. "I'm sorry."

Roxy inclined her head. "She's actually why I'm getting this tattoo. She always loved the beach. A tropical one, not like Oregon's. I flew to Tahiti and spread some of her ashes there."

I waited until the back of my throat no longer burned so I could speak normally to my client. Except she'd never be just a client to me anymore. She was a woman who shared the experience of what I'd gone through. There was a connection in that. Even if she didn't have it herself, she'd witnessed it, lived with the aftermath. Fear crept over my body. It wasn't fair that someone beat it only for it to come back somewhere else. No person should have to fight it twice and with worse odds.

Would I need to? Right now cancer could be growing in my body. It could be targeting somewhere new. I wouldn't know. It could be too...

A hand landed on my shoulder and I turned to find MJ standing next to me.

"How old was your mother?" she asked Roxy.

"Sixty-five."

MJ glanced at me. "Retirement age."

Staring into her dark eyes, so strong and confident, helped calm me. I took a deep breath. I was okay. I was healthy. I was going to do all I could to make sure I stayed that way. I would get tested and if anything was going on, hopefully it would be caught in time. After another breath, I nodded both to let MJ know I was okay and to thank her. She was standing by my side just as she had been when she made me tell the other artists I wouldn't be helping them. I might not always like her methods, but each time she pushed me I came out stronger and she was there for me in her own way.

MJ resumed her seat and I went back to working on what I could control—the tattoo.

"This is a beautiful way to honor her." I stared down at the seascape I was creating on Roxy's side. "What if we put her initials in the sand. I don't have to do them big. I…"

"Yes. Yes." Roxy reached out and wrapped her hand around my wrist. "I would love that."

I patted her again. "Then that's what we'll do."

For the next hour I laid each drop of ink with the certainty that I was supposed to do this tattoo. Finished, I pushed my seat back, a sense of peace flowing through me that I'd only ever achieved with meditation before.

MJ approached, but my heartbeat stayed the same. I didn't even need her evaluation, didn't fear it. I knew this was perfection.

"Looks good." MJ held out her fist. After a second of hesitation, barely noticeable, I bumped my fist to hers. "I think this calls for a celebratory drink."

Chapter Eleven

MJ

We walked into the bar where the beat was loud and the bodies were pressed close. Just like I liked them. Glancing over my shoulder, I watched Cassie's wide eyes as she took everything in. Was this her first visit to a queer bar? Nothing like pushing Cassie past her comfort zone to perk up what was already looking to be an awesome night.

An arm slipped around my hips and then a female body was plastered against me. I'd almost forgotten about our tag-alongs. Impossible now with gorgeous Sabrina rubbing her large breasts against my arm. Her pebbled nipples were no match for her barely-there shirt, and I could feel their outline against my skin. Yes, this had been a good idea. Maybe even brilliant.

To my right Cassie stopped at the edge of the bar, Roxy behind her, half shielding Cassie's back. It was a bar. What did Roxy think was going to happen? At most Cassie'd have to fend off an advance, or if she stuck around me long enough, I'd teach her not to. To let go. Stop thinking and have fun. That's what I was going to do tonight, have some fun. It'd been too long.

I hip-checked Cass. "This round is on me. What will it be?"

"A club soda with cranberry, please."

I twisted to stare at her. "A club soda."

"Yes, please."

I opened my mouth and closed it right back up at the lift in her eyebrows. That was the thing about Cassie. She might be fake with people and all about getting them to like her, but sometimes she stood her ground. She wore her old lady sweaters even though we all ragged on her, refused to grab a ride with me, and always pestered me to hire a piercer even though I told her no every single time.

With a sigh, I looked at the waiting bartender. "A cranberry club soda and a whiskey sour."

Still hanging onto me, Sabrina leaned forward, gripping me tight to keep her balance. To be fair she was pretty top-heavy to be reaching like that. "I'll take a Negroni."

Well, damn. I didn't mind paying for hot thing's drink but now I'd have to get Roxy's too. Normally I didn't give a shit about being rude, but I made it a general rule to at least try not to do it to my clients. Since she'd gotten a tattoo at my shop that made her a client.

I jerked my chin at Roxy. "And you?"

The woman looked amused at what, yeah, could've been a nicer tone, but hey, money was tight. That was one less drink for me. Or Cassie.

"Apple martini," Roxy said.

The bartender handed Cassie hers before getting to work on the rest of ours.

She picked up her glass and took a sip out of the little red stirring straws. "Mm, so good."

"Yeah, nothing like some fizzy water to really let loose with."

"Come on." Sabrina grabbed my glass in one hand, hers in the other, and tilted her head toward the center of the busy room. "We'll show her how it's done."

She made her way to the dancefloor, hips swaying to the beat.

I shot a glance at Cassie and then Roxy. I had no reason to say no, and all the reasons to say yes. Sabrina had my alcohol, she was beautiful and she wanted me.

Catching up to her, I wrapped my arms around her from behind, my fingers quickly finding their way to the bare skin of her stomach. She leaned into me, plastering her ass to my front.

I curled myself around her and reached for my whiskey sour, draining most of it in one gulp. She shimmied in a circle until she faced me.

"You smell so good." Sabrina pressed her hips against mine. "I don't think we need these anymore." She snatched my glass.

I turned, keeping her in sight as she deposited the glasses on an empty table. On her way back she made sure to give me a show. With her to focus on there was no thinking about the shop. Or an apprentice that I couldn't get with.

She stepped all up in my space and wound her arms around my neck. "There. That's much better."

As we turned I spotted Cassie. She and Roxy remained in the same spot, nursing their cocktails. They were talking. Talking in a crowded bar with multiple couples going full tongue down each other's throats around them. I lost the beat as Cassie shrugged out of her sweater. Good. Her ink deserved to be admired and it would be because it was on such creamy skin.

"The second I saw you, I knew we were going to fuck."

I dragged my attention back to the woman who was all over me.

"Is that so?" I squeezed Sabrina's hips and drew her even closer.

"Oh yeah."

The growl that came from my throat lacked the rasp that should have been there. We made another circle, my gaze snagging on Cassie. She stared right back. She'd angled herself in her chair and was staring at the dancefloor. Even from the distance I could see the longing on her face. That's not the only thing I saw. No missing the way Roxy's arm draped across the back of Cassie's chair, her body crowded close. I growled again and this time the rasp was in full effect. Luckily, Sabrina obviously thought it was for her and pressed her ass into my hips. I pulled her closer and kept moving. It was the reason we were here after all, to dance and drink and have fun. Actually no, the reason we were here was sitting at the bar sipping expensive, pimped up water instead of celebrating what an awesome job she'd done. She should be out here, not watching us like a kid that didn't get invited to play.

That was enough stressing over her. She was an employee. Even if she wasn't, she wouldn't be my type. I needed a woman who was independent, successful on her own and couldn't take anything from me. I was done being used for what I could do for people. If the person who had started the shop with me, been there for every milestone could betray me and leave me in the lurch, then anyone could. I needed someone like Marissa, someone who had her own career that was in no way associated with me. Except of course, Marissa did nothing for me.

Leaning forward, I put my mouth near Sabrina's ear. "I'm thirsty. Let's hit the bar."

"Good idea. We'll sweat it out later."

We made our way to the bar. The seat next to Cassie was taken, so I wedged my way in and stood at her shoulder. Pathetic how winded I was from some dancing. Hell wasn't even much dancing, more grinding. That's what happened when I worked all the fucking time.

Like the awesome bartender he was, ours came up right away. That or I looked so fucking out of breath he feared I was going to pass out. "Another round?" he asked.

"Yes. A whiskey sour." Cassie's glass was down to melting ice. "Club soda with cranberry juice." I nodded my head at Roxy to give her order to the bartender and then looked over my shoulder at Sabrina. "What was yours again?"

Earning his tips, the bartender started putting down glasses in front of us in no time. Behind me, Sabrina pressed herself against me and with the way we were both sweating, I expected her to have to peel herself away from me to get her Negroni.

I nudged Cassie with my shoulder, our skin making contact. Before I started panting again, I took another gulp. "You want to go out there?"

Her eyes darted out to the floor, and up this close the longing was even more obvious, but she shook her head. "Is that what you want me to do?"

Yes. I wanted to be out there with her. I wanted her to have some fun and let go.

"I want you to do whatever the fuck you want. If that's watching people fine, have fun. But if it's not and you actually want to be out there and you're letting what people might think or some shit keep you here, then yeah."

Cassie's large eyes stared at me, the dim lighting in the bar making them look like they were an ordinary brown when I knew that was not true.

"Anything else, ladies?" The bartender set the last of the drinks down, his attention already snagged by some guys on the other side of the bar.

"No, we…"

"Yes," Cassie interrupted over me.

"What'll it be?" the bartender asked.

"Um…" Suddenly her chest was rising and falling as bad as mine when I'd got off the dancefloor. She zeroed in on our drinks lining the bar. She grabbed mine and took a sip. Her face scrunched. Next she took Roxy's who handed it off with a laugh. After Cass drank she licked her lips.

"Go ahead," Sabrina said, gesturing to her glass.

One swallow of the Negroni and Cassie hacked. Tears in her eyes, she wheezed, "That one please," pointing to Roxy's apple martini.

"Good for you." I squeezed the nape of her neck, my fingers staying against her bare skin.

Her martini arrived. She swallowed it down and put the empty glass on the bar. She pushed to her feet. The tight space meant her body rubbed against mine. I shuddered. "You're right," Cassie said. "We're here because I did a bomb ass tattoo."

I laughed, both at her words and her fierce face as if she were daring me to disagree.

"I'm going to have another one of those yummy concoctions," she said. "And then we're dancing."

Cassie

Sabrina led our line out to the dancefloor with MJ behind her, then me, and Roxy bringing up the rear. People pressed in from all sides, their bodies moving to the beat. Men ground on each other. Women on women. I stared. They didn't care about anyone who might be watching. They were focused on having fun.

I didn't know what that felt like.

A hand slid along my hip and I jumped. Roxy leaned forward, her head lowering to mine. "You don't have to do this. I'm more than happy to keep you company at the bar."

Yes. I wanted to be back at the bar. Back to watching everyone else. Safe from doing something I was inexperienced with. When had safe become a dirty word?

"No, I need to do this."

"Then relax." She squeezed my hip. "It's a lot easier to dance when your muscles aren't locked up."

I nodded even as my heart attempted the Guinness World Record of most beats per minute. Sabrina had already carved a little spot on the dancefloor and was dancing with her arms above her head, her butt and breasts shaking. Next to her MJ swayed, staring at me as if waiting to see if I'd bolt.

I'd give it a sixty percent chance.

Behind me Roxy began to move. That left me, standing out here. I needed to move. Everyone else was. I was sticking out. But what if I stuck out more by doing it wrong? I didn't know how to dance. I didn't know this song.

MJ danced her way closer, crooking her finger at me.

My feet obeyed before my brain could get involved with the decision and my reward was MJ's satisfied smile.

I was sure my movements didn't match the music. What was I supposed to do with my arms? They felt ridiculous hanging at my sides while the rest of me moved. My eyes darted around, trying to get ideas, trying to see how others…

"Hey." MJ's voice cut through my panic. She put her finger under my chin, holding my gaze. "Look right here."

I sucked in a shaky breath. Under her steady stare, the frantic thoughts started to recede.

"Nowhere else." MJ smiled at me. "We're dancing. Nothing matters but having fun and letting loose."

I tried to listen to the music and get my body to match it. My hips shook a little faster. But my arms what did I—

"Nope. No more thinking." MJ tapped the side of my head. "Feel the beat. Do what's natural."

Nothing felt natural. That was the problem. How could it be natural when I didn't know what I was doing and I was in a room full of people who would quickly realize the same thing?

"Okay, we're going to try something else." MJ looked over my shoulder and then put her hand on my hip.

I sighed, my mind no longer on the mistakes I might be making and instead on how good her touch felt, how grounding it was. Now this… I gasped as breasts crushed against my back, and then my butt was cradled by someone's hips.

"Yes." The word was lost in the noise of the music, but I read it on MJ's lips.

I craned my neck to the side to find Sabrina smiling at me. Her hips nudged me forward, right into MJ at my front. I had no choice but to move or I would be a ping pong ball between them.

Sabrina's arm wrapped around my waist. She pulled me against her until she was partially supporting me. "There we go. Now dance."

When Sabrina stepped forward, I was still going backward and our legs collided into each other. My butt kept crashing into her. In no way could that be considered sexy. I was like an out-of-control bumper car while all the people around me were sleek racecars.

Sabrina's arm dropped and she looked at MJ. "This is hopeless."

I stopped altogether, not caring that Sabrina caught the heel of my foot. She was right. I was hopeless at this. If I'd known we were going to be dancing I could have watched some YouTube videos and tried to practice.

"No, it's not," MJ said. "Just need to try something different." The right side of her mouth kicked up as she looked me over. "I didn't know someone could be so stiff and still be moving."

Stiff? My body went to full-blown rigid. I knew I looked out of place. Did she think I didn't know? It didn't help pointing it out.

"I'm trying," I gritted out.

MJ's body brushed against mine at the same time her hand trailed down my face. A dual caress. "I know."

"Here. This might help too."

I blinked and then seized the glass Roxy held out. "Thank you," I told her.

Roxy smiled at me. Her hips rocked to the beat, but she wasn't using her arms and still managed to look cool.

"Bottom's up." MJ tapped my glass.

I dutifully drank. It went down easily, the taste of the alcohol buried under the sweet apple. Surely since I didn't usually drink they'd be hitting me soon. Hopefully they'd either loosen me up so I looked like I knew what I was doing or fogged up my brain enough that I didn't care.

MJ took the empty glass from me while Roxy danced in front of me. She nodded encouragingly as I tried to mimic her actions.

The nape of my neck tingled and I caught the scent of pine before an arm slid around my waist and hauled me back. Sharp hip bones pressed against my butt and I could feel the slight curve of breasts brushing against my shoulders. I breathed in deep, taking in the scent of MJ. I wrapped my hand around the arm that held me, right over her grim reaper tattoo.

"There you go," she said in my ear. "Lean into me. We got this."

I dropped my head against her shoulder. Then I did as she said and let her take control. I let her rock me until we were moving to the music together. Our skin touched as my shirt rolled up. The tingles were instantaneous. I let my eyes close and left it be. With all the flesh on display in this bar, male and female alike, no one would be looking at my ghostly skin.

Heat registered at my front. I opened my eyes to see

Roxy right there, smiling at me, keeping rhythm with us as her leg slid between mine, our knees brushing.

I was dancing. Not with one but two women. Sabrina pressed her butt against Roxy and ground all over her. Make that three women.

MJ's arm tightened on my waist, pulling me closer, her hips digging deeper against me. MJ bent her knees, lowering us. Unprepared for the motion, I stumbled. MJ's strong arm was right there, keeping me upright.

"Come on, let go."

This time when she dipped, I went with her.

"Yes." Her breath was warm in my ear.

I tilted my head until her lips brushed my ear. "This feels good."

MJ ground against me. "Hell yeah, it does."

I lost track of how many songs we danced to, me sandwiched between MJ and Roxy.

"I think it's time for another round," Sabrina said, her annoying voice intruding on my dancing.

I opened my eyes. Sabrina stared at me, her cheeks flushed and rosy. She looked so healthy. I hoped she stayed that way. I hoped we all stayed that way.

"So how 'bout it? Another drink?" She wagged her brows.

The thought of another one of those sweet cocktails had me nodding. Good idea. I was starting to sweat, probably from the heat of MJ pressed against me. There were a lot of bodies here. Because I was in the middle of the dancefloor in a gay bar. I was doing it. I giggled. "Yes, please."

Sabrina shook her head and laughed. "Actually I think it's your turn to get them."

MJ stiffened behind me and for the first time in…a

while, I lost the rhythm. I turned my head and opened my mouth to complain, because hey, she was supposed to be the expert here, but I stopped when I saw her in some kind of eyes talk with Roxy. Yes, I was sure of it. Their eyes were talking to each other and they seemed to understand what the others' glances and slight head jerks meant.

"OK, I've got this round," MJ said, obviously satisfied with her discussion.

I stopped, motionless and confused without her guiding me.

"Now, none of that." Roxy danced up to my side and nudged me with her hip.

Right. I was dancing. Dancing. I gyrated my hips and my arms were doing something at my sides. MJ should hurry back though. I was thirsty and it was more fun when she was here.

She returned and I drank the yumminess and kept on dancing. We made our own little circle with MJ by my side. We'd occasionally bump hips, share a smile, but we didn't get as close as before. That was okay. I had my cocktail and I'd found my rhythm somewhere. No one was staring or pointing or laughing. I was doing it.

I danced so much it felt like the room was moving with me. I blinked and kept my eyes wide as I looked at my new friends. Sabrina and MJ were dancing together. Sabrina's breasts were pillowed against MJ's chest and MJ's gaze kept dipping down at what was right there. Why wouldn't she? They were gorgeous.

My stomach lurched. I lost the beat, but then I found it and kept going. That's what I did, I kept going. Except the room was really spinning and I stumbled.

"Hey." Roxy put her arm around me.

I leaned against her. It was much easier to stand when she was helping.

I spoke in the general direction of her ear. "I'm not feeling sooo good alls of a sudden."

"Okay. Let's take a break. We'll go sit down."

I nodded and instantly regretted it. It was loud and hot and spinning. I didn't like it anymore. "I just really wanna go home."

Roxy's cheek brushed against my hair as her arm tightened around me. "We can do that."

She turned us so we were facing the edge of the dancefloor. In the distance I saw the door. Yes, that's where I wanted. Out. Cool air. Space. No more bodies pressed against each other. No more having to see it.

"Hold up. I'll be the one taking her."

Chapter Twelve

MJ

I extracted myself from Sabrina's hold and turned toward Cassie and Roxy.

It was hard to see much of her with the way she was tucked up into Roxy.

I squatted down to get a look at Cassie's face. Hell. Her eyes were glazed and the perspiration on her forehead looked blue in the dancefloor lights.

I held out my arm. "I've got her."

After a long look, Roxy stepped aside and I slid into the space at Cassie's side. Whoa. I braced my feet. This was more than helping steady her, this was holding her up. Cassie tucked her head right into my neck in the exact same place she'd been against Roxy. Her lips grazed my skin and the hum that had been going through my veins turned to a howl.

"I don't feel so good."

She smelled like the martinis she'd had. Like it was leaking out of her pores.

"I know. I'll get you out of here." I brushed her hair back so it'd stop tickling my chin. Free of product, her hair was soft and the scent reminded me of my mom's kitchen after a day of baking, but crisper thanks to the sweat.

Whether Cassie wanted it or not, I would be getting her home. No one else.

"Is she okay?" Sabrina put her hand on my arm.

"Yeah, just had too much. We're done for the night."

Sabrina's lower lip popped out. "I was really enjoying our time together."

"Yeah, me too." I tightened my grip as Cassie listed to the right. "These are hitting her hard. I need to get her out of here before they all catch up."

"Here." Roxy handed me a cold bottle of water. "Give her some of this."

"Thanks."

"Are you sure you have to go?" Sabrina tilted her head to the side, her smile an invitation into her pants. "Roxy could take her home." She trailed her finger down my chest to my stomach. "Then we could continue to party."

The appeals of this chick were shrinking fast. She was cute and yeah, getting off would be awesome, but she could see the condition Cassie was in. I wasn't going to just thrust Cassie's warm weight into someone else's hands.

"Nah. She's my responsibility."

I headed for the exit. Cassie was getting heavier by the minute. Granted that didn't mean shit since she weighed practically nothing, but if she'd been strung tight about dancing on a dancefloor, she would lose her shit if she puked in public.

Roxy went around to Cassie's other side, sliding her arm around her waist. "I'll help you get her outside."

Whatever would get Cassie out of here fastest. Cassie

walked with her head down, watching her feet. When the lights from the dancefloor hit her shoes, she'd give an "ah," like she was seeing fireworks.

Yup, she was going to be needing some help tonight.

Once outside we steered her away from the door and I motioned Roxy with a tilt of my head where I wanted her. We rested her against the wall of the building where it was lit by a streetlight, away from the crowd smoking outside the door.

I opened the water bottle and handed it to her. "Drink some of this."

Cassie grabbed it and took a sip. She made a face and stuck her tongue out. "Ew. This doesn't taste good. Not like the others."

"It doesn't have any taste. That's good right now."

She started to shake her head and then seemed to think better of it. "I like the others. They're sweet." She held the water bottle out in front of her and frowned at it.

I kept my hand around her waist, caressing the bare skin near the waistband of her black jeans. "Yeah, well I don't think you're going to be liking the others in a little bit."

"Yeah." She sighed and tucked her head against my shoulder.

Roxy laughed and looked at Cassie like she was the cutest thing ever. I couldn't even blame her. She *was* the cutest thing ever.

Roxy bent her knees until her face was level with Cassie's. "It was really nice meeting you. I love my tattoo. I'll be back for another."

Cassie's face was as serious as someone in her condition could get. "That would be nice. I hope that happens."

"It will."

"Okay." Cassie closed her eyes and leaned her head against the wall.

Roxy turned to me. "You going to be okay to get her home?"

"Yeah. I didn't have anything the last couple of rounds."

She turned to glance at Cassie. "Hey, can you give her this for me? In case she wants to hang out. Or you guys do."

I stared at the napkin with what was obviously her phone number written on it, making no move to take it. "Sorry, no can do. Shop policy. No dating the clients."

Roxy stared at me for a long moment, not looking like she believed me. I stared right back. I'm sure if I'd ever gotten around to making an employee manual it would be in there.

The woman finally shrugged. "It could be just hanging out."

Snatching the paper from her hand, I stuffed it in my pocket. "Yeah, okay."

"It was nice meeting you. I'll recommend you guys to all of my friends." She smiled and nodded to the club with her head. "In fact, I have a feeling Sabrina will be getting one and she doesn't do pain."

Damn. Now I had to put on my business owner hat. "That would be awesome and appreciated. You guys are welcome any time."

Roxy raised her hand in farewell and then headed inside. I turned my attention to Cassie who looked like she'd fallen asleep against the wall. Not so bad, except her skin was so pale it worried me. The rosy alcohol flush was gone.

"Come on, Tink." I slid my arm between her neck and the wall and pulled her into me. "Time to get you home."

As I drove to Cassie's place, I snuck a quick glance at her. Like last time I checked, she was pressed up against the door, eyes closed. Only Cassie would be a sleepy drunk. She was missing out on the full drunk experience of letting loose and living it up.

I tapped my fingers on the steering wheel, my rock music turned low so it wouldn't disturb her. Shifting, I stretched my left leg out, tapping my boot.

"Oh my gosh." Cassie jerked upright. "I have to text her."

I jumped, cursing as the Jeep almost swerved into the opposite lane. Next to me Cassie frantically pulled her phone from her pocket.

"What the fuck?"

"I have to send her a drunk text. She'll be so proud of me."

"Who?"

"My mom." She said it like that was completely normal.

I looked back at the road as she typed on her screen. Sighs and then grumbling came from her way. Hitting the wrong letters, I was guessing.

"There." Cassie relaxed back against the seat with a satisfied smile and closed her eyes again. A few minutes later her phone dinged. I glanced at her, but she was asleep. My leg bouncing at the next light, I stared at her phone. Fuck it. Snatching it, I hit the home button.

Mom: That's my girl. I'm so proud of you. You can hold your own hair tonight.

I chuckled. Her mom sounded like a trip. Then the "hold your hair" bit sunk in. Since it was obvious Cass had no experience with drinking, her mom had obviously been holding back her hair for something else. No big guess what. Cass had said the cancer made her really sick.

With her pixie cut there was no hair to hold back. Could it grow or would it always be like that? Unable to resist, I ran my fingers over her hair and down around her ear. It suited her as it was, showing off her sweet face.

Coming to a stop at the apartment, I noted the few people hanging outside of their doors as well in the parking lot.

How did I want to play this? I could handle them. What I didn't want was them seeing me have to support Cassie to her door. They might take her for an easy target.

Another option would be to lift her in my arms. It'd look like we were so hot for each other that we couldn't lay off long enough to walk. Problem with that was I could be opening her up to a different kind of harassment.

She shouldn't have to live in a dump like this. She shouldn't have to wait for some stupid test to start tattooing. She should be doing it now and making money.

"Fucking cancer," I grumbled as I made my way around to the passenger side.

I opened the door and she blinked at me and then smiled. "Hi," she said, her voice soft and sleepy.

Damn. A smile that sweet should give me a toothache, not a lady boner. "Hi."

"I don't think I like this cele...cele...celebration thing."

Jennie Davids   *141*

"It's not the celebrating you're having problems with. That would be the alcohol."

"Yeah." She sighed, her eyes closing. "No more bars."

"I don't know." I unbuckled the seat belt. Our eyes locked. "The dancing was pretty nice."

"Yeah." Her eyes closed again, her body swaying as if she could still hear the music. "Yeah, it was."

She held her arms up in front of her and it reminded me of the way my siblings used to do that when they were waiting for me to get them out of their car seats. But in all the times I did that for my brother and sisters, I never pulled them to me and held them because I liked the way it felt.

Cassie tucked her head into my neck, her arms tightening around me.

"I like dancing with you." She hummed something off key in my ear.

My arms circled her tighter. "You think we're dancing now, don't you?" I was standing perfectly still and her toes were barely touching the ground.

"Mm. It's nice."

Someone yelled for their kid to come home and that got me moving again. I wanted Cassie behind a locked door. I propped myself under her shoulder and wrapped my arm around her waist. I gave it a squeeze. "I like dancing with you too."

"More than you liked dancing with Sabrina?" Her eyes widened and she slapped her hand over her mouth.

I winced and pulled at her hand. "Hey, now careful." Swallowing my laugh, I kept us walking. "Now what were you saying?"

"Nothing," she said. She looked up at me, her eyes

still wide. "I don't like drinking. It makes you do things you shouldn't."

I tilted my head to the side, making room for her to tuck in close. Fuck her neighbors. I'd take her home each day if need be. I slid the side of my face against her soft hair. "You haven't done anything to be regretting. You danced. You relaxed. Now you're speaking your mind. I might start spiking your drinks."

She stopped, my arm around her the only thing keeping her from pitching forward. "Don't you dare."

I chuckled and grabbed onto the stair rail. There was little chance of that. Yeah, I liked seeing her like this. Liked her all open and relaxed. But man, there was nothing like when she sassed me. She made me work for those moments, work hard. Unlike so many things in my life that hard work paid off.

I jostled her and nodded toward the door. "You're either going to have to open that or give me the keys."

"Okay." She blinked up at me.

"You're something else."

Damned if that hadn't come out sounding like a compliment. I slid my hand into her front pocket and wiggled her keys free. Not exactly the way I'd imagined having my hand down her pants.

I had her inside and on the couch in no time. Surprised at how cold it was in her apartment, I draped her sweater over her shoulders. She looked up at me and for once her hazel eyes didn't have a filter that made sure she blended in and nothing stood out. Right now it was her. Bare.

"Thank you," she said. She brought her knees up to her chest and rested her cheek on one. "You were so nice to me tonight."

I jerked my gaze from the curve of her ass to her face. She stared at me with a soft smile. "Nice?" People didn't accuse me of that. Ever.

"Uh-huh." She reached out and put her hand on my knee. "And patient. I had fun."

She was looking at me like I'd hung the goddamn moon. I shouldn't get a thrill from that. It's exactly what I didn't want. I didn't want anyone looking to me for anything. Yet her soft, admiring gaze had me wanting to go hunt down the choicest cuts of meats. Or for Cassie, the freshest vegetables. It was so much more powerful than the lusty looks Sabrina gave me.

"Me too," I finally responded.

She chewed on her lip, still watching me, driving me insane with the way she was working over her pink flesh. She released it and I searched for any dampness, any marks, anything I could lick.

"You never answered me."

After giving her coffee table a quick glance and deciding the wood looked sturdy enough, I sat. "Answered what?"

"Who you liked dancing with better."

I gripped my hands on my knees. Yeah, I would've been dead not to be turned on by Sabrina's curves rubbing all up on me. But I'd had Cassie in my arms. I'd felt the moment she went from stiff and on-edge to relaxed and unchained. "There's no comparison."

Her face fell and she hunched over her knees. "Yeah."

I grabbed her chin, bringing her head up until she met my eyes. "You. It was you."

She hid her face in her hands. "That makes this worse."

"What?"

But I knew. It was hell being attracted to her. It'd been bad enough since that kiss. But now I'd spent even more time with her, time for me to discover how damn much I liked her. Tonight just added on to the hell. All those hours of touching her, breathing her in, wanting to take her to the bathroom and tear off all her clothes. It made it all so much…

"I took this," she said.

My chain of thoughts came to an abrupt stop. Cassie held out a crumpled piece of paper toward me.

It was Sabrina's name and number.

Hell.

"I took it from your pocket while you were helping me up the stairs."

That didn't bother me as much as not having felt Sabrina put it there in the first place. My brain had deemed Cassie no threat, but I hadn't come to any such conclusion with Sabrina. Yes I'd danced with the woman. When had I become distracted enough for her to stick something in my pocket? Scratch that. Hell it could have been any time. I'd barely been able to take my eyes off Cassie all night.

"I'm sorry," she said, staring at the slip of the paper and then back to me, frowning and chewing her lip again.

Jesus. This little Tinkerbell of an apprentice was trying to kill me. If it wasn't enough that she'd spent hours keeping me aroused, now she had to go and do something like this. So sneaky. So manipulative. So sexy. Was alcohol bringing the true Cassie out?

"Are you mad?"

I shook my head and scooted closer to the edge of the coffee table, knocking my knees against hers. "Nope."

"Oh, good."

I reached out and caressed her bottom lip with my thumb. "You were jealous, huh?"

"Very. I wanted to pull her away be her fake eyelashes."

I tried to recall Sabrina's eyes. "Were they fake?"

"I don't know, but it sounds better."

I laughed. Even after I stopped Cassie still stared at my mouth and I realized I was smiling. Of course I was. Cassie hadn't liked me being all up on Sabrina any more than I'd liked her with Roxy. Roxy, whose number was still in my pocket. Now would be the time for me to come clean and give it to her. I didn't dig it out. I couldn't take the chance my little rule-follower would chose the "no dating clients" rule to be the first she broke.

Cassie ran her tongue along her lips and flicked her gaze to mine. I groaned, holding her stare for another long second. Fuck it. I launched forward and captured her mouth with mine. Her lips opened eagerly, her tongue darting out.

I could taste the sweet drinks she'd had. I kissed her harder. I didn't want the taste of lingering alcohol. I wanted her. I wanted what I'd been obsessing about since the last time I got to kiss her.

Our tongues stroked against each other. Yes, that's what I wanted. My blood zinged and I leaned closer, pulling her tighter to me. I wanted to devour her, swallow down every moan, groan and cry.

Many kisses later, we broke apart, panting. She rested her forehead on my shoulder, her breath ghosting against my neck.

"This isn't working," I said.

"What?"

"Staying away from you. It's not working. All I want to do is kiss you, touch you, take you."

She let out a little sigh and then pulled away, her hands leaving my thighs from where she'd been balancing herself. "You might have a point." She leaned back against the sofa, staring at me. "It was much easier when you were mean. I don't feel much like kissing you then. But when you're nice you become irresistible."

Cass was becoming irresistible to me no matter what. I didn't know how much longer I could hold back. If I was denied something it made me want it more, didn't matter if I was the one doing the denying.

"Then I guess I'll have to be nice more often."

"You won't get any complaints from me."

She leaned close again, her eyelids lowering and those sweet lips pursing. Ready for me.

I clenched my fists. She worked for me. She was around the shop. She relied on me. She'd had a lot to drink. Fuck. Fuck. Fuck.

"So how bad do you want to be a tattooer?"

Cassie's eyes snapped open.

"You keep in touch with your old job, right?" I scooted closer to her as I warmed up to this idea, my fingers twitching with the need to get back to touching her. "Or there's other good shops. With working for Zan and a reference from me I'm sure you could apprentice with one of them."

She chuckled. "What?" It died abruptly as I nodded encouragingly. "You're serious. There's a reason I quit my old job. I'm not going back. I'm not going to move to another shop. I'm staying right where I am and finishing."

Her eyes flashed at me, cheeks red. Sick puppy that I was, her temper turned me on almost as much as the dancing had. "You are so fucking sexy right now."

Her mouth dropped open but it was definitely not an invitation for my tongue. She rocketed up from the sofa. She staggered, but the anger seemed to be clearing the alcohol pretty fast. "Well, you're not. You're back to being mean."

She reached past me, her elbow knocking against my hip in a way that didn't seem all that accidental. "Here." She thrust the paper with Sabrina's number at me. "I think you're going to need this."

I covered my hand over hers, not taking the paper. "But she's not who I want."

For a moment her face relaxed and I could see surprise creeping in, but then she thrust her chin up, eyes hard as they stared into mine. "You say that now. Trust me I'm a much better apprentice than a lay."

I opened my mouth because holy hell I couldn't let that go, but she thrust her arm out. She staggered to the left before quickly righting herself. "I've had enough celebrating. It's time for me to go to bed. Alone."

Two hot women had been into me tonight and I still managed not to get off. Fuck my life.

My little people pleaser stood with her head held high and finger pointed directly at the door. Warmth spread deep in my chest. Ignoring the slip of paper she continued to hold out to me, I tipped my chin. "You are a great apprentice. But I think you're selling yourself short and would also be a damn good lay."

Chapter Thirteen

Cassie

I scanned the webpage and finding nothing, clicked back out. One of them had to have answers. My eyes slowed over the words. My heart pounded. Yes, those were my symptoms. I leaned closer, jumping down to the prognosis and treatment section of the article. It gave the oh-so-helpful advice to call your doctor.

"I'm trying!" I clutched the sides of my head.

A knock came on my door.

I ignored it, clicking onto the next site.

The knock came again.

Really? I didn't put the volume of my TV over a four, I never vacuumed before ten even though I woke up early, and now when I make a peep, *a peep*, they were going to come to my door. Not answering. Screw them.

My phone rang. I snatched it up, my heart pounding so loud I had to raise my voice to drown it out. "Yes. Hello?"

"Answer your damn door." The call ended.

Taking my phone with me, I opened the door. MJ pushed past me, stomping to the middle of the room. She looked me over from the top of my unbrushed hair to the tips of my fuzzy socks.

"What the fuck is this? Why are you calling in sick?"

"Because I don't feel good."

"You can feel not good at the shop. We've got a full day."

"I can't. I'm waiting for my doctor to call in case they have any cancellations."

MJ frowned. "The doctor for a hangover?"

"I'm not hungover." The pounding of my head and the queasiness in my stomach begged to differ. "I mean, yes, I'm hungover, but that's not what I called about. It's not about last night."

I walked into the living room but didn't sit. I didn't think I could stay still long enough. I needed to be doing something. If it wasn't searching websites for information I already knew, then it could be pacing. "I'm sorry I can't come in today. I know it's inconvenient. That's why I left you a message as soon as I knew."

"Eight. You left me a message at eight."

"That's polite. I gave you as much notice as I could."

"It ain't polite when it wakes someone up. I don't need notice, I need your ass at the shop."

"I can't." I stared into her thundercloud of a face, knowing that what I was saying was displeasing her and yet I'd keep saying it. Maybe later the panic would come, but right now I was at max capacity.

MJ snatched my arm, keeping me still.

"You're feeling good enough to do a damn marathon in your apartment, so what's wrong?"

"It hurts. Right here." I heard the fear in my voice, felt it in every cell in my body. I pointed toward my chest, to the left of where my breast used to be. "Deep inside. It aches."

"Here?" MJ put her hand right over the spot I indicated.

My muscles seized and I stayed frozen. Her hand was on my chest. She had to feel that there was only flatness where there should be the softness of a breast. Unlike a lot of women who chose not to do reconstruction surgery, I didn't wear breast forms.

Breaths coming hard and fast, I met MJ's gaze. I found no pity or disgust there. They were still filled with frustration and impatience.

"That's where it started before." My words came out a whisper. Like if I didn't give them too loud of a voice, I denied them power. "Now it hurts there again. Like an ache when you've worked out. I ignored it last time. I can't this time."

MJ's hand remained against me, the warmth of it penetrating the cotton of my shirt. "Hold up. You did work out."

"No, I didn't."

"You danced last night. Toward the end you were doing some interesting moves with your arms. You probably worked some muscles you don't normally use."

Hope flared and almost as quickly extinguished. "It feels exactly the same. The same spot. Triple negative is more likely to recur. I have to catch it fast. It's not caused by hormones. Treatment options are limited."

MJ pressed her hand tighter against me and then pulled away, her expression fierce. "So you're going to stay here all day and hope your doctor can fit you in?"

"Yes."

"No."

"Um, yes. I called out."

"Get your stuff. We're leaving."

"I can't." I walked into what served as my dining area, putting the table between us. "You don't understand. I can't think. No, it's all I can think about. I can't deal with clients."

"Uh-huh. Now like I said, go get your shit."

"I can't."

"Yeah, you can." MJ crossed her arms over her chest. I was doing the same thing and yet I knew I looked like I was hugging myself, while she looked ready to take on anything, including one freaked-out apprentice. "I'm not messing around."

"MJ, please…"

"Cassie, sitting around working yourself into a panic isn't doing you any good. I'll drive you to the urgent care."

Shaking my head, I backed away. "No, they won't have my records. They don't know my story. It's different for me. I need my doctor. She was the one who was with me last time. She's the one I trust. If I'm going to get bad news, I want it from her."

"You're not going to get bad news." MJ put her hands on my shoulders and bent until our faces were level, her eyes looking right into mine. "Breathe," she ordered.

I took a deep breath. She stayed hunkered down with me. I tried to soak up some of her strength from those brown eyes, that seeming ability to face anything.

"Good," she said after a few minutes. She squeezed my shoulders and then stood to her full height. "Now go get your stuff. We're doing things my way."

If her way included standing in front of me, I might go along. She had an insulating effect that made me feel like nothing could get me.

"Come on. There's nothing to think about. Go get your stuff."

I swallowed and reluctantly moved. "If I get the needles mixed up, it'll be all your fault."

"Like I'd let that happen." She jerked her head in a "get moving" gesture.

I gathered my bag of tattooing supplies and then I grabbed a sweater, the motions repetitive and requiring very little thought.

I went for my bike, but MJ took it out of my hands and leaned back against the wall. "You're riding with me."

"If the doctor calls and they can get me in I…"

"You still have a license, right?" At my nod, she continued, "Then you'll take my Jeep. It'd be a hell of a lot faster than the bus anyway."

I couldn't argue with that. It would be faster. With the state my brain was in, I'd be lucky if I could figure out the bus routes. So instead I was going to work on people getting permanent artwork on their bodies. Maybe I was hiding my meltdown pretty well if MJ thought this was a good idea.

She nodded toward my feet. "Want to get some shoes?"

Then again, maybe not.

I changed my socks, since my flats wouldn't fit over my bright, fuzzy ones, and then followed MJ out.

My phone in my lap, I stared out the window as MJ drove to the shop.

"I didn't think I'd find you in worse shape than last night," she said.

Last night. In the panic this morning I hadn't given myself much time to think about last night. But oh, yes, last night. The memories were all there. The alcohol hadn't affected those. I remember confessing to being jealous. I remember making out with MJ on my couch. I remember she suggested that I could quit so we could hook up.

"Me either, actually," I finally spoke.

"I thought you were calling out because you were still mad at me."

I turned away from the window. "I am."

MJ's mouth twitched. "Really? I can't tell."

"You would have. I would have walked in today and been all smiles, and no matter what you did, I wouldn't have let it get to me. I would've been so sweet and fake you would've wanted to wring my neck."

"I was supposed to get that you're mad out of that?" She shook her head. "Have I taught you nothing?"

"What? I should have come in and hit you?"

"Yeah, if you think I deserve it."

I snorted. As if I'd ever do that. Still the picture of doing it was nice. "Sorry, I only do things like that in my imagination."

MJ took her right hand off the steering wheel and pressed it against the side of my head. "Don't keep it all up in here. We gotta get you to let others see it."

"Trust me you don't want to be anywhere near the clusterfuck my mind is today."

"That's where you're wrong. I want to be right up in there and see what makes you different. Different is interesting. Different is sexy."

MJ

The day was nothing but a shitfest.

I stared down at my client's hip and for one second I

seriously forgot how to do a leaf. A leaf. Tattoos didn't get more common than that.

Nothing was as easy as it should've been. One, I didn't have my apprentice and dammit, I'd gotten used to her having everything set up and waiting for me. Two, I couldn't stop staring at her. I looked for any sign that the fucking cancer could be in there, growing, trying to take her again.

No. I refused to believe it. It was a muscle twinge or some shit. She was so unused to having fun that when she finally went and had some, she sprained something.

I rubbed at my neck. I was practically losing my shit and Cassie was putting strokes down on paper, all Zen-like. She'd gone from nuclear meltdown to comatose.

I tore my gaze away and got back to the damn tattoo. In double the time it should have taken, I finally finished. As my client checked out his new ink, I stood and stretched my back. I started to strip off my gloves, the skin at my nape prickling. Looking up, I found Cassie tracking my every move.

Heat blasted through me. It was damn welcome after the chill of the helplessness I'd been rocking all day. She continued to stare, her eyes narrowed in that way they did when she was thinking about kissing. Hell, I only had to look at her to be thinking about her soft lips, the way she was so eager and aggressive when our tongues were getting into the action. Pink filled her cheeks. Oh yeah. Tossing the gloves, I took a step forward, scanning the room and snagging on Jamie, who was watching me. As soon as our eyes connected, she started my way.

Jamie nodded in greeting. "You look rough."

I snorted. "I bet."

"Long night?"

"Went out to a bar last night."

"Ah, that'll do it."

"It wasn't even the bar that's got me like this. Woke up with cotton mouth and got some water. Thirty minutes later I'm getting out of bed to pee."

Jamie laughed. "Isn't getting older grand?"

"It's like I'm eighty or some shit."

"I give you credit." Jamie patted my shoulder. "I don't even try anymore."

"I'm not quite ready to throw it all in and fall asleep on the couch watching the news like you."

"Fuck you. And I say that 'cause it's true."

I laughed and leaned my hip against the wall, getting more comfortable.

When was the last time I'd just chatted with Jamie? It'd been a long damn time.

I liked her. Hell, she'd been to my house. We used to hang out after work. She and her daughter would come over with the other women from the shop and I'd barbecue in my backyard. And there it was. The reason I didn't hang out with her or any of my remaining employees. The reason Jamie's daughter Riley had probably sprouted another six inches since I'd seen her last. Because half of the people that used to come over had ditched us. I'd thought we'd been tight, a family, and they'd left with Heidi, taken their clients with no word or explanation, leaving me to pick up the pieces and on the brink of closing. I made sure it wasn't a line between work and personal, but a deep trench.

In making sure that I never let someone betray me like that again, I hadn't let myself miss her friendship and moments like this.

"So I wanted to bring something up," Jamie said.

Because it'd been all of thirty seconds since I'd looked at her, my gaze went to Cassie. Today she didn't look away. Her eyes stayed locked on mine. My nipples tightened. Eager little fuckers.

"Yeah, that's actually what I wanted to talk to you about."

My attention snapped back to Jamie. "What?"

She tipped her chin in Cassie's direction. "What's going on there?"

"You've got to be kidding?" I folded my arms across my chest and didn't even bother keeping the "back off" out of my voice. "Nothing."

Jamie stared back at me as unflappable as ever. "You've been really nice to her."

I relaxed a bit. "I can see why that'd confuse you. I'm just trying to keep her from having a heart attack and suing my ass. She's wound tight."

"You sure that's all there is?"

It was damn hard to keep my gaze locked on Jamie and not straying to Cassie. But I couldn't look at her, not with Jamie watching. I was afraid of what she'd see. She'd been my first hire and known me for a long time. She'd seen me cry at her daughter's adoption ceremony before I could wipe away the tears. She'd been the one to step up in her quiet way the day when half the staff deserted us, while I'd sat stunned in my office until the anger, the blessed anger, came.

"I'm not stupid. Not like I've forgotten the last time I got too close to people I work with. I'm not letting that shit happen again."

Instead of her expression easing up at my words, she frowned. "You know that wasn't it, right? It wasn't because you got close to people that Heidi and the others left. It's because they're shitty people."

"Can't argue with you there. But I'm never letting that shit happen again."

Jamie nodded, the frown finally going. "Good. You're the boss, but things have been tense for a while and now things seem to be lightening up. We'd just hate for some…thing to mess that up."

The "we'd" had my muscles tightening. I didn't like the thought of the other women getting together and talking behind my back. "You all've got nothing to worry about."

"Good. If you ever need some help, you…"

"Nope, I'm good."

She didn't look surprised at me shutting her down. "I'm out." She flashed a peace sign. "Don't stay too late."

"Yeah, okay."

I turned to face the shop, which was mostly empty. Just Cass at the table and Vivian still shooting the shit with her last client. I could always count on Vivian to be here almost as late as I was. She treated the shop like it was her second home. It'd be nice if it was because of her dedication and not so she could get away from her large Vietnamese family. Not that I exactly blamed her. They sounded intense. But it only took one hard look for her to get the clue and clear out.

I locked up the front door after her and then went to the back door and did the same. I returned to the main floor to find Cassie packing away her supplies.

"Glad to see you've calmed down."

She tilted her head to keep me in her sights. "Mm hm. Art is amazing."

Her gaze did a thorough sweep of me. The kind of

gaze the girls noticed and had brought Jamie chatting.
Fuck. How did I tell her to stop looking at me like that
when it was the best part of my day?

"Do you want to see my drawings?"

Uh, there'd been no doubt I'd be seeing them. I'd just
been expecting to have to grab them from her, like I did
pretty much every day.

I held out my hand, wiggling my fingers. "I do."

Her skin brushed mine as she placed them in my
hand. Had her skin felt hot? Was she running a fever?
I didn't want to bring it up and scare her when she was
all chill. How the hell was I going to put my hand on
her forehead and check?

"Well?"

Right. The art. I flipped the first one over. Damn.
She'd drawn a large tree with a laughing woman at the
base. Behind the tree a dark shadow loomed over the
woman.

Setting that one aside, I moved on to the next.

It was of a woman's face. One side was beautiful
and normal but the other side had the skin ripped off,
revealing the muscles and sinew covered in maggots.

I wanted to tear it up, throw it away and incinerate
it. My thoughts must have shown on my face. Cassie
plucked it from my grip and put it behind her, out of
my reach.

"There's one more," she said, tipping her head toward my hand.

The air whooshed out of my lungs like some invisible hand had crushed them. She'd drawn a woman's
naked leg bent at the knee. Coming up from the bottom
of the sketch a hand stroked the woman's inner thigh.
The detail was incredible, right down to the scar on

my third knuckle from when I had been dared to leave some "artwork" on the school building. I hadn't let a barbed wire fence stop me.

Jesus. I couldn't look away. It was like she'd reached into my brain and plucked out a fantasy. One of my tamer ones for sure.

I lifted my gaze to Cassie. Passion flared in her eyes. Holy hell. If someone touched my forehead right now, I'd be the one with the fever.

Cassie pushed away from the table, starting toward me. Each step sure and so fucking sexy. I stiffened, my pulse a bombo drum at the side of my throat. I lost sight of her when she stepped behind me.

"What do you think?" she asked, pressing her body against my back.

The hair on my nape stood straight up like it was trying to get as close to possible to her. "I'm thinking my hand looks damn good on you."

"I thought so too."

Her fingers trailed up my arms, up to my shoulders, and she started kneading. I groaned, dropping my head forward and arching into her touch. I could feel the strength in her hands as they traveled over me. She was here and she was strong and that's what was important.

"You're so tense."

"Mm hm." Her breath hit my ear, her beautiful mouth so close I could hear it open, hear her tongue slick across her lip. "I think I need to do something to fix that."

Chapter Fourteen

Cassie

I moved my massage from MJ's neck to her shoulders. I'd never really considered myself a shoulder gal, but there was something about the way she always had them thrown back, ready to handle whatever was coming her way. Only now, with my fingers working there, I could feel her bones beneath, as fragile as anyone else's. Feeling that humanness gave me hope that I could be just as strong and brave as her.

"Does your mom know about the pain you have?"

My hands froze. The layer of numbness that blanketed my brain started to lift. No. It needed to stay right where it was. "Mm hm. I called her this morning."

"What does she think?"

"She told me not to worry. That it's probably nothing."

"It is nothing." MJ twisted to look at me over her shoulder.

Any other time I'd have appreciated her fierce "I've said it so it will be" look. Right now I didn't want her looking at me with anything less than a "get ready, I'm about to bend you over this table and make you come" look. I needed to see it again. If only tonight. I'd passed on that opportunity last night. I didn't want to pass on anything else.

What if...no, I wasn't going there. I just didn't want to regret not being with someone who reminded me my body was capable of giving me pleasure.

"What time is your appointment Monday?"

"One thirty."

"I don't have anything going. Want me to take you?"

What was she trying to do to me? She couldn't be sweet. Not now. I'd seen the glimpses, knew from the way she was concerned where I lived, that there was hidden kindness. But I didn't want to see it tonight. I needed the woman from last night. The one who had callously suggested I work somewhere else so she could sleep with me. That woman I could remain immune to. That woman I could use to remind me that I was alive and could go after what I wanted. And I wanted MJ.

"Thank you, but my mom is going to do it."

MJ nodded and faced forward again. I stared at the nape of her neck, specifically the spot right below her shaved hairline. Leaning down, I kissed her there. MJ's muscles tensed under my lips. "Please," I silently begged her, pressing more kisses down her neck.

She leaned away from me. "Hold up."

I stopped and stared at her, willing her to listen to her body, to feel the same desire I felt. To let this happen. I needed her to make me feel something good.

MJ twisted in the seat, looking at me over her shoulder. "What are we doing here?"

The answer was so obvious to me, but yes, I could see why it wouldn't be to her. For normal people a shoulder massage and some closed-mouth kissing weren't an invitation to sex.

"Fucking." I stumbled over the word.

She rubbed her hand over her face and let out a loud, long groan. "Cass."

Her hand fell away and we stared at each other some more, that strange calm still in me, allowing me to hold my head high as I waited for her answer.

MJ slowly rose to her feet, her eyes searching mine. "That's it? That's all you want from me?"

All? It seemed like a heck of a lot. "Yes."

She growled and stepped up to me. "It doesn't change anything. No special favors. No special treatment."

"Sh." I covered her lips with my fingers. "Don't ruin it. I'm not asking for anything. And you're right, nothing's changing. I'm not quitting. I'm not apprenticing for someone else. This is about sex. This is about me shutting my brain off and enjoying sex. Just sex. Two bodies."

Between one pounding heartbeat and the next, MJ's lips slammed down on mine.

I wrapped my arms around her neck and tugged her even tighter. She tasted of coffee. Mixed with the taste of her, I didn't mind the hint of bitterness. I gripped the back of her neck, holding her where I wanted so I could take more of her mouth.

"How do you taste so good?" I licked at her lips.

Her hands gripped my hips hard enough to bruise. Good. I wanted bruises. I wanted proof that she desired me as much as I desired her.

Desperate to feel more of her, I yanked her tank top from her pants.

For one torturous moment she remained tense, separate from me and then she pressed her forehead against mine. "Let's do this." She pushed away, pulling her top off and revealing the black thin strap sports bra she wore underneath. "I'm done. I fucking want you."

She stood unashamed, not seeming to care that her head and shoulders would be visible if anyone were lurking outside the front windows. I took in all of her golden skin. Until my hand came into my view, I didn't realize I'd held it out toward her, the need to touch so strong. She remained still as I pressed my palm flat against her collarbone.

"Warm," I said, curling my fingers. "I'd wondered if your skin was as warm as it looked." I kept my hand there, trying to soak some of it into my body. I was always cold.

MJ's knees knocked into mine, a cocky grin on her mouth.

I trailed my fingers to the edge of her sports bra, running them up and down the strip of fabric, hoping I'd get a chance… No. I wasn't going to wait for a chance. This was it. My chance.

I slowly lowered my head to her neck, inhaling her outdoorsy scent. I followed the ridges of her collarbone with my tongue. In my excitement my teeth grazed her. She shuddered. If I didn't stop, there'd be a mark. I sucked harder, wrapping myself tighter around her. Even if everyone saw it, they'd never guess it'd come from me. Never me.

MJ gripped the back of my neck, pulling my head away. "I'm a big believer in payback."

I nodded eagerly, exposing my neck. My only regret was no one would ever see it with the clothes I wore.

While her mouth worked at my neck, she bent me

backwards. Her arms went all the way around my waist and slipped below my butt, lifting me up. She set me on the edge of the drafting table. The fluorescent lights backlit her as she stood in front of me, making her appear even more imposing.

I moaned. I'd never have thought I'd like being maneuvered like that, but it was strangely freeing. I didn't have to worry about what she wanted me to do, she just did it. Another moan broke free.

"You like that, huh?" She pulled my thighs apart, making room for herself.

Wetness gathered between my legs. I was ready. My body was ready.

When she took a step back, I clutched at her with my hands, my thighs, everything.

"This has got to go." She tugged at the sleeves of my sweater.

Yes. Yes, that was a good idea. Not relaxing my grip from around her waist, I pulled my left arm free while MJ worked on my right.

She tossed my sweater to the side. "Much better." Crawling over me, she used her body to push me down to the table. She deployed her tongue like a weapon, seeking out all the places that made me gasp. Wrist. Elbow. Ear.

"Oh god." She kissed a path from my ear to my neck. Instinctively, I tensed, wanting to protect that vulnerable spot, but I forced myself to relax, to experience the sublimeness of her lips against my skin.

"Jesus, do you bathe in sweetness?" MJ's tongue made another long stripe. "Mm. You taste so fucking good."

"Natural olive oil soap with cinnamon," I said, my

voice throaty as my eyes rolled back and she continued to suck on my skin.

She pushed herself up. Her look was another variation of the "are you for real" one she loved to give me, but this time her eyes were dilated and...fond?

She groaned and pressed our crotches together. "Fuck, you're hot."

My hips lifted towards her. "You too."

Her lip quirked at the corner and I couldn't stop myself from pressing my finger against it. "Is that what you were really thinking?"

"In my head I used the word 'sexy.'"

"I'll take sexy." She reared up and grabbed my lower lip in her mouth, nibbling on it. "And I'm gonna take a whole lot more."

Her tongue parted my lips, demanding entry. Instead of just opening to her, I nipped the tip of her tongue. Then it was on. Our tongues dueled and our teeth grazed and nipped. There was no space for worries or self-consciousness. It was all about keeping up with her.

Breathing hard, I pressed my head against the table. I wasn't sure who'd won that battle of a kiss, but it'd been fun.

Her quick grin my only warning, MJ rolled me until she lay beneath me and I was straddling her. Slowly her grin faded, glee lingering in her eyes.

She slid her hands up my waist. Up her hands went until she reached the edge of my camisole.

I jerked, pressing my arms tight against my body to stop her from raising it any further. "It stays on."

MJ froze. I'm sure it was only seconds, but it felt

like decades before she pulled her hands from under my shirt and slowly lowered them to my thighs.

I curled my hands into fists and pressing them into my stomach.

Let her take my shirt off and watch her become disgusted by my scars? Or keep it on and have her constantly reminded of what she was missing out on?

"Is there anywhere else?"

I looked at her miserably. "What?"

Her face was completely expressionless. If not for the slight flush to her cheeks and the slight pull of strain around her mouth, it was like these last incredible minutes had been all in my imagination.

"Anywhere else off limits?"

I shook my head, hating every second of this. I hated that we were even having to speak of it right now.

"All right then. There's still plenty to work with." She grinned up at me.

Acid burned the back of my throat. I knew what her real grin looked like, had seen it mere minutes ago. She was being phony, the thing she detested most, the thing I never associated with her. Because of me.

Fingers trembling, I reached down and cupped her face. "I'm sorry."

Chapter Fifteen

MJ

The lust pouring through me shifted to something softer. The hands that had been gripping, cupped. Instead of grinding, I held her. I turned my head and kissed her palm. "Nothing to apologize for. I'm not a one spot woman. There's plenty of other places of yours to keep me entertained."

That earned me the saddest excuse for a smile I'd ever seen. Oh hell no. Only thing I wanted on her face was a blissed-out look from all the orgasms I'd given her.

Was she a screamer? Tonight she would be.

I hooked my leg over her hip and rolled until her back lay against the table. "I like this view," I said, staring down at her.

Her gaze dropped away. The rosy color on her cheeks was not the soft pink that so often happened when she caught me being a creeper and staring. This was deep and festering. This was shame.

Tonight had become about more than orgasms. It was also about proving to Cassie she was still a sexy woman.

I went back to the bottom of her tank top, waiting

until her muscles relaxed before I inched it up to her belly button. Watching her reaction, I slowly lowered my face until I could kiss her stomach. Her muscles jumped but when she made no other move, I flicked my tongue in her innie.

"Think I need to switch up. Start calling you Snow White." I licked at her pale skin. "Fairest of them all."

"Your tough girl image is on the line with all these…" She gasped as I kissed her again. "Disney references," she finished.

I unbuttoned her jeans and then moved on to the zipper, the metal warm from her body. "I think I'm safe. Got just as many *Suicide Squad* references. They just don't fit for you." I tugged at her jeans. "Lift up."

Her hips arched and I slid her jeans down. The fabric moved easily, revealing her legs. Some pants were so damn tight I was tired and sweating before I even got to see the goods.

My mouth salivated at all of her creamy skin. My gaze skimmed over her hips and stopped at her panties. Her white panties with palm trees all over them.

She met my incredulous stare with a blush and tried to turn her hips to hide them. A move I quickly blocked.

"I can't believe I'm going to fuck someone wearing palm trees."

"Hopefully I won't be wearing them when we get to the fuc-fucking."

Ah, Jesus. She was going to kill me with the way she kept stuttering that word. I rubbed my thumb across the skin of her stomach. "You're right. Time for them to go."

I pulled her underwear down and nuzzled her belly before detouring to her hipbones. Then I went lower, to the triangle of light brown hair. She jerked, her knee skimming my chin as she tried to close her legs.

She rose to her elbows, staring down at me. "Um. It's untrimmed. I... That is... It all fell out with chemo. Now that it's grown back, I've kept it."

I ran my fingers through the coarse hair. I'd never cared much one way or another if a woman was all bare or kept some. Now I knew I never wanted to see Cassie bald down here.

I slipped my finger to the slit in her folds to find her wet. More. Give me fucking more. I slid down and widened her legs with my shoulders.

"Look at you all wet for me. So beautiful." I lowered my head and licked her. Her taste burst in my mouth. Spicy and sexy as hell. With the next swipe of my tongue her moan filled the empty shop. It sounded even better than the buzz of my tattoo gun.

I ran my tongue over her, varying from hard to lighter, judging when her hips rose, the way her breath stuttered, learning the rhythm that set her off the most. Two quick swipes and then one long, deep lick.

Her hands gripped the back of my neck, pulling me into her. I centered on her opening, gathering the wetness and swallowing it down.

"Oh god, MJ." Her voice broke in the middle of my name.

I licked and sucked and fucked her with my tongue and fingers until she was grinding against me, head thrown back, cheeks flushed pink, desperate cries urging me on. Everywhere our skin touched mine blazed. I was on fire inside, burning.

"MJ. MJ... Ah." Her thighs locked against my head, her muscles trembling and then she was coming.

As the aftershocks racked her, I gentled my mouth. Her fingers loosened their tight grip in my hair, and I missed the sting. I gave one last, soft, lingering swipe and then turned to kiss her thigh. Wiping my mouth on my arm, I moved up her body until I straddled her thighs.

Damn. Eyes closed, skin glistening, she looked like something out of a fairytale. An X-rated one. Which happened to be my favorite.

I reached up and laid my head against her forehead. Her skin was warm and a little sweaty, but I was the cause of that, not some fever.

Her eyes opened and she gave me a dreamy smile, and yeah I didn't care about the whys of why I was looking at her instead of trying to get off.

"Hi," she said.

I was pretty sure my answering smile was even cheesier, seeing as I hadn't just come. "Hi."

Her face was so damn relaxed. It was like the orgasm had shut off all the extracurricular activities of her brain.

Her head lolled to the side, taking me in. "You've still got your boots on don't you?"

"Uh, yeah."

Her lips twitched. "Why don't you take them off now? It's safe."

I frowned as I crawled off of her and got to my feet. "You're pretty bossy for someone who just got off."

Her smile widened and she angled her head, keeping me in sight without lifting it. "You're pretty grumpy. But we'll fix that."

"Hell yeah, we will." Inspired to hurry the fuck up, I unlaced my boots and kicked them off. Yup, standing in my socks, my toughness factor went down ten points. Thank god I never had to shed my tattoos.

Of course it was Cassie who had to point out that I felt all naked and shit without my boots. Even blissed out, the girl noticed so much. Too much. I slid my pants down, taking my boxer briefs with them.

"Wait." She rose up to her elbows. "Pull those back up."

I started to grab my cargos, but she shook her head. I let them go and instead grabbed the waistband of my drawers.

"Yes." She drew the word out in a breathy way that would do Enchantress proud.

She licked her lips, her gaze riveted to me.

This was different. Usually the women I was with put on the show in some delicate lace number or a matching set.

I slipped my finger under the wide elastic band of my not delicate lace underwear and let it snap against my skin.

A tiny whimper came from her throat. That needy sound scorched my remaining patience. I grabbed my sports bra. I froze. If she was keeping hers covered, should I?

In the split second of my indecision, Cassie's smile faded, the shadows returning to her eyes.

Nope. None of that. Keeping the bra on, I pounced. I straddled her and had my mouth on her fast enough to swallow her startled umph. It took two swipes of my tongue before she responded. Then with a moan she let me into the sweetness that was her mouth.

"Touch me," I panted.

She palmed me through the outside of my boxer

briefs. I groaned and pressed into her hand. I'd been expecting a shaky caress down my back, maybe my hip. No, she went straight for it and I couldn't have been more grateful.

Wasting no time, she wedged her hand into my underwear.

"Fuck. Yes." One of her fingers entered me, stroking my wet flesh. "Faster."

She sat up, her other hand wrapping around my waist. Her lips found my neck, sucking at my skin.

"Yes, there. Right there." I flung my head back, squeezing my legs around her hips. Another of her talented fingers entered me while she circled my clit with her thumb. So close. So close. Just…

"Fuck, yes." My eyes slammed shut as the orgasm hit me. For a few damn good seconds nothing else existed but the high of a fucking good orgasm.

At first my own harsh pants were the only thing I could hear, but eventually the indie band playing at the cafe down the street registered.

Cassie's fingers slipped from me and I groaned. The moisture from my orgasm glistened on her finger. Grabbing it, I licked it clean.

She jerked, her mouth falling open. "Um, wow." Her fingers twitched. "That's really sexy."

I bit the tip of her finger. "This is nothing. I've got so many moves to make those eyes go big."

"Many?"

"Many," I confirmed, crawling up her body. "Where's that notebook of yours? You can write down which one you like best." I lowered my head, swallowing her gasp of my name.

Who knows how long later, I flopped back on the

table and wondered if I'd be able to peel my sweat soaked skin off it. My chest struggled to get enough air in. A mind-blowing sixty-nine would do that to you. Next to me, Cassie was panting just as hard. Like me, she lay on her back. For some reason I'd pegged her as a cuddler. But nope, the arm that I'd flopped down next to her wasn't being used as a pillow.

I sighed, content. "Fuck, that was good."

"Uh-huh."

"I think that puts to rest you're a bad lay crap."

The woman might not use her mouth to speak up, but holy hell could she use it to eat me. I'd never be able to sketch on this table again without thinking about our sixty-nining. If my pants were closer, I'd pull out my pocketknife and carve something into the table.

I lay there, the thought of ordering supplies not even enough to get my ass moving. I could stay here all effin night with Cassie's warm body next to me all...

Cassie jumped off the table, lurching forward a few steps and then catching herself on a stool.

"You okay there?"

She bent over and snatched up her underwear. "Yeah, I'm just really tired and the table's not that comfortable."

I grunted in agreement and sat up, twisting until my back gave a satisfying crack. Cassie bent over to pick up her jeans and I stared at her beautiful ass before it was covered with the clothes she was hurriedly putting on.

Guess there wasn't going to be a round three. I scooted to the edge of the table and pushed to my feet. I stared at my clothes for a long moment before actually making the effort to get them.

"Well, I'm going to go," she said, her hand gesturing to the door.

I hopped in place, one leg halfway into my boxer briefs. "I drove you."

The leftover pink in her cheeks deepened. "Oh, I forgot."

She hadn't been kidding about only wanting some fucking. What'd she think I was going to do? We'd relieved some stress and it'd been good. I wasn't going to be showing up with a U-Haul. If we were only going to have one time, it would've been nice to draw it out.

I snatched her arm as she went to pass me. "Why are you getting weird?" I asked.

Cassie

"Weird? I'm not getting weird."

MJ dropped my arm. "And now you're back to this shit."

What shit? All I wanted was to go home. I needed to get home. I needed a cup of tea and a warm blanket. I rubbed my hands up and down my arms. Even though I was dressed I felt cold, exposed.

She shook her head while she buckled her belt. "You think I can't tell something's off? Instead of giving me some 'everything's fine' bullshit, how about the truth?" She shot me a knowing glance as if she read me from cover to cover and knew all the contents.

"The truth? You want the truth? Fine. The truth is while you lay there—" I pointed to the table "—with your smug smile, my mind was bombarding me with all the things I should do to make it up to you."

MJ stopped tying her laces, giving me her full attention. "Make what up?"

She could not be serious. "For this." I waved my

hand in front of my chest. "I know what I'm missing. Unlike you I couldn't just lie there and enjoy what we'd just done. No, my mind was filled with what it'd take to make you forget what you weren't getting. How many orgasms? Did I need to start yoga so I could try some crazy position."

"Cassie…" MJ stepped toward me.

I shook my head and backed up, pacing a tight circle around the table. "I'm backsliding."

MJ planted herself in my pacing path and grabbed on to my shoulders. "I'm not missing out on anything. Now explain this backsliding thing."

"I was doing better." I twisted my hands in front of me. The calm that came from drawing, the peace after the orgasm—gone, all gone. This was worse than this morning. The pain was still there, I knew it might be back, but now I got to add that I hadn't changed. Sex was still a failing for me.

"Before tonight, I was doing better. Those thoughts in my head telling me I need to do more, that if I only do this someone will like me—I didn't hear them as often. Now they're as loud as ever."

MJ squeezed my shoulders tight. "I've got some facts to shut them the hell up. I don't come hard like that for everybody. I don't want to kiss and touch and fuck someone I don't find hella sexy."

I shook my head. It didn't matter what she said. I didn't believe it. I didn't believe that MJ wouldn't miss what I no longer had. I didn't believe what I had left was enough to make up for it.

"It doesn't matter." I crossed my arms over my chest. "I want to go home."

Chapter Sixteen

Cassie

I lowered the kickstand of my bike, propped it on the porch, and smoothed my hands down my pants. I really wished my nerves would give me a break. After this day that I'd intended to just spend freaking out at home, they should be all worn out. Yet here they were making my hand tremble as I rang the doorbell. It was ridiculous to be nervous to visit my own parent.

The door opened and there stood my dad. His eyes went round. "Cassie. What are you doing here?"

"I wanted to visit." I swallowed. It was late. I always kept it between nine and seven, business appropriate hours. "I hope that's okay."

He stared at me for another long second before opening the door wider. "Of course, come in. You surprised me. You've never come over without calling before."

True. I'd inherited my aversion to spontaneity from him and had always been considerate of that. Also if you asked beforehand you were assured of your welcome. "I was close by and wanted to see you."

His scrutiny landed on my bike. He looked up and down the street before motioning me forward. If it wasn't dark out, I'm sure he would have had me wheel it around to the back.

"So…we're watching some TV."

I followed him to the living room, his shoes tapping on the tile floors. Even though he'd gotten off work hours ago, they and his tie remained on.

My stepmom, Lesley, tilted her head back on the sofa. "Who was at the do…?" Her eyes widened as she spotted me. "Cassandra."

I flinched. Had I really thought that calling myself Cassandra—even though my given name was Cassie— would make me sound more sophisticated and endear me to his new wife? It wasn't about a name. As soon as I'd quit my job, my father had reverted to calling me Cassie. If only I could go back and shake my fifteen-year-old self. Or maybe hug her.

"Cassie came to visit for a little while," my father said.

"Oh."

I lifted my hand in a wave. My half brother and half sister glanced at me, and I received a nod and a half-hearted smile before they went back to watching the TV. I shifted my weight, searching for a place to sit. They'd changed the furniture since the last time I'd been here. My father and stepmom looked comfortable on the couch. My half siblings took up the only other chairs in the room. That left me taking a seat on the edge of the fireplace.

I stared at the screen because that's what everyone else was doing, but I didn't recognize the show. Not surprising since I only had basic cable and worked late most nights so MJ could take as many clients as possible.

I gripped my hands tighter, the silence uncomfortable. At least for me. Maybe no one else was wondering whether they should fill it or leave them alone and not interrupt.

"So is everything all right?" my dad asked, staring at me expectantly.

"Yes, I just…" I trailed off as Abigail, my half sister, glared at me over her shoulder and put her finger to her lip.

Lesley patted my father's thigh. "Why don't you and Cassandra go into your study? I'll fill you in on what you miss later."

"All right." He stood and inclined his head, heading toward his study.

At least this room was the same. I took my customary seat across from him at his desk.

"How are you? Is everything going well in your recovery?"

I swallowed down an inappropriate laugh. He made it sound like I was getting over an addiction. "Everything is good."

He cared, I reminded myself. He'd visited me in the hospital. He'd called. He'd even arranged for a cleaning service to come to my house once a week when I'd been too sick to take care of it myself.

Still, that care wasn't evident as we silently stared at each other. Did he feel the wrongness of this? We were father and daughter. I carried half of his genes. Yet we still couldn't talk to each other.

"Right, well." My father cleared his throat. "You must have had a reason for coming here this late. Did you need something?"

I needed so many things. Money, security, but right

now, more than anything I craved a hug. I wanted him to wrap his arms around me and assure me that everything was going to be fine. That I was fine. I wanted the one thing he would never provide.

I shook my head and smiled. "I had a bad day at work and wanted to see you."

No, that wasn't true. Work had been the one positive in this terrible day. Not exactly hard when it had started with the unalleviated terror that my cancer was back. My foolhardy idea to prove I was alive and strong by having sex with MJ hadn't improved anything. Voicing the specifics of my day to my father would be pointless. I could predict his reactions to those events—empty platitudes about my cancer recurrence fears and condemnation for sleeping with my boss.

He looked confused by my words, like he couldn't fathom why I would seek him out for a bad day, but then his brow smoothed. "I imagine that is going to happen often with the new...career path you've chosen. The tattooing industry is unstable and not at all what you're used to working in. Not to mention the type of people you're in contact with."

I pulled up the sleeve of my sweater, baring my "diamond with a flaw" quote. "People like me?"

The first time he'd seen one of my tattoos, he'd actually paled. My stepmother had shaken her head and asked when I would be done rebelling.

Done? That had been my start. Not much of one for a woman who'd been twenty-six. I'd been too busy blending in and achieving a 4.0 and trying to earn a place with them. Fat lot of good it did me. Tonight was a prime example of that. I'd conformed and twisted myself and it still wasn't enough. All I'd wanted was to be

included. To be part of this family too. Yet I never was.
I was always the guest, not the member.

"That's different," he said. "You were going through
some life-changing events. It makes sense you wouldn't
think of all the repercussions."

After sex with MJ, I'd been desperate to make it up
to her for being so lacking. That desperation had felt so
natural. It'd felt right. And I'd known I needed to come
here. I needed to see what happened when I gave into
that desperation. I'd done it with my father my whole
life up until my "life changing events." I'd done everything I could to make sure he remembered me, the
daughter he saw on the weekends. I'd followed all of
his advice, excelled at everything. Now I needed to see
what it had gotten me.

"Actually the reason I'm upset is because of my actions, not the other way around," I said.

"Today, but it's only a matter of time before a place
like that rubs off on you."

I was fairly certain he thought I worked in some
biker gang shop like they portrayed on TV. If he'd ever
taken time to come see either Zan's place or Thorn &
Thistle, he might be surprised at how professional the
space was and how "normal" our clientele was.

"So your suggestion is to go back to my other job?"

"Yes."

"Isn't that giving up?"

My father shook his head. "That doesn't matter."

"Why?"

"Because you were good at what you did."

I had been good. My brain's ability to foresee every
possible way something could go wrong had been an
asset. I'd had a plan A, plan B, plan C for every even-

tuality. And yes, I'd taken satisfaction in being needed. "But I wasn't happy."

My father snorted. "A job isn't about being happy. It's about having security, the ability to provide for yourself. The pride of knowing what you do and that you do it well."

I tilted my head back to stare up at the ceiling. I'd had all of that. I'd met his definition of success. But still I hadn't been welcomed into the fold. Still I was held at a distance. I'd been so careful to follow the path that would please him and still I couldn't get what I wanted.

I'd done the same at the shop. I'd tried so hard, done everything to make the girls like me. They didn't. No matter what I did, I wasn't getting what I wanted. I wasn't happy.

The thread that led back to my unhappiness was my actions.

If I went back to the corporate world, I'd regain my father's approval. But it'd never be the love I'd wanted, the sense of belonging. Not if it could be given and taken away by no more than what I did for a living.

"Cassie." My father's sharp voice drew my attention back to him. From his impatient look, I guessed it wasn't the first time he'd said my name. "Why did you come to me? What is it you're wanting?"

That was the question wasn't it? Why had I come to him when it was usually my mom I'd seek out? Tonight it'd seemed imperative to come to him in my shaken state.

I stared across the desk at the man who'd given me my eye color and underbite, but that I hardly knew.

"I wanted to see if I'd wasted all those years trying to get you to like me and be proud of me. I wanted to see how important it is. If all that effort makes a difference." I sighed. "It doesn't."

"Cassie…"

I stood and motioned for him to stay where he was. "I'll see myself out. You stay with your family."

MJ

I jumped to my feet as the blond of Cassie's hair came into view on the stairs to her apartment.

She froze and then obviously recognizing it was me, continued forward. "What are you doing here?"

"I needed to talk to you." I shoved my hands in my pockets and rocked back and forth on the balls of my feet.

"Sorry I had my phone on silent." Cassie had one hand on her bike and the other digging around for her keys.

I stood at her back, shaking my head. For fuck's sake. Her keys should be out and ready. Someone could come up behind her while she was distracted and vulnerable. Though the only thing I'd noticed in the hour that I'd been waiting for her was the neighbors' curtains fluttering as they kept peeking out at me.

I took hold of her bike, freeing her other hand up so she could hurry up and get inside.

"I didn't call," I said in response. "This needs to be done in person."

"Okay," she said.

Okay? With the way I'd spit that out, Cassie should be all panicky and thinking the worst. I couldn't help it though. I'd made it halfway to my house after dropping her off before I turned around, unable to leave her alone—only to find her not here.

"Do you want to come in?" She held the door open.

"Yeah."

Cassie went over to the couch and took a seat, staring up at me with a slight smile. What the hell? The woman who'd demanded to be taken home had seemed seconds from a breakdown.

"What did you want to talk to me about?" she asked.

"About what happened tonight."

"I'm okay now."

Ah, yeah, her yoga teacher vibe kinda clued me into that. All namaste and shit. Well, I wasn't okay. Yeah, we'd done exactly what we agreed to do, but I couldn't leave it like that.

"I didn't feel right after I dropped you off," I said.

My mind couldn't shake the hopeless expression she'd been wearing as she practically jumped out of my Jeep.

Her hand landed on my knee and she patted it. "Thank you. That was very sweet of you." She smiled at the frown I flung at her. "Don't worry. I won't tell anyone about this side of you."

I rubbed my hands over my face. Fuck it, my eyeliner had to be trashed after this crapfest of a day. "Okay what the hell happened after I dropped you off?"

"I'm taking my power back."

"I'm glad that we got that cleared up. What does that even mean?"

She lifted her chin. "It means that the only voice I'm going to listen to is the one that has my best interests at heart. The one that speaks for me, not what I think others want from me."

There was a strength in her voice, in her words, in the way she met my eyes that I'd only see brief flashes of before. My chest expanded with pride, but also a slight prick. "I guess you won't need me mentoring you for anything other than tattooing. Good on you."

"I wouldn't go that far."

"No? Hell maybe you need someone else. Someone who was nice probably wouldn't have caused your back-sliding or whatever."

She tucked her face against the cushion and brought her knees up to her chest. She'd toed off her shoes, leaving behind pink striped socks. My apprentice might wear boring-as-hell clothes but she had a thing for colorful socks and shoes. Some type of foot fetish or just where the least amount of people would notice? Before I was done with her, I'd have her in some of those colorful leggings. Ones with skulls and crossbones.

With a small smile on her face she continued, "I had a mentor that was gentle and nurtured me."

I dropped my gaze down to my boots. I might be looking at the scuffed black leather, but it was Zan's face I was seeing. Would she be disappointed with the way I'd handled this apprenticeship?

Cassie's hand landed on my thigh, drawing my attention back to her.

That small smile remained. "It worked for me then. You're the mentor I need now."

My throat seemed to shrink, making swallowing damn hard. "For tattooing?"

"Yes and more. Tonight I'm determined, but I know that I'm not going to suddenly stop caring what other people think or stop wanting to make them like me. I'll still need your help."

"Okay, yeah, that's good." I cleared my throat and licked my lips, feeling uncharacteristically nervous. "I think I could help you with something else. I thought about it tonight after…" My hand flopped around in a stupid back and forth motion until I stuffed it under my thigh. "Anyway I think I can help out."

Her smile dimmed. "With my reaction after sex."

"Yeah, but to the whole thing. I wanna help you believe that you're hella good at sex—which you are."

Behind her eyes I could see the gears churning. Knowing her she had some chart in her brain where she was trying to figure out who it would benefit more, some risk analysis thing.

"Wouldn't you like to enjoy your climax and have your brain shut the hell up?"

Her eyes flared, her body swaying closer to me.

"I can see the answer in your face." I ran my finger down her flushed cheeks. "That's where I was going wrong. I was all about getting you to stop giving a shit what other people think about you. I need to add 'stopping you from listening to the fucked up stuff you tell yourself.'"

"What is your plan?"

"Practice. Lots and lots of practice. What do you call it when you keep doing it until you believe how hard you get me off?"

She licked her lips and it was hard not to lean forward and capture her tongue. "Desensitization."

"Yeah. That. That's what I'm going to do to you."

"I think this idea of yours has merits."

"Hell, yeah it does." I scooted closer, my hips bumping hers.

She held up a hand. "Not tonight, though. It's been a long day."

"One fucked up day," I said over her.

We both laughed. A peace settled over us. One that should have been there after the sex.

"Yeah, I'm exhausted and can't do another...session," she said.

I held up my hands. "Didn't think you would." I was attracted to Cassie and I couldn't imagine a time if she said "I want sex" that I wouldn't be rearing to go, but right now this was nice. Real nice. "So what are your plans for the rest of the night?"

She shot me a look out of the corner of her eye. "I was going to watch the news."

I nodded like that was something I did at the end of the day too, not watch YouTube videos until I fell asleep. "Sounds good."

She grabbed the remote and soon her TV was filled with a fuzzy picture of newscasters, their droning voices already having me tuning out.

Nothing was said about me leaving, so I settled more comfortable, my shoulder close to Cassie's head. Close enough that I could feel the prickle of a few of her hairs. The peace of this moment was cruel when so much could be happening unseen in Cassie. The reminder was there trying to steal this moment.

"It's going to be okay," I said.

She nodded, more of her hair tickling my arm.

I rested my hand on her thigh. "I mean it. You're fine. It'll come back nothing."

It had to.

Chapter Seventeen

MJ

My laptop perched on my thighs, feet kicked up on my coffee table, I inputed the totals into the program that was supposed to make doing the bookkeeping easy. Easy for who? Obviously not someone who scraped by high school with C's. I hit enter and frowned. Wait. That wasn't right. I knew that much. But not enough to know why it wasn't right.

I looked down at my cat, Snickers, on the cushion next to me. "Do you know which of the bajillion steps I did wrong? Because I have no fucking cl…"

My cell rang. I lunged for it, catching my laptop before it slid off my lap, but not before startling my cat. Snickers scrambled from the couch, tearing down the hall. I'd probably be paying for that later by her pissing somewhere other than the litter box.

Snatching up my phone, I glanced at the screen and deflated. Usually seeing my brother's name was a good thing. Today I really needed it to be Cassie's name. Cassie, who was at her doctor's office.

"Hey, bud, what's up?"

"Mom and dad suck."

"Uh, yeah, tell me something I don't know."

My brother, Javier, sighed with all the gusto of a teenager sure they had it bad in life.

"So what are they being sucky about this time?"

"Dad's making me go to the sites with him. I don't want to learn all that stuff. I just want to play my games."

All that stuff. Had he really called to bitch about having to go to the one place I used to love above all others? Not only had I loved the work, I'd loved doing it with my dad, the way he'd introduce me around to the guys on site, pride in his voice. In the end that hadn't been enough. All those years, all those memories, hadn't been enough. No matter how skilled I was with power tools didn't make up for me being queer.

Pain shot through my jaw. Okay, time to ease up on the clenching. That was the past. It wasn't worth tooth surgery. Needles in the gums were just as bad as piercing ones.

I wiggled my fingers trying to entice Snickers in coming back. "What's mom done to go on the shit list?"

My brother snickered at my cussing. I worried about him. He was sixteen. He sure as hell better be cursing by now or I'd completely failed as an older sister.

"She's making me go."

"Ah, you poor thing. Hey, I have this crazy idea. You could say no." I glanced at the clock. Two thirty. Still nothing from Cassie. I rolled my shoulders trying to get rid of the tension that'd set up shop there today. "It's not like they're going to tie you up and force you to go or withhold meals or something."

"I can't do that." The words came out in one long whine. "I'm not like you."

No, he wasn't. That's why our father still took him to the site and wanted to be around him. Hell, that was probably why they had Javier and my two other sisters. My mom and dad hadn't been able to have any more kids after me. They'd always seemed okay with it, but it wasn't too long after I came out, after everything changed, that they'd adopted Javier and his sisters. All coincidence of course. I couldn't even blame my parents. They were damn good kids. Better than I'd ever been.

"So you called to bitch?"

Another long sigh. "No."

"Uh-huh."

"Okay, fine. Maybe. But it wasn't the only reason."

"Hit me with it."

"I'm trying to get Mom and Dad to let me come see you this summer."

I snorted. "How's that going?"

"Not so good."

I bet. Imagine how much I could corrupt him.

Since I'd moved to Portland, they'd visited a grand total of zero times. I'd returned a few times. There was nothing like going back home after a long absence to make you feel like the leftover ratty chair in a roomful of new matching furniture.

"I'll be back for your graduation," I said.

"I'm not giving up yet."

"So everything else going okay?"

"Yeah. Everything is the same. It's so boring here."

Ah yes, the joys of being a teenager in small town Arizona. I remembered it well. Unlike me, he didn't have being queer to spice things up. Queer in our conservative town made things very interesting. "That's why there's video games. A client of mine told me about a really cool one, *World of Warcraft* or something."

"That's a subscription Dad doesn't let me do that. I have to have the game."

Jesus, I really was getting old. Didn't they all have those plastic games that you shoved into the slot? That's what was happening when I last stopped paying attention. "Go outside and explore."

"It's too hot out there."

I looked out the window to the cloudy skies. "You don't know how good you have it." I could barely remember what it was like to go outside and not have a layer of goosebumps on my skin. It was my winter coat.

"Ugh. Yeah, yeah I know. Just think of lots of fun stuff for us to do when I get there."

Fun. What the hell did I know about fun? I owned a business. My back ached all the time. The mail was something to be avoided because it now came color-coded so I'd know how past due I was on utilities. The only person I was qualified to show a good time to was a straight-laced apprentice who didn't know any better.

"I'll get right on that." On the nonexistent chance my parents said yes, he could spend the day at the shop with me. Tattoos. Women. Bare skin. Hell, he'd think he'd died and gone to heaven. I used to.

"I don't know why they won't just let me. I'm sixteen now. Maybe it'll help if you ask too."

Ha. I hadn't asked for shit from them since I was seventeen and graduated high school. I wasn't going to start now. "Sorry, bud. You're on your own."

Just like me.

We hung up after that. I flung myself back on my

couch and scrubbed my hands over my face. Enough. I was done being patient and waiting for Cassie to call.

I snatched my phone and didn't go the polite route with a text. Whatever the response, I wanted to hear it, not see some words on a screen. One ring. I rechecked the clock again. Did the simple math in my head. Over two hours. Two rings. Damn, she must have it silenced, which meant she was probably still in the doctor's and couldn't answer. Three rings. Or she'd gotten bad news and wasn't answering.

"Hello?"

My breath rushed out of me and I was hella glad I was already sitting down. Damn old knees might've gotten weak. "Hey, it's MJ."

"Hi."

"Any news?"

"Yes. I got an all clear." Then in a muffled voice she said, "It's my boss."

"Hi, sorry," she said, coming back on the line. "I'm all good. She, uh, thinks I probably overexerted myself."

I pressed my hand down on the cushions to keep myself steady. She was okay.

I shook my head. Of course she was okay. There was no need for me to go getting messy about it. "Yeah? Like from dancing?"

"That's one theory."

I bet her cheeks were as red right now as they'd been on Friday night when she'd been splayed naked on the table. "So how long you been sitting on the good news?"

There was a long pause on her end. "We left the doctor's about an hour and a half ago I think."

"Ah, so you would have gotten around to telling me tomorrow at least."

"I didn't want to bug you on your day off."

Right. My day off that I'd spent sitting here not being able to get shit done because I knew about her appointment. I should be glad she didn't call. I should be giving thanks that she didn't know I'd sat here worrying over her. What she didn't know, she couldn't use against me. We weren't in a relationship, weren't ever going to be. But damn it she should have called just so I knew whether she was going to be at work tomorrow. She was into all that considerate shit.

The silence stretched between us and in it, the background noises on her end became much louder. "Where are you?"

"My mom and I went out for lunch to celebrate."

"A celebratory lunch."

It hadn't been a question but she answered it like one. "Uh-huh." And damned if she didn't sound happy.

The woman just found out she didn't have cancer again and her idea of a good time was lunch with her mom.

It was an odd mix of pathetic and sweet.

"Well, I'll see you tomorrow," Cassie said into the silence I'd let linger too long.

Still eighteen hours before I got to see for myself that she was really okay. Eighteen hours to feel things out and make sure she was still cool with the second part of our deal.

"So when you're done with your lunch, what are you up to?"

"I don't have any plans." Another long pause. "Why?"

"I was thinking I could come by and show you how I like to celebrate. Spoiler: it involves getting naked."

I could hear her gulp through the line.

My leg bounced as I waited for an answer from her.

"I'll text you when I get home," she whispered. The call ended before I could even respond.

I pumped my fist in the air. I was liking this math. I'd cut my wait from eighteen to just a few hours.

Cassie

The smile that popped up as MJ pulled into my complex dipped as she frowned at me through the windshield. It'd been five days since we'd seen each other outside of work. Five days of making sure I didn't look at her like I'd seen her naked. Five days of me not being able to celebrate that I was still in remission in my new favorite way. Five days of me anticipating today. All for her to be frowning at me.

I'd jumped at the chance when she'd invited me to go antiquing with her. We'd been naked, well, half naked in bed, but there'd been nothing romantic about her invitation. I knew it was probably a teaching opportunity. That didn't stop the flutter in my stomach. I dared to hope that any embarrassment awaiting me would be small at an antique mall. It wasn't like an improv comedy club, which I wouldn't put past MJ. It'd be worth it to be near her. There was no one that made me feel more alive.

The frown hadn't left when she came to a stop at the curb in front of me.

Utilizing some soft belly breathing, I reached for the door.

She didn't even let me get all the way in before saying, "You didn't have to wait out here. I would've come to your door."

My shoulders relaxed. "It's broad daylight and it's truly n…"

"Not that bad," she finished for me. "Yeah, so you say."

"Hey now, you're not doubting your teaching skills, are you? I think a badass like me can walk to the parking lot."

"Mm hm." She shot a look around. "It wouldn't hurt to get you some backup pepper spray."

Buckling my seat belt, I chanced a look at her and my tongue tied itself an intricate knot. In the place of her tank top and cargos, she wore a gray T-shirt that bunched at the waist of her sweats. I didn't know if it was the casual look itself, or the fact that I was seeing something new that captivated me so.

I'd seen what was under those clothes, touched her. Fabric should be less of a distraction.

I transferred my attention to my phone. "So since I had extra time this morning I checked the reviews of Thorn & Thistle. The false ones have stopped. Now the worst ones coming in are about Kayla."

MJ looked at me out of the corner of her eye. "I'm not firing her. Take that off the plan. I need her."

"I didn't put that on my plan." I showed her my phone screen so she could see firing Kayla wasn't there. Firing Kayla was so obvious I hadn't bothered writing it down. "I disagree with your needing her. I can see why in the beginning you were desperate for bodies and to bring money in. But you need someone good. Someone who will bring in their own clientele. In the long run she's costing you more than she'll ever make you."

"Why don't you say that to her face? It could be a lesson on being assertive and speaking your mind."

"It would also be a lesson in me getting my eyes clawed out."

MJ laughed, pulling out of my complex. "She does seem the type to scratch instead of punch. You on the other hand…" She did a quick scan of me. "You'd probably have some sneaky Jitsu move and take her down by touching a pulse point or something."

I smiled, liking the image of responding to her next snippy comment with a flip that landed her on her back. Maybe I should take a class. "No. No, jiu-jitsu. I could probably find a neat trick online."

She snorted. "While you're searching I'd have to step in and save your ass."

"Probably," I conceded.

"We'll get you there."

"Hopefully not. There's quite a spectrum between not caring about someone's opinion and wanting to fight them."

"Eh. They're pretty much one and the same for me." She went around a car that dared to be going the speed limit.

"Well, they're not for me, though I have made some strides."

She stopped at a red light, the front end of the Jeep taking up almost half the crosswalk. "Yeah, how's that?"

Immediately my mind went back to my bed where we'd spent hours touching and licking and getting each other off. I'd been too exhausted to let my mind ruin my orgasms. From the way her nostrils flared, I could tell her thoughts had veered down the same path. But it wasn't that side of her influence that I'd been talking about.

"Last week at the doctor's office I didn't worry what others would think about the mark you left on me."

Her gaze drifted to my hip where my caterpillar tattoo was covered by my jeans.

"Not that one. The one your mouth left on my stomach. I'd forgotten how much you liked that spot until I was at the doctor's getting examined with my mom in the room."

MJ's eyes widened much like my mom's and the oncologist's had. "Your mom saw it?"

Was that horror I heard in her voice? I settled deeper into the seat, keeping my face neutral. "No missing it really. It's so big and bright. Then there's the location…"

She held up her hand. "I get the picture." She peeked another look at me. "What'd she say? Was she freaking out?"

Freaking out the way MJ was because my mom saw a hickey on me?

"No. She didn't care. If anything, she looked happy it was there." I reached out and nudged her with my elbow, careful not to hit her hard since she was steering. "That woman has cleaned me up after I puked on myself and has been around me when I couldn't find the energy to shower for a week. We're well past the point where she gets squeamish."

MJ's scandalized expression faded into something much more serious.

Dang it. I wanted to enjoy her company today as… friends. Whatever we were, she was not my cancer confidant. I had a support group for that. "My doctor on the other hand…"

"Did she ask for all the dirty details? Is that how I made a difference? Did you tell her exactly how you got it?"

My cheeks flushed, not in embarrassment. No, it was all the heat surfacing from remembering us pressed together. "I did. I told her all about the way you went down on me and got distracted by the area above my belly button. How you couldn't get enough of me."

MJ steered with her left hand and bopped me on the end of my nose with her right. "You're cute when you're lying."

At one point in my life I'd like someone not to have to question whether I would do something so outrageous.

"Yeah." I released the word with a long exhale. "But hey I didn't get all embarrassed and stutter up false stories of how I got it, so progress."

MJ smiled, appearing satisfied. She turned, the blasting music not enough to hide the sound of her tires squealing as she pulled into a drive-thru coffee stand. She ordered a coffee for herself and a hot chocolate for me.

"Um…" I started to speak up to let her know that I avoided sugar, especially in liquid form, because of all the studies linking sugar with cancer cells multiplying. Her "don't bother, I know it's going to be lame" look stopped me. She was right. It would be lame. I was okay. It wasn't back. I should get to celebrate that.

She passed me a Styrofoam cup—also a no-no— with whipped cream coming out of the top. "Enjoy."

For today, I'd live a little. I sipped at the chocolatey piece of liquid heaven. I moaned. Oh, wow. So good.

MJ stared at me with the same intensity I'd stared at erotic lesbian pictures I'd discovered when I was fifteen.

Unblinking. Intrigued. She shook her head and took her coffee from the woman in the drive thru. "See? That tea you drink tastes like piss."

"How would you know, hmmm?"

"I accidentally sipped out of your cup one day. Almost sprayed that shit."

I'd have taken a drink after her and I hadn't even known her lips had been there. How had I not been able to taste her? It'd been five days since we'd hooked up at my place, but I still remember the lingering taste of the coffee she drank.

MJ pulled into a dirt parking lot and followed the directions of a guy in an orange vest.

"You ready?"

I nodded, grabbing my bag and hot chocolate. Rows and rows of stalls were set up with people displaying their wares. "Do they do this every weekend?"

MJ shook her head. Today she wore a beanie down low, strands of her dark hair sticking out. "No. Once a month."

I'd never really been interested in antiques. If it was used, my mind spent too much time obsessing about who owned it before and what they'd done with it, on it, or in it, depending on what it was.

Shopping with MJ was exercise. She bounced from stall to stall without any rhyme or reason that I could discern. Her eyes scanned quickly and then she'd move in another direction. Personally I would have started on one end and gone row by row until I reached the last one.

As I was her guest, I just did my best to keep up.

A red rug with threads of gold spun through it caught my eye and I slowed. It was beautiful. Not lacy and delicate like I'd always associated with antiques. If it was bold for nowadays, what must it have been like back when the original person owned it? That was a person's feet I wouldn't mind walking all over the rug. I'd like to follow in those footsteps.

MJ back-stepped until she stood even with me. "Are you getting something?"

I shook my head. As nice as it would be to cover the worn, stained carpet in my apartment, I didn't even need to look at the price tag to know I couldn't afford the rug. I couldn't afford anything.

"Okay, then we can come back if you only want to look. I want to get to my favorite vendors first."

That at least answered why we were bouncing around. I gave the rug a long last look and then followed behind MJ as she growled and dodged around two women with strollers who'd stopped in the middle of the walkway. Her mission to get to the best stalls also led me to believe that the purpose of this trip wasn't some lesson to uphold our bargain. I put my hand on my stomach, trying to keep the flutter from becoming an all-out ripple. I needed to make this outing my own lesson on how to keep my feelings for my mentor separate from my sexual partner. These glimpses of the considerate, kinder MJ would be good for when we were working for years to come, hopefully, but our bedroom antics would not last near that long.

Down the next row, MJ darted into a stall. For the first time since we'd arrived she came to a full stop.

A middle-aged woman approached with a smile. "Hello, I remember you," she said.

MJ had drifted to a cherry desk with an inkwell that

sat on a top. She didn't even bother to look up as she spoke. "Yeah, I bought a lace fan a while back."

The woman nodded. "It was a very nice piece."

MJ inclined her head toward the inkwell. "Tell me about it."

Walking up to it, the seller lifted the small silver pot in her hands, angling it so MJ could get a better look. "It's from the 1850s. It belonged to a woman who had wanted to marry the man she loved, who was going south to look for gold. Her father only allowed them to marry with the promise that she would write to him, and he gifted her with this."

MJ looked back at me with the exact look my mom got when she saw a baby, like she could already picture her grandchild in her arms. "Isn't that cool?"

"It's a lovely story." I transferred my attention to the stall owner. "Is there a certificate of authenticity that comes with it?"

The woman shook her head. "No. Like so many pieces of history there is no record. The great-grand-daughter of the original owner sold this piece to me and told me its history."

MJ ran her finger along the wood base. "I'm touching something that that woman touched over a hundred and fifty years ago."

Uh-oh. I dug my phone out and started typing.

"I'll take it."

Too late. MJ was already pulling her wallet out of her back pocket, the chain attached to it sliding down her hip.

Wasting no time, the owner grabbed the cash. "I'll get this wrapped up for you."

A satisfied smile on her face, MJ came to stand next to me while she waited.

I showed her my phone. "I could have got you one for cheaper."

"It's not the same at all."

I rechecked to make sure the image hadn't changed. It was still a quill and an inkwell. "I can't see a difference and this one is twenty-five percent less."

"But I don't know the history of that one."

I slid in front of her and tried to keep my voice down. "You don't know this one's. She could've totally made that up."

MJ shrugged. "I like it."

"You like a probably fictitious story?" I wasn't quite succeeding in keeping my voice down.

"I didn't make it up." MJ cocked her head and smiled at my outraged growl.

I... I didn't even know how to process this. I showed her the picture again, specifically the price in large numbers. That should be enough.

MJ lowered my phone and patted my hand. "I like knowing that I'm getting something someone's family decided wasn't important enough to keep. I'll remember the info."

Oh, MJ. How she was testing me today without even intending to. The way she lifted her chin and squared her jaw as if embarrassed she'd said that, weakening me even more.

I think it was a relief for both of us when the stall owner returned.

"Here you go." The charlatan handed MJ her purchase. "It was nice seeing you again. I hope you come out next month."

I bet she did.

As MJ left, I stared at the woman, my mind whirling with all the things I wanted to accuse her of, and of course none of them came out, except a frustrated sound. Shaking my head, I followed after my surprisingly gullible mentor.

"I can feel you glaring. We can separate and meet in an hour if you want."

"Oh, we're staying together. It's the only way I can make sure you don't get swindled. Apparently anyone can tell you anything and you'll believe them."

Was she whistling? She'd let herself get taken advantage of. MJ. The woman who went full-on rant about people wasting her money when someone left the breakroom without turning the light off. It didn't make sense.

It made about as much sense as leaving a secure job to become an unpaid apprentice in a profession that had been flooded with new artists and was notoriously hard to get started in.

I'd always viewed MJ as an impenetrable fortress with no vulnerabilities, besides the glaring exception of the shop. Today's display of weakness was a balm to my insecure heart.

As I followed her, the March sun broke through the clouds. It wouldn't be long now before the tulips started blooming. We were even supposed to hit sixty degrees today, though we weren't even close yet and MJ was out with bare arms. For someone who was always cold, she hardly ever wore a coat. I was pretty sure she thought it made her look tough.

"Hold on."

She turned, her face exasperated. "I'm not returning it. All sales final."

"Yes, I realize it's hopeless to try to talk some sense into you." I swung my bag around my shoulder and rooted in it until I found my sunscreen. "I need to re-apply."

Finished, I approached MJ with the bit left on my hands. "Do you want me to get your exposed areas?"

"Nah, I'm good. It feels nice on my skin."

"You'll still be able to feel it, it's just your skin won't be absorbing the rays."

She sighed. "You're going to have some comeback no matter what I say, aren't you?"

"I am. You should be grateful. Skin cancer is no laughing matter."

Mouth snapping shut, she turned and presented me with her back, her head bent so I could reach her neck.

I leaned up and spread it around her neck, rubbing every bit into her smooth skin. Even after it was absorbed, I continued to rub my thumbs across her tendons, reveling in the feel of her under my fingers.

MJ groaned. "Damn, didn't know putting sunscreen could be sexy."

My hands froze because yeah, my rubbing had turned to caresses. "Sorry. I didn't mean to."

I put some space between us, conscious we were in the open in a public market. Portland was a progressive place as far as same-sex PDA went, but I didn't want to push it. Yes, I wanted to live a little today, but I knew myself enough to know one person's side eyes still had the power to ruin it for me.

"No sweat," MJ said, turning to face me. "But you didn't have to do all that. You're wanting sex, you just say the word. I told you the more we do it, the better you'll start to feel."

I didn't know why I was so surprised that'd she bring it out in the open like this. That was MJ. Unlike me she wouldn't pussyfoot around something. "I'll, um, keep that in mind."

MJ sauntered up to me, her hips swaying, and a very satisfied smile curving her lips. "You do that." She closed the remaining space between us until our hips bumped. "I bet if I put my hand down your pants right now, you'd be wet."

That was a bet she'd win.

I nodded, though I was pretty sure I didn't mean to, but I was already under the MJ spell. "I think we might need to hurry if we're going to work on my, um, problem. We only have two hours before we need to be at work."

Chapter Eighteen

Cassie

"I still don't see why we couldn't go back to my apartment," I said. In the two weeks since we'd started my sexual liberation, as MJ called it, I'd managed to prevent this from happening.

By going to MJ's home it felt like we were crossing a line. We'd already had sex at my apartment, but if we went to her place I'd see more of the woman behind the hard exterior I saw at work. The more I got to see, the more difficult it became not to notice how much I liked about her.

MJ didn't even look at me as she negotiated a right turn. Just as well. I liked her eyes on the road, especially when she was turning since she didn't seem to realize that most people applied the brake while doing it.

"Because my bed's more comfortable and my back is fucking killing me."

"My bed isn't that bad. It's a Sealy."

That earned me a quick look. "How old is it?"

Hm. She had a point there. My mattress had been very nice when I bought it eight years ago. Now it had that slight, very slight, dip in the middle—my favorite place to lie.

"Mine's memory foam," she added, as if that clinched the argument. She pulled into a driveway and shut off the ignition. "Plus we don't have to worry about sharing a wall with any neighbors."

I unbuckled my seat belt. "I can't look them in the eye. Your obsession with not stopping until they're banging on the walls is unhealthy."

MJ grinned. "Hey, just making sure they get their money's worth thanks to your thin-ass walls."

Getting out, I stared up at a lovely bungalow. I followed her toward the bright porch light, illuminating a well cared for yard.

"Are you coming?"

I jerked and realized I'd stopped at some bushes. Bushes. I started again, walking under a wooden arch with vines woven in it. They were bare now, but I could envision how beautiful they would look come spring. What I couldn't envision was MJ here.

Even when she put the key in the door I didn't trust this wasn't some prank. I waited for the real owners to come rushing out, threatening to call the cops. The door swung open, squashing that worry. She'd left a light on and I could see the large living room, a wide curio filled with knickknacks that appeared very old and hardwood floors. It all looked so normal.

MJ pressed herself against my back, lowering her chin to my shoulder. "You look disappointed. What were you expecting?"

Not so long ago, days even, I'd have smiled and said it was beautiful and sidestepped the question. But a lot had changed. I'd changed. I might not blurt out every thought, but if someone asked for my opinion, I was going to give it. "Black. A lot of black. Some kind of old warehouse with exposed pipes. Filthy. Dishes, clothes everywhere."

MJ lifted her head and out of the corner of my eye, I could see her amused expression. "I'm not here enough to get it dirty. I never cook, so no dishes to worry about." She shrugged. "I would've been fine at some place like you described, but when I walked in here I knew it was meant to be mine." Reaching out, she stroked the wood trim around the door. "It was built in 1922."

I ran my hand across it as well, skating my fingers along MJ's. "It has history. A story."

"Exactly." Her free arm locked around my back and she dragged me close.

I tilted my head back and stared at the wood trim. I don't think I'd ever noticed if a place had trim, and upon first meeting her I never would've thought MJ would either. But now I knew she was a woman who liked antiques and indie rock and things with a story behind them.

My body swayed closer. Sometimes I still couldn't believe I was doing this with her. MJ Flores. Opinionated, strong, queer woman, who wasn't afraid to go toe to toe with anyone. And her dark eyes flared with desire as she stared at me, conformer, afraid of everyone.

Her tongue flicked against my lips and I eagerly opened. I relaxed as our tongues twirled and stroked against each other. It'd only been a matter of hours since we'd been in my bed, but my body responded like it was starved for touch. Her touch.

MJ's arms encircled below my butt, lifting me. I happily wrapped my legs around her hips and looped my arms around her neck. "I like when you manhandle me."

"Yeah?" She loosened her grip, letting me drop several inches before she hauled me back up tight. "You probably shouldn't tell me that. Gives me all kinds of ideas."

Laughing, I squeezed my legs tighter around her. "I can handle them." And I could. I'd found my voice and I was prepared to use it for more than telling people what they wanted to hear. I'd tell MJ if she did something I didn't like.

A slow smile spread across MJ's face. "I guess we'll find out."

As she carried me through a doorway a flash of gray fur went by. Ah, there was the one responsible for all the hair on her dark clothes. I'd have to meet the pampered feline later. I had no doubt it was pampered. Anyone that cared about antiques and safe neighborhoods and buying me yummy drinks would take care of their pet.

I squealed as MJ toppled us down toward the mattress, expecting to bounce. Instead I was absorbed by softness. I patted the surface beneath me.

"You really do have a memory foam mattress."

MJ reached over and flipped on a light. This close I could see her individual eyelashes and the dark beauty mark underneath her lower right eyelid.

She nipped my bottom lip. "You thought I'd lie to you?"

"In a second if it meant sex."

MJ's chuckle sent her hot breath against my face. "You think so little of me."

"Mm, but I think highly of this bed." I sank into the mattress more. I didn't know if it really was the magical mattress or starting to shed the shame of my body I'd been carrying around for the last four and a half years, but I felt weightless.

And more than ready to take advantage of that. What better way than to do it with the woman who inspired me to "grow a set," as she would put it.

I pulled her shirt from her waistband. "How about we get to work on my hang-ups with sex? I made a lot of progress today, but that still needs a lot of work."

I matched MJ's sly grin with one of my own. It felt good to be daring. More so than denying myself to please someone ever did.

I trailed my fingers down under her pants. Wanting more access, I went to her belt buckle. I ran my fingers all along it, trying to find where it unlatched. Ugh. The metal rectangle buckle engraved with a dragon might be nice to look at, but it was a modern-day chastity belt keeping me from what I wanted.

Dropping my hands, I growled, "Will you take this damn thing off?"

She rose up, straddling my thighs. Her long fingers made quick work of the belt. Such talented, talented fingers she had.

She trailed her hands down the front of her body, dragging her nails over the tips of her nipples through the fabric of her shirt and then stopped at the hem.

I thrust my hips up against hers. "Do it. Show me."

As if my words were what she'd been waiting for, she dragged her shirt up over her body. She tossed it aside, baring all of her gorgeous brown skin.

"You are so beautiful," I said in awe.

The left side of her mouth kicked up and she put her hands on my shoulder. "You know what I like?"

I licked at my lips. "What?"

"When you take what you want."

Swallowing, I held her dark gaze. "I want you."

She pushed up and spread her arms out to the sides, a wide smile on her face. "Then take me."

It wasn't challenge in her voice, but invitation. An invitation I was eager to accept. No second guessing, no worrying. Just me taking what I wanted, what she wanted.

I pulled her sports bra over her head. I stared at her breasts, beautiful like the rest of her. Irresistible. I leaned up and licked her nipple, sucking the tip into my mouth. It was me lying flat on my back with her weight on me, but I was the one who felt powerful, more so with each moan I pulled from her.

I released her nipple with a pop. "Take off the rest of your clothes. I want to see all of you."

She pushed off the bed and dropped her pants. She twisted, letting me get a good view of her black boxer briefs.

"God, your ass looks amazing in those." My gaze dropped down to her thighs. She was thin, but so toned. She'd have to be, stomping around in those heavy boots.

She stuck her finger under the waistband. "Do you want me to keep them on?"

"No. I want to see all of you."

"Do I need to give you a show?" She pulled her underwear down her hips inch by inch.

Her movements captivated me. Focused on her, the other parts of my brain were silenced. "You do without even trying."

Her lips curved in a true, genuine smile and she climbed up onto me.

I clasped her hips in my hands, but that wasn't what I truly wanted. I trailed my hands further until I could cup her butt cheeks and pulled her even tighter against me.

She kept one hand braced on my shoulder. The other hand she wiggled between us, down into my pants all the way past my underwear until her finger slid into me.

I moaned, lifting my hips as she hooked her finger. Her thighs tightened on me to keep from being bucked off. She pulled her hand free and brought it to her mouth.

"Mm. You're about the hottest thing I've ever tasted. You want to try?" She held her finger in front of my face.

I stared at it and then opened my lips, letting her put it inside my mouth. I sucked on it, catching a faint taste of myself.

"Good, isn't it?"

Anything that brought that look to her face was good. "Yes." Because the word had come out so soft and timid, I added, "I like tasting myself."

Her eyes flared and then she gave me a hard, fierce kiss. We were both panting when she pulled away. "What next?"

"I want to be naked with you."

"Mm." Her finger walked down my chest and over my stomach. "Do you sleep naked in your bed, Cass? Do you like to feel the sheets rubbing against your naked body?"

I gulped, my toes curling. "I will be now."

"You should." She leaned down and over me until my vision was filled with only her. "It's so freeing."

So was being in this bed with her. Like we were in

our own safe space and I could do what I wanted with no judgement.

What I wanted was to be naked skin to skin with her.

I wedged my hand between our bodies, trying to get to the button of my jeans.

She pushed my hands aside. "Let me." Far more dexterously than me, she undid my button and then lifted her weight away from my thighs, crawling backwards down the mattress as she dragged my jeans down my legs.

"Ah, fuck yes." MJ dropped to the bottom of the bed and curved her fingers around my legs, drawing them apart. She placed a smacking kiss to my hip. Next she nuzzled my inner thigh. She audibly inhaled. Oh god. She was smelling me. Where once there would have been embarrassment and frantic questioning if I should have used douche or perfume, now it only turned me on. All of the wetness there was for her.

Her hair tickled my sensitized skin as she lowered her head closer.

"Wait."

MJ reared back.

I swallowed and pushed myself to my elbows. "I'm not naked yet."

Her gaze immediately went to my chest. "You don't need to. It's…"

These were my battle scars. Tonight I was owning them. "I do need to."

Her fingers curled tight around my thigh and I could feel the tremor in them. I laid my hand over hers. She was making this into a big deal because I had.

I released a breath and then guided her hand up to the edge of my camisole. She gripped the hem. An endless second passed before she slid it upward. It skimmed over me easily. No nipples or curves to get caught on. Only a lot of ugly scar tissue. And then my covering was gone and the cold air hit my naked skin.

My ragged breathing echoed in the room. To keep from covering myself, I fisted my hands in the sheets. I squeezed my eyes shut, not wanting to see MJ's reaction.

No. I was not a coward. This was me now. No hiding. I snapped open my eyes.

"You're beautiful," she said.

Chapter Nineteen

MJ

With my thumbs I brushed away Cassie's tears until it was a straight shot to stare into her hazel eyes, the green so damn bright. She took a quivering breath. Slowly her lips lifted and she smiled up at me. It didn't matter that it wobbled at the edges. It was the most beautiful thing in the world.

Drawing her top all the way off, I set it to the side where she could still see it. I kissed her, trying to tell her with my lips that nothing had changed.

I pulled back and let my gaze drop.

A large bright Aztec design covered her chest where her breasts once had been. Directly in the middle was a sundial, the flames bright red and orange. This wasn't a piece, it was a tribute. I leaned closer. Were those...yup. I could make out middle fingers incorporated through the design. A fuck you to cancer. My throat burned and I blinked rapidly. God bless Zan.

"Fucking beautiful," I repeated, my voice husky.

Below me Cassie remained tense, her eyes searching mine. Waiting for a rejection, I knew. Not going to happen. Hell, she knew I loved ink. I'd probably get more pleasure out of this than I ever did some mounds of flesh.

I wanted to touch and explore, but I was afraid if I did, she'd up and have a heart attack on me. I pressed myself over her, letting my chest rest against hers so she knew I wasn't scared off by what she showed me.

I kissed her. Again and again. Her soft mouth was as addicting as anything I'd experimented with in my younger days. I moaned as she finally joined in the party, her mouth opening and her tongue circling mine.

I was pushing her deeper into my pillow. Later her scent would be all over it and I knew I'd be sniffing it like a junkie. Had she done the same after I left her place?

"Touch me," she panted, her hands curling into my back, nails too short to even sting.

I ran my palm down her leg and then pressed against her curls. Never would I take them for granted. I stroked my fingers through the hair. I couldn't resist any longer. Her clit received a tap as I passed, but it was her wet heat that I craved. I groaned as my thumb sank into her.

Cassie arched into me, her arms clinging to my neck like I was the only thing keeping her from levitating off this bed. I lowered even more of myself on her. She wasn't going anywhere.

"Mm." She bit her lip, cutting off the sound. Before I could even protest she released it again. "Yes, ah, yes. Feels sooo good."

I ground myself against Cassie, her increasing cries making me so fucking wet. Her movements—hell, her fast breaths—had me bucking against her. Her muscles tightened, becoming rigid, her cries turning into one moan. She pushed up into me as she came. Fuck she looked beautiful, all red-cheeked and wild-eyed.

Slowly the tension eased from her body. Her legs dropped down to the mattress, freeing my hand. Her chest heaved with her harsh breaths, but everything else about her was still, peaceful.

I'd done that.

My gaze ran over her, snagging on her breasts—or where they'd once been. A stark reminder of how much was riding on me not fucking this up. This was about more than orgasms. This was helping Cassie like her body. This was her coming to me to show her how. I liked knowing she was needing me for something. Fuck.

Cassie's eyes opened and she smiled at me, looking blissed out. "That felt so good."

I grunted.

Her lips twitched and she patted the mattress next to her. "No need to sound so grumpy. I know you need yours."

My mind might still be spinning, but my body happily responded to the sexy promise in her eyes. I lay next to her, spreading my legs.

No dummy, Cassie pushed herself up and then crawled to the space I'd made for her. There was no room to stress about how this had become deeper than sex and how to rein it in when she was kissing her way up my body. Her tongue flicked against my nipple. When she sucked it into her mouth I about shot off the bed.

I groaned, arching into her mouth. "Feels so good. I…" Shit. I didn't want to be rubbing it in. Luckily Cassie didn't pay any mind to my flub, her mouth not slowing on sucking what little bit of breast I had.

Even with my brain deciding to take a break, I managed not to be too vocal. Yeah, the tingle in my nipple felt good, but it was her touch that had me soaked.

Once again my brilliant apprentice read the signs of my hips humping the air and slid a hand down my body until her finger parted me.

"God, yes." I dropped my legs all the way, spread them as far as I could, offered myself to her.

Her thumb circled my clit while at the same time her mouth switched to my other breast. So good. So fucking good. I fisted the pillowcase in my hands. Just as quickly I released it. I didn't want to be touching fabric, not when I could be touching Cassie. I clutched at her sides. Much better. My palm rested perfectly into the curve of her waist as if the indentation had been molded for me.

I...no that wasn't right.

My fingers twitched and I slid them down between our bodies until I was parting her lips and stroking. There. This touch could be explained. It was all about sex.

The rhythm of her fingers faltered as her hips pressed against my wrist, a strangled moan coming from her. It wouldn't take much. After already coming, her body would be primed for another.

Cass released my breast with a pop. "Wha...what are you doing? Your...turn." She thrust herself on my hand. "Right there. Uh."

I jacked up into a sitting position and latched onto the bottom of her ear, nibbling. "Don't worry. I'm keeping count."

I continued to work my finger inside her, my thumb

brushing against her clit in the soft, slow rhythm she preferred.

Cassie groaned, stopping any attempts at trying to get me off. Now her fingers were just moving spastically as her body humped against my hand. She threw her head back, panting.

I hunched over her, quickening my pace. I trailed kisses down her neck, her collarbone. Lower. I pressed my lips against the bright ink. Fascinated by the different textures, I explored. Some areas were smooth under my lips and others were rough, raised scar tissue that the tattoos concealed.

Cassie stiffened, her growing cries no longer filling my room.

Oh hell no. I added a second finger and flicked her clit with my thumb.

"Oh god." Her legs squeezed my hand.

"Beautiful," I whispered against her flesh.

"MJ," she cried out, her body squeezing around my fingers.

Her eyes were darker than I'd ever seen them, pupils blown. Lines branched out from the corners of her eyes, tense as she reached for it. They eased when our gazes met, as if trusting that I'd get her there. I did.

Her body twitched in the aftermath. I waited until her breathing evened before sliding my fingers from her. God how I wished I could draw sound. The contented moan she gave should be memorialized.

Once she blinked, I held up my hand to show her glistening wetness on my fingers and then lowered my hand to myself. I rubbed my clit.

The beautiful ink on her chest came to life as she took a deep breath. She leaned forward and then kept

moving, sliding down my body until she rested between
my thighs, her feet dangling off the mattress. At the first
swipe of her tongue, my hips bucked.

"Fuck."

Cassie moaned against my flesh and I could feel the
vibration against my sensitized flesh. Hell, she didn't
even have to lick me. She could probably talk and I'd
get off.

It only took minutes for me to be clutching the back
of her head and grinding myself against her fucking
awesome mouth. My muscles trembled and a groan
burst from me that sounded damn close to a whimper.
Jesus, it was so much. Not just the lash of her tongue
against my sensitive nerves, but flashes of the day.
Her being so outraged at the market. Her blushing and
glancing away every time our eyes met at work. Showing me her scars. Owning her body. It all combined
into one powerful surge and with the next swipe of her
tongue, I came.

God only knew how much later, I blinked and
brought the room back into focus to find Cassie kneeling between my spread thighs, wiping her mouth on the
back of her hand. A damn hetero apocalypse could start
and I didn't know that I'd have the strength to get up.

Cassie stared at me, lifting her arms up like she was
going to cross them over her chest and then dropped
them back down. She sat there and I could feel the tension start to fill back in and worse, it was trying to
creep my way and ruin the good buzz I had going on.

I grabbed her arm, tackling her to the mattress and
throwing my leg over her hips from behind. "No messing with a good orgasm. Turn your brain off." No doubt

she was wanting to put her shirt on, or worrying that she was too loud, or who knew what else.

Bit by bit and a hell of a lot faster than I thought she would, she started to relax until her back actually touched my stomach and there was some spooning going on.

"Two," she said.

"Huh?"

"Two orgasms."

I curled closer to her, resting my chin on her shoulder so I could speak into her cute little ear. "Don't think I've forgotten. You still owe me one."

"Well, a goody-goody like me always pays her debts."

A yawn caught me by surprise.

She nudged me with her shoulder, probably so I'd stop doing it in her ear.

I nuzzled down into her neck and hitched my leg higher on her. "It'll have to wait until I recharge. I'm fucking exhausted."

Her hair tickled my nose as she attempted to turn to look at me. "So you're saying you're holding me hostage until you're ready for me to make good on my debt."

"Yup, that's it exactly."

She settled back against me and let out a yawn of her own. Hers much quieter than mine. "Okay. I'll agree to that, but only because of your bed."

"Ah, my bed. It all comes back to the bed."

We settled in, the light still on, but that wouldn't stop me from falling asleep. Hell at this point I didn't think anything could. Not when I had Cassie's warm weight pressing against me, feeling so damn good. Yeah, I could stay here for... Whoa. That she barely cleared five feet and looked like a pixie tricked you into thinking she was harmless. But holy hell she was dangerous. She had me thinking of sleepovers like they were a good thing.

"This doesn't mean anything," I said.

The pillowcase made a scratching noise as she nodded. "I'd never expect anything different."

Cassie

"Everything okay?" I asked as MJ checked her phone again. This time she'd at least waited until her client had taken a restroom break.

MJ typed a quick response and then put her phone back on the counter, screen side down. "Yup." She tapped her fingers on her thighs, her gaze bouncing around the room. Not so unusual because she liked to keep tabs on the shop, but I didn't think she needed to look at the ceiling or the empty wall behind me.

My chest pinched. Where was the woman who'd had her arm wrapped around me in bed and kept me so close we didn't need her king? A sleeping bag would've been roomy.

She was gone. Instead this version of MJ had walked into the building. Either she had a very serious vision problem or I'd managed to become invisible.

I understood it in a way. It was hard for me to meet her eyes and not think of them looming over me, so fierce as we kissed and caressed each other. It was hard to ignore that the hands that sometimes brushed mine when trading sketches were the same ones that had been inside me, bringing me incredible pleasure. The only other time I'd been sexual with a woman, I'd been in a relationship. I'd known I might have a difficult time separating the two.

What I didn't understand was why it was suddenly a problem for MJ. She'd been fine the previous times we'd had sex. What had changed for her last night at her house?

"Is there anything you'd like me to do?"

She looked at me. No, close, right over me. I knew when she was actually looking at me. There was no charge right now.

Who knew I'd long for when she snapped orders at me?

Her fingers pressed flat on her thighs and she started to shake her head. "Wait. Yes." She jumped up from her seat and held up her finger. "I'll be right back."

Mere seconds later, her long strides brought her right back with some papers in her hands. "You can drop these off at the painting place down the street for me."

There was a colorful drawing of a wine glass painting in front of the easel and the name of the shop on the painting. "What are these?"

MJ shrugged, pushing her hands in her pockets. "They needed a new logo. I drew up some ideas in my spare time."

Spare time? There was no such thing with MJ. "It's very good."

"Yeah. Hopefully they think so." She shrugged. "They've already paid me. You just need to give them to them and make sure they like 'em okay. If they give the go ahead, they'll be in by next week."

I held the papers carefully so I didn't wrinkle them. "Okay. I'll be ri…"

MJ shook her head. "Nah. I'm almost done and then

got some paperwork. Everybody's finishing up. Hand them off and go home. You can text me what they say."

That answered the question if we'd be seeing each other after work tonight. I bit back a sigh. This could be a good thing. Maybe we needed a full eight hours outside of each other's presence and everything would go back to normal—normal, where she looked at me and I didn't feel quite so alone.

I grabbed my bag from my locker and then got my bike. Not bothering to put on my helmet, I walked my bike down the street to Bubbly and Paint.

"Hi," a woman said, smiling at me across the counter. "Can I help you?"

"Hi, I'm Cassie. I work at Thorn & Thistle. MJ Flores asked me to drop these off for you. She has clients booked late tonight but wanted to make sure you got these." It sounded better than "I think she needed an excuse to get rid of me because we were uncomfortable around each other."

The woman took the papers and gasped. "These are amazing."

They were. I still hated them. MJ shouldn't have had to make them. The shop should be making enough money that she didn't have to spend her precious time making art for something she didn't love.

"So I can tell her that you like them?" I asked.

"Definitely." The woman ran her finger over the graphic, smiling.

"Then she wanted me to tell you that it'll take about a week and you'll have your banners."

I said my goodbyes and sent MJ a text message that they were approved. When no response came, I swung up on my bike and headed home. I needed to redirect my brain from thinking of the places on MJ's body I wanted to explore and instead come up with more ideas for the shop. I had my part of the bargain to uphold. If the shop were more profitable, MJ wouldn't need to be taking on side projects.

I turned onto my street, my backpack sliding along my back. My too-light backpack. Crap. My notebook with all of my research and ideas was still in my locker at the shop. I'd definitely been distracted by sex.

It'd only been forty-five minutes. Jamie might not have finished her last client or was still there cleaning up. Maybe I'd be able to slip inside and grab it without MJ even knowing I was there. If she caught me returning after she'd told me to go home, it'd look too pathetic, like I was making excuses to be around her.

I arrived at the alley and sighed at finding Jamie's car gone. MJ's Jeep was there. Parked next to it was an Outback I didn't recognize. These parking spots were reserved for Thorn & Thistle.

I walked up to the door, letting out a breath when the knob turned. Not exactly safe for MJ but it would allow me to sneak in and get my notebook.

"So that's it." MJ's voice came from the main floor of the shop.

"It's very nice," a woman responded.

Had she done another client? She wanted me gone so bad that she wouldn't even let me do my job and help?

MJ's heavy footfalls headed my way, followed by softer ones.

Panicking, I stepped back outside. Before the door closed, I caught a glimpse of MJ coming into the room followed closely by a dark-haired woman.

I rushed back to my bike, knowing there was no way

I'd be able to make it out of the alley before they stepped out. I'd make this as natural as I could. Seconds turned into a minute and still the door didn't open. Which meant they'd been headed to MJ's office.

I shakily put my helmet back on my handlebars. In all the time I'd worked here, MJ had never brought a client to the back.

Puzzles had never been my thing, but there were sure a lot of pieces coming together. Shop closed. Strange car parked next to MJ's. The texting she'd been doing. Wanting me gone. I clutched my chest. I wouldn't need to call the doctor for the cause of my pain this time. Had MJ been setting up some kind of hookup?

I gulped in more of the night air. MJ was allowed to be with whoever she wanted. We weren't in a relationship. We were two women who had sex together in an almost clinical way to get me comfortable with my own body.

Now she might be doing it with someone else.

My stomach clenched, a sharp pain radiating through my midsection with the force of the worst menstrual cramp I'd ever had. I didn't miss that part of not having a uterus.

My notebook wasn't that important. I needed to get on my bike and pedal away with my sanity.

I took a step.

In the wrong direction.

I opened the back door and not seeing anyone, slipped inside.

I inched my way down the hall until I stood in front of MJ's door. Muffled voices filtered out. Talking? There were stretches when no sound came out. Because they were eating a late meal? Kissing? Touching?

A gutting thought.

I stared at the dark wood door of the office, wanting to know what was going on behind there. There was a scraping sound, followed by another one. The metal chairs being pushed back. My heart launched in my throat. Oh god. I raced toward the lockers. MJ's office door opened just as I crouched down.

This was bad. Very bad. My pulse pounded so loud, I couldn't hear their approach, but I knew they were getting closer. I could feel it.

Jesus why had I trapped myself here? I should have gone into the bathroom. Or even better not hid at all and just gone home. My mind was not good at making split-second decisions.

"Thanks again for stopping by," MJ said.

"My pleasure. I think we could have a really good thing here."

I bit my lip hard, curling tighter into myself.

"Me too."

I snuck a glance in time to see them shaking hands. I got a better look at my comp...the other woman. I'd guess her to be in her early thirties, and the ear I could see had piercings all the way up it. She had dark hair with pink streaks. She looked hip and vibrant. My lip curled.

Opening the door, the woman looked back at MJ with a warm, wide smile. "I'll call you and let you know what I decide. We could discuss a test-run then."

I jerked my head back down. Test-run? That didn't sound very hookup-ish.

A car started and then the back door closed. I uncurled my fingers. No goodbye kiss. The lock turned and then MJ's heavy footsteps rang on the concrete floor. Coming closer. Closer. The tips of her boots came into view.

I slowly tilted my head back. I lifted my hand in a feeble wave. "Hi. I forgot something."

"Did you?"

Technically the words were a question, but the tone went straight to calling me a liar.

MJ folded her arms over her chest, her eyebrows one dark unhappy slash on her forehead. "FYI even kneeling, you can be seen if someone is say standing over there." She pointed to where she and the mystery woman had been. "Not to mention your bike is outside."

"Right." I nodded like I appreciated that helpful bit of information and rose to my feet, my cheeks burning hot. "I didn't want to interrupt."

"Yeah, it'd make it hard for you to try to spy on us."

And now my ears were getting into the embarrassment action. My first attempt at a covert operation was a flaming failure.

"What the hell?" MJ asked. "We sleep together a few times and you're gonna start spying on me? That is not okay."

"No. No, I didn't come here to spy. I came to get my notebook. I saw you going to the back with that woman and I stayed because I had to know."

MJ stepped closer, arms still crossed tight. "Know what?"

"If she was the one you were texting earlier."

"How is that not spying? Now you're keeping track of who I'm texting?"

I shook my head. This was so much worse than the measly "pathetic" I'd feared she would think if she saw me at the shop. "It wasn't about the who, it was about the why. I wanted to know if that was why you've been acting so different today."

"It sounds like you were jealous and thought I was getting down and dirty with her on my desk."

Another stomach-contracting pang hit me, both because she didn't deny it and because they could make plans to do exactly that in the future. I wisely kept my mouth shut. I'd done enough damage tonight.

She shook her head and dropped her hands. "Which would be stupid because you already know the answer. I don't hook up at work."

"Uh, may I point out that table?" So much for me keeping my mouth shut. "The one right there in the middle of the shop. I'm pretty sure what we did on it would be considered hooking up."

Chapter Twenty

Cassie

MJ stepped closer to me and snaked her finger through my belt loop. Nowhere did our skin touch, yet my nerves danced.

"Yeah, but you're an exception," she said. "Look how well that worked out."

I swallowed and rocked on my heels when all I wanted was to thrust my hips at her. No, I could go one night without touching her. There'd been so many nights before her that I spent alone. "I'm glad."

"You were jealous." Her finger stroked around my belly button over my shirt.

Yes. She couldn't go to someone else yet. We weren't done. Last night was the first time I could even show my scars.

"I... I am." I kept my head up, surprised to find I didn't feel weak admitting it. Quite the opposite. It took courage to be honest.

"What would happen if you saw her again?"

I tilted my head, trying to read her expression, but she'd gone in to lockdown mode. "Will I?"

"Yes. All the time, if we can work things out."

The breath knocked out of me, I staggered back. I'd known that was a possibility. But to hear it, to have it confirmed. I... No.

MJ's hand landed on my shoulder and she gave it a squeeze. "If you hadn't hid, I could have introduced you to Gina, hopefully our new piercer."

The words slowly penetrated the cloud of misery shrouding me. I jerked my head up. "Piercer?"

"Uh-huh." She waggled her brows. "I don't want to tell anyone until it's a sure thing, but yeah, she came and interviewed. I looked over her stuff. It looked good. Real good."

I bounced on my toes. MJ had been interviewing, interviewing, nothing more.

"Oh my gosh. You're going to do it. You're going to become full service." I put my hands on her shoulders and shook her. "Finally."

"We'll see."

"Too late. I saw that smile."

She grunted, but it didn't dim my enthusiasm. This would work. It'd bring in revenue and help take some of the burden off MJ. Maybe she could even come out of that ten-by-ten room of disorganization she called an office.

"So what finally convinced you? My numbers? The articles I left on your desk? The tally?"

She shrugged, her fingers sneaking up under my shirt and caressing the skin of my belly. "You. Okay. You. You wore me down."

I threw my hands in the air and danced in a circle. "Yes. Yes. Yes."

After I'd completed my victory spin MJ was staring at me like I was the most ridiculous thing ever. I didn't care.

I didn't care.

I'd done it. I'd convinced MJ to take my advice. And she wasn't attempting to get horizontal with Gina on her desk.

Shaking her head, she crooked her finger at me. "Get back here." She snagged me around my waist. "Let's channel this energy another way, hm? I think this calls for another round on the drafting table."

Oh, how tempting. By hiring a piercer she'd taken away my urgency to work on ideas tonight. Plus there was the added benefit that she was back to looking at me, and she seemed to like what she saw.

But what about tomorrow? Would it be a repeat?

"I think that might cause more problems."

"Problems?" She pressed her hips into me. "We'll see if you're still saying that when I'm licking you until you come."

I stepped back. If I was going to have any chance of making sense of today, then she couldn't be touching me. "Things are already getting complicated keeping work and after hours separate."

"Ugh. We've talked about this." MJ wiped her hands down her face, smearing her eyeliner, but on her it just added to the smoky effect. "Yeah, we shared an incredible night, but nothing changes once we're here."

"But it did change. You hardly spoke to me today. You didn't even have me do my actual apprentice duties."

Her dark eyes staring into mine sent tingles of anticipation through me, my body equating the prolonged contact with the pleasure to come. Proof that I could never put enough distance between us for her not to affect me. "Maybe it seemed like it because last night was so intense."

"Maybe it seemed like it because that's exactly what happened. Ignoring me and not even letting me do my job is the opposite of nothing changing when we're at work."

Her mouth opened and I could see almost to the exact second when she swallowed down the automatic argument and instead took in what I was saying. "You're right."

"Say it again, this time without the surprise."

"You're right." She stepped up to me and then shocked me by tucking her head against my neck. "I was so damn focused on making sure I didn't show you any favoritism, I went too far in the other direction."

Amazing how voicing what was bothering me and having her acknowledge it could bring me instantaneous peace.

I rested my cheek on the top of her head. "Okay."

She turned her head and pressed a gentle kiss to my chin and then because it was MJ, she licked me. "I'm sorry."

I wrapped my arm around her shoulder. "It's okay."

MJ lifted her head up and placed a smacking kiss on my cheek. "I suck. Think you can forgive me?"

Was there a doubt? She might be getting less powerful, but the people-pleaser was still alive and well inside of me. "Yes."

"Yeah?" She bumped her hips against mine. "On the table?"

"No. I need to eat. You need to make it happen."

MJ slung her arm around my shoulders, leading us

toward the back door. "Come on. Let's feed you. Sex is always better when the only eating your partner is thinking about is going down on you."

We walked two streets over where some cafes and pubs were open late. I chose the diner because my stomach took one whiff of the grease and decided that's what it wanted. We ate, stealing fries off each other's plates. Somehow hers were better than mine.

Taking the back way to the shop, we passed the art gallery that had a show going on.

"Let's go in." MJ said.

I grabbed the back of her shirt. "We can't go in there," I hissed. "We're not dressed appropriately." I pulled MJ to the side as a woman in a cocktail dress came out the door as if to prove my point.

MJ's lips kicked up at the corner and she bopped the tip of my nose. "You're cute." She linked her hand through mine.

I stared down at her, her long fingers surrounding my pale ones, my mind going blessedly blank.

She gave my hand a tug. "Come on. The paintings don't care what we look like."

We were most definitely the least well-dressed people in the room. As we walked around, I remained tense, waiting for the tap on my shoulder asking us to leave.

MJ's finger stroked the side of my hand. Her head was tilted back, staring up at a painting as if how the artist had made that particular shade of green was her biggest concern.

I let out a breath and followed suit. The artist's use of colors was amazing.

If someone was going to judge us because of our clothes, or our tattoos, or that we were holding hands, it was going to happen. Whether I worried about it or not, it would happen. I could leave and wait for her outside so I didn't have to suffer the humiliation on the chance of that happening. Or I could stand here and get a glimpse inside of this person's world through their use of oil paint.

I didn't want to miss out anymore.

I had MJ to thank for that.

I clutched her arm, leaning up to whisper in her ear, "Thank you."

She turned to look at me. "For what?"

For so many things. I clutched her tighter. "For bringing me here."

Her expression softened, and she squeezed my hand. It was as if she got that I was talking about more than this room we were in, but here, this place in my life.

MJ

"Wow, look at this one."

Part of me really didn't want to, but the other couldn't resist. I flinched.

Yeah, I'd known I shouldn't look. Just like I shouldn't have looked at the last ten.

"Holy shit, why would anyone do that?"

Cassie turned to me, her eyes twinkling. "No plans to get one, huh?" She stared at the picture of a VCH piercing. "I think it's beautiful."

I turned to face her straight on. If it meant I didn't have to look at that picture anymore, I was all for it. She was serious. My crossstitching, sweater-wearing apprentice liked the looks of a clit piercing. As much as I'd like to be on the receiving end of the look she was giving the picture, holy shit I couldn't even imagine a needle going through my skin there. I shuddered.

Since we sat shoulder to shoulder at my desk, Cassie obviously felt it. She grinned at me. "I'm guessing that's a hell no to getting one yourself."

"No. What about you? Any plans?" If I could get over the horror of getting one, I could see her point that it was pretty. Cassie would look good with a little jewel there.

Her head tilted and she pursed her lips. "Maybe. I'll have to talk to Gina when she starts."

Not a surprise anymore. Cassie might look fragile, but she was far from it.

"As much as I love that part of you, I won't be watching."

She laughed. "Not going to be there to hold my hand, huh? That's okay."

Well, shit. Now it wasn't okay with me. I didn't like the thought of her going through that pain alone. She'd been through enough pain already. Yeah, she'd had her mom there for her then, but a piercing like this wasn't exactly something you invited your mom to. I'd have to buck up. What the fuck was up with that? We weren't going out or shit. We were fuck buddies. No, that wasn't right. We were…hooking up. It didn't feel like that's all it was. Mentor and mentee? Hell, that sounded kinky.

She nudged me with her shoulder. "No problem. I know your liddle, queasy stomach can't handle it."

Oh hell no. She didn't just break out the baby talk. "Fuck off. My stomach is just fine. I'll have you…"

I broke off as Cassie flipped the page of Gina's portfolio. Of course it would be a scrotum piercing. I stuck my tongue out at the wrinkled skin. "Ugh, I did not need to see that."

Cassie laughed. The sound petered out as she met my gaze, but I could still see it in her eyes and the way just the ends of her lips curved up. "I never knew you were so squeamish. I mean come on these aren't even hairy."

I raised my eyebrows at her. "Seen a lot of balls, have you?"

"Not…"

My phone vibrated in my pocket. After reading it, I put it away to find Cassie still staring at the picture. If I didn't know she was trying to give me some privacy I'd be worried about her interest in the guy's balls in the pic. "My client just canceled which means I've got some free time." I hooked my arm around her waist and drew her closer so she was half sitting on my seat. "I wonder what we could do with that time."

Cassie gasped as I nuzzled her neck, her body leaning into me. I was just making my way around to her front when she gasped and pulled up straight, nearly knocking me in the chin.

Her gaze flew to the door. "We can't. Not here."

I laughed. She looked so scandalized. "It has a lock," I said, tilting my head to the door she still stared at like it was going to bust open. "Besides everyone is busy with clients."

She slowly turned toward me, her eyes huge. "Someone could still hear," she whispered.

I laughed again. Cassie slapped her hand over my mouth. "Shh."

My whole body shook. How could one person be so cute? I took her hand from my mouth and put it on my thigh. "Why do I have to be quiet? We're not doing anything."

"I know that, but if someone walked by they might

think we were. There's not usually laughter coming from in here."

I grunted. That was true. Most of the time I was in here, I was doing paperwork or making phone calls. Not much to laugh about.

Cassie pushed off of me and returned to her seat.

"I take it there will be no making out?"

"No." She shot me a look out of the corner of her eye. "Later."

Slightly appeased, I leaned back in my chair. "So we're going to spend the time going through more pictures." I grimaced at the one Cassie had left off on.

Cassie closed the book. "No. I've got a better idea."

I perked up at the excitement in her voice. "Yeah? Hit me with it."

"Shading."

"What?"

She stood and reached out, grabbing my hand and pulling me to my feet. "You're going to give me a lesson in shading. I want to be as good as you."

I lifted my eyebrow at her as she propelled me to the door. "No one is good as me."

"Yeah, yeah. I know. Come on."

We made our way out to the floor of the shop. A quick check showed all the girls had a client except Kayla. Not a surprise. Right now she filled the need of being available for walk-ins who wanted small, quick tattoos. I didn't want to turn anyone away who wanted ink and had the money to pay for it.

I took my seat and Cassie rolled up the extra stool next to me. "What was the last thing you were working on?"

"The T-Rex."

"All right, bring him out. Let's get to work."

Cassie and I set up our supplies and then she brought out the latest tattoo she'd been working on a sheet of synthetic skin.

I looked at the realistic T-Rex and felt a thrill. Damn, but Cassie was an amazing artist and getting to help her be even better was fucking awesome.

"All right. I'm going to do the front leg. Watch me. You'll do the other one. I'm going to go for light and subtle and darker at the bottom."

Cassie leaned right next to me, her warmth against my side a heck of a lot better than the little space heater I brought in on the really cold days.

I turned off my machine and pushed my chair back. "Your turn."

She turned to look at me, her pupils large, her lips parted.

I got it. There was nothing sexier than when she was laying down ink. It was damn nice to know I did the same for her. I bumped her with my shoulder. "You sure you don't want to spend the time in my office?"

"No." She shook herself. "No. I want my lesson." She straightened her shoulders. "I got this."

Her lip between her teeth, Cassie got to work, trying to mimic what I had done. I pressed closer to her side, not happy until we touched from knee to hip. I glanced up to find Kayla watching us like a visual ruler, checking the distance between us.

Jesus. When was Cassie going to put this chick in her place? Only thing chaining my tongue was that if I unleashed, it would definitely be special treatment. I didn't get involved in any petty bullshit between my employees. When it was against Cassie, it didn't seem so petty.

Her arm brushed mine as she shifted. Thank god Kayla wasn't close enough to see the shudder that went through me from one brush of Cassie's arm.

God help me if Cassie ever discovered how much power she had over me.

Chapter Twenty-One

MJ

A repeating buzz woke me. I went to fling a hand out to shut off the alarm when the weight against my side registered. Groaning, I lifted my head, my neck protesting with a sharp pain. Shit, we'd fallen asleep on the couch.

The buzzing started up again and I was awake enough now to identify it as my phone. Five o'clock in the morning. Fuck. No good call came at this time. Trying to not jar Cassie, I pulled my phone out of my pocket.

My brother's name flashed on the screen. Cold invaded my body. He was sixteen. He didn't get up before noon if he could help it. "Hello?"

"Hey, it's Javier. Um…"

"Tell me."

"Dad's in the hospital."

The words looped in my head as I stared at the glow from the infomercial on TV.

"MJ?"

Swallowing down the bile my brother's words unleashed, I clutched the phone tight. "How bad is it?"

"He's not dying or anything. He crushed his leg. José says it got caught under the concrete mixer."

Cassie stirred, but I continued to stare at the man cleaning floors on TV.

"He's got to have surgery," my brother continued.

"When's the surgery?"

"Tomorrow. He ate breakfast this morning so they have to wait for it to clear out of his system or something before they can do it."

"All right, I'll see when I can get a flight. He's at Regional Hospital?"

Cassie squeezed my thigh, her hand a warm, welcome weight.

"Yeah."

"I'll text you my flight info."

I hung up and tossed my phone next to me.

Cassie turned to face me, drawing her knees up to her chest and wrapping her arms around them. "Family?"

"Yeah, my dad." My voice broke and the sound surprised me. It was a sound you made when you were scared or sad. He wasn't dying.

She reached for my hand. I gave it to her.

"He busted his leg and needs surgery."

"Okay." Her fingers squeezed mine. "You get in the shower. Go pack. I'll look for flights. Which airport are you flying into?"

Shower. Pack. The words stood out in the whirling in my brain. I could do those things. I needed to do those things. Before I got up, I turned and wrapped myself around Cassie. I took a deep breath, her scent helping to clear the chaos. "Thank you."

"Go," she said, her arms dropping away. "I'll check flights."

I hurried down the hall. Thank god for Cass. No asking me to describe how I was feeling or patting my hand and telling me everything was going to be okay. She was helping me do shit that needed to get done.

In record time I was packed and dressed and printing out a boarding pass. I handed Cass the keys to my Jeep so she could drive me to the airport and bring it back.

"I'll be careful with it."

"I know." I held out my other set of keys. "Be even more so with these."

She took them, staring down at the keys as if she couldn't understand what she was seeing.

"Those are the shop keys," I said.

She curled her fingers around the silver ring. "I'll give them to Jamie as soon as we open tomorrow."

"No." I shook my head, cupping my hand over hers. "I want you to keep them. I want you to open and close the shop."

Cassie inhaled sharply. The keys jangled as her hand trembled. "Thank you for trusting me."

"I do trust you."

I held her gaze, needing her to believe me, to see the truth. I trusted her. I didn't know when it happened or how, but I trusted her not to screw me over. She wasn't using me for some endgame. Everything was out in the open with us. The only thing she was using me for was my body and I happily gave it to her. As part of our deal, because I was getting something too.

She swallowed hard and then visibly pulled herself together. "Thank you."

I wrapped my hand tighter around hers. This moment

was everything I'd avoided since the day I'd been betrayed. I'd vowed to never let anyone have any kind of access to me or my business. Here I was handing the keys, the entry to my livelihood, to Cassie.

And I was okay.

Cassie released a shaky breath, stepping back. "Come on, you have a flight to catch."

"Yeah." I swung my bag on my shoulder and cast a glance at my living room before shutting the door. For some reason it felt important that I see it now, like it would somehow be different when I got back. Like everything would be different.

While Cass pulled onto the highway, I called Jamie.

"Hello?" she answered, her voice thick with sleep.

"Hey, sorry for waking you. Listen, I have to leave town for a family emergency."

"Everything okay?"

"Yeah. Well, no. My dad needs surgery. I'm leaving the keys with Cass but I need you to be in charge of everybody else."

"Shit. I hope he's okay," Jamie said. "I'll watch the shop for as long as you need."

"Thanks. Appreciate it. I'll call and keep you updated."

"Focus on your family. Don't worry about us."

Of course I'd worry. The last time I hadn't paid enough attention I'd gotten fucked over and was still paying for it. Now I was going to be hundreds of miles away. It helped knowing Cassie would be there. Hell, the way she watched and listened to everything, she'd know if anything was going down.

"I mean it," Jamie said. "We've got this. You focus on your dad."

"Thanks." Jamie'd been with me this whole time. She'd stuck with me. I could trust her. Amazingly it didn't feel like me repeating shit to make myself feel better. I was actually starting to believe it.

My gaze slid to Cassie. She'd been quiet the whole time. Shoulders up around her ears, hands tight around the steering wheel, she was obviously tense, but that could be because she was driving. She took driving someone else's car seriously.

At the drop-off section, Cass got out of the car and gave me a hug. "Go. Don't worry. We'll take care of everything."

I clung to her for a second longer before stepping back and reaching for my bag. "Use the Jeep as much as you want. I'll call you when I get there."

Her eyes widened and she shook her head. "Don't worry about that. You'll be busy."

Why, because a phone call would be too personal? Crossing a line? Maybe it was time that line be crossed. The announcement over the loud speakers, even if it was just the TSA spiel, got me moving. I had other shit to deal with first. Lifting my hand in a final wave, I stalked toward the airport entrance. I'd be seeing my family in a few hours. Rumor was for some people that was a good thing.

Lucky people.

MJ

Miracle of miracles my flight left and landed on time. I'd barely settled in to try to catch some z's before we were bouncing on the runway, and then I was standing in a half crouch with every other person onboard as we waited for them to open the damn door.

Beating the rest of my plane mates, I burst out into the arrivals area. The hot air blasted me. Home, sweet home. A car horn blared as someone laid on it. I glared over my shoulder and squinted. Was that…? Yup, there was my brother in a truck, waving.

I tossed my bag in the back. "I told you I'd catch a cab."

Javier shrugged. "I was just sitting around anyway. Nothing's happening yet."

Uh-huh. Or he was a normal teenager and would take any excuse to drive, even if it meant going to the airport, which most smart people avoided at all costs. Even people who normally could drive lost their god-damn minds near airports.

"Thanks." I reached over and gave him a one-armed hug.

He updated me on all that had been going on, starting with my dad and his condition and then into the normal everyday stuff I'd been missing. He spoke like I was supposed to know who and what he was talking about. Not being near them, I missed out on all the little stuff and all that stuff added up to feeling big.

At the hospital, I followed Javier as he went down the corridors, tapping his shoulder to redirect him when he would have turned toward the ICU. They might have given the walls a coat of solstice blue paint and put up some new lake pictures, but I remembered this place well. I'd been here when I broke my arm and again when I'd jumped from the coffee table to the couch and needed stitches on the top of my head.

Too soon we were turning into the surgery depart-

ment, our shoes squeaking on the linoleum. I curled my
fingers into a fist and then straightened them, trying to
give them something to do besides tremble, which was
stupid. As stupid as me wishing I had someone's hand
to hold. A certain tattoo artist with delicate fingers.
Yeah, that'd go over great. Getting his leg in a concrete
mixer might not have killed off my father, but seeing
me holding hands with a woman would sure do the job.

Javier pointed unnecessarily to room 202. The voices
of my family spilled out into the hallway. About the only
time my mom could ever keep us quiet was in church.
A hospital stood no chance.

I stood corrected. All it took was me stepping into
the room.

My sisters froze, their eyes widening. I took them
in, hardly believing how much they'd grown. I'd missed
these munchkins.

Blinking at the dryness of my eyes—damn airplane
air—I looked to the hospital bed and the man lying in
it. My chest squeezed tight. When had my dad gotten
so old?

"Maricela Joy."

I swiveled to my mom, grateful to turn from the
man in the bed who looked nothing like the father I
remembered.

"Hi, Mama."

She blinked at me.

Thankfully, my other siblings broke the awkward-
ness and surrounded me, giving me big hugs and talking excitedly over each other. It'd be a miracle if we
didn't end up kicked out.

"What are you doing here?" My father's harsh tone
broke through the noise.

Dropping my arm from around my sister Louise's shoulder, I turned to the hospital bed. "Javier called me."

My dad transferred his glare to my brother. "I told you not to tell her."

I squeezed my lips tight, locking them down. I wouldn't let him see his words had made a direct hit.

My brother thrust his chin out. "I thought she should know."

With a grunt my dad looked back at me. "There was no need for you to come."

Yet here my stupid ass was. I'd hopped on a flight that by some miracle my credit card hadn't declined.

You'd think since the years he'd shut me out outnumbered the ones where I'd been his shadow, I would think of his disapproving look when I thought of him. But no, when I pictured him it was with the wide, proud smile he'd given me back in the day.

I took in his leg propped on the bed. Red spots dotted the bandages where blood had soaked through the dressing. "That's not exactly a sprain."

He made a face. "I'll be fine. They're going to fix it."

"Since I already made the trip…" I gave a casual shrug. "I think I'll just hang around to make sure you make it through surgery."

"Maricela!" My mom covered her mouth with her hand.

I channeled Cassie and went for big, innocent eyes. "Isn't that what family does? Wait around to make sure no one kicks it? Sorry I must be a little rusty on this family stuff."

My father shook his head. "I don't need you…"

"Yeah, you've made that real clear."

"Would you let me finish." He slammed his hand down on the sheet. My mom rushed over and grabbed his fist, probably afraid he'd forget and pound his own leg. "You've got a business to run elsewhere. I've got insurance and José to fill in. We're going to be okay."

"Are we? Are we ever going to be okay?" Damn it, where the fuck had that pathetic tone come from?

"I don't know what you want me to say."

I wanted him to say that he loved me. That it didn't matter who I was attracted to because it didn't change me. I wanted the fucking impossible.

"Forget it." I whirled around ready to search for the next flight out, surprised to see the room now empty. "I don't want you to say anything. As long as I like pussy, then you don't like me."

"You didn't even give me time to come to grips. You tell me and then all of a sudden you change."

Was he seriously saying given some time he would have been a-ok with it? Fuck that. I'd been a kid. He'd known me. He should've loved me no matter what. Hell, if I'd confessed I killed someone that day he probably would've visited me in jail, but instead I'd admitted to liking women.

"The only thing that changed for you was my sexuality and I'd known about it for a while."

"No. You changed. After that day you changed."

I tried to think back to those days after I told him. I didn't let myself go there often. Why the hell would I want to relive how scared and devastated I'd been. Had I changed? Hell, yes. Not every day you realized the man you'd worshipped wasn't a hero after all.

"You got mouthy," he went on, pointing his finger at me. "Disrespectful."

I had. I'd thought I was his sidekick who could do no wrong.

So yeah, I'd gotten a little "mouthy." What the hell else was I going to do? Cry? Let him see how much his approval meant to me?

His jaw working as he ground his teeth, he stared down at the white sheets covering him.

"I do love you, you know."

I jolted. "No." I waited a dozen heartbeats, giving my voice a chance to recover so it didn't sound so broken. "No, I didn't know."

My dad's gaze met mine and I collapsed into one of the chairs my little sister had vacated. Holy shit. He had tears in his eyes.

"Well, I do. I never stopped."

Chapter Twenty-Two

Cassie

I gathered my notebook and pencils and headed towards Jamie's station. While she finished up with her client, I hung back and took the opportunity to admire the art around her station. She had the prerequisite sketches and tattoo pictures that all of them had, but also had photos of her daughter.

Giving the stencil one more press, she glanced at me. "Hey, what's up?"

"I'm heading out. Wanted to let you know."

Jamie nodded. "Okay, thanks. I'll lock up. Say hi to MJ for me."

"I will." I turned and almost stepped into Kayla.

"Leaving early?"

"Mm hm."

Kayla's eyes narrowed and she thrust her hip out. I'd seen her do this move many times, in what I figured was a way to show off her curves. In my case I was pretty sure it was to take up more room and make it hard for me to go around her.

"MJ's flight doesn't come in for another two and a

half hours. You only get there early if you're flying out, not when you're on chauffeur duty."

Did she really think I didn't know down to the last minute when MJ was getting back?

"Thanks for the tip." I smiled and slid sideways, brushing past her hip.

Most people probably wouldn't understand the satisfaction found in meeting her snideness with pleasantness, in carefully passing by her instead of giving her the hip check she would've no doubt given me. In this moment it really felt like God's work I was doing, one unruffled smile at a time. MJ might not approve of the methods, but surely she would agree with the sentiment.

I gathered my bag from my locker and then went out to the back parking lot. As I slid into the Jeep, I inhaled deeply, catching the lingering scent of MJ. I knew I shouldn't take such comfort in it, that it wasn't healthy, but like a true addict, I couldn't stop myself.

After starting the Jeep, I pulled out of the parking lot. I'd miss having a vehicle. It was more than just the convenience of getting in and going where you wanted. It was not having to research if somewhere was close enough to bike or look up bus routes and times. A car gave you freedom and independence, not two things I'd expected to miss so much.

Or I hadn't until MJ Flores had come into my life. I guess more rightly, I'd come into hers. I'd gained a hands-on tutor to show me that the only person I needed to please was myself. She'd made me believe that I was desirable, that my body, as is, was enough. I'd come so far with her help. How much was left? When did the lessons end? When the shop was making more money? When MJ decided?

However it happened, the time was getting closer and closer and I needed to prepare myself. Nothing had brought that home more than these last few days. I missed her so much. My day didn't feel complete without her in it. And that was a problem.

I needed to be ready. Ready for the day when I wouldn't feel her touch, wouldn't be the recipient of her sly smile, wouldn't share the bliss of orgasms. Not working on strategies hadn't been a conscious decision to delay the inevitable.

These last few days had not only been a wake-up call, but had also required a renewed action plan. I was on my way to put another check mark on it.

I leaned down and tried to read the street signs while still going with the flow of traffic. I don't know that MJ could ever get me to the point of not wanting to piss off the drivers behind me.

The parking around my destination was all taken so I ended up parking two blocks over, which negated some of the convenience of a car. My stomach fluttered at leaving MJ's precious Jeep out of my sight. I did not want anything to happen to it on my watch.

This section of Portland had an edgier, more industrial feel than the artsy street Thorn & Thistle was on. No cafes with chairs outside or brightly lit galleries. This was dark. Dark colors. Dark street. Dark tinted windows. I squinted trying to find the numbering on buildings. I felt like I was searching for a place that didn't need any signage because it was so cool people knew about it by word of mouth. I spotted the word Chaos in "Raven" font on the next storefront and knew I'd found it. A quick tug on the sleeves of my sweater, and then I opened the door.

The type of place my father pictured me working probably looked like this, with its decor of dungeon chic.

"Hey," a heavily tattooed and pierced guy greeted me.

I pretended not to notice how many glances were being cast my way. Ignorance was bliss.

I pulled my lips up into a smile. "Hi, my name is Cassie and I'm here to speak with Rusty."

"His office is down there." He pointed to a hall to my left, away from the main floor of the shop.

"Thank you." I walked down the hall he'd indicated, pleased to see how clean it was. The burly men didn't look the tidy type, but then I didn't look like the type of person to come in a place like this and request a meeting with the owner. But here I was, knocking on an office door.

Seconds later it swung open to reveal a man with frizzy gray hair and a long white beard braided to his chest. His eyes did a quick sweep of me that ended with a grunt. "You Cassie?"

"Yes." I really wished my voice had that forceful quality that MJ's had. Maybe then he wouldn't be frowning at me quite so fiercely.

"You said you had some questions you wanted to ask."

I held up my notebook. "Yes."

He motioned with one huge hand. "Out with them."

Here? Right now? No small talk and pleasantries so I could get comfortable? I flipped open my notebook, suddenly very conscious it was bright pink with a unicorn and a rainbow. A gift from my mother. Wonderful.

It didn't matter. I wasn't here to make friends or impress him. I needed answers. To get them I had to ask my questions. I took a deep breath and clicked my pen.

"What do you think the owner's role is in artists' happiness? Do you only do marketing for the shop or for some of your individual artists to build up their clientele? Having now been in your shop, I see that your website is very similar in feeling. Was that intentional? Are you targeting a certain type of clientele? What…"

He held up his hand and then stroked it over his long beard. "All right then. Take a seat. This might take a while."

It did. Rusty was accommodating and let me stay over the allotted thirty minutes we'd agreed on. My hand was cramped and my unicorn notebook was full by the end.

Walking out of the shop, it wasn't the neighborhood or the worry that something might have happened to MJ's car that were responsible for my hurried steps.

It was time to go pick up MJ.

Cassie

I scanned the crowd, passing over a woman power walking with her suitcase. Over a father and son. Over an unsteady elderly man who kept his hand out, touching each pole to balance himself. Come on. Where was she? I sucked in a breath, energy bursting through my body. MJ. She shouldered her way past two people who'd stopped, her boots pounding the pavement. Our eyes met through the windshield. Her stride faltered and then she started back up faster.

I clenched the steering wheel. Four days without seeing that face. The delight bubbling in my veins only reinforced I'd made the right decision to wait in the car. The nightmare parking and traffic at PDX had been my excuse, but the truth was there was no way I would've been able to resist running and launching myself into her arms. Which would be bad. Very bad. Way over the top for the return of your mentor, quasi-friend, and... I still hadn't come up with a term to describe what we became after hours.

"Hey," she said, sliding into the passenger seat. The Jeep rocked as MJ closed the door.

I breathed in her scent, getting it as deep in my lungs as I could. Even mixed with the airplane staleness, the pine scent I associated with her relaxed my muscles.

"Hi." Embarrassed at how breathy that'd come out, I adjusted the rearview mirror and the side mirrors and looked over my shoulder. Time to get mov...

"Hey." She cupped the sides of my face and pulled me toward her. Her lips landed on mine, her tongue thrusting into my mouth.

I moaned. Thank god I hadn't put it in Drive. We'd probably be ramming the car in front of us about now because I couldn't feel my feet. Couldn't feel anything but MJ. Her mouth. Her lips. Her tongue.

I'd missed this. Missed her hands on me, missed being surrounded by her, and yes even missed the bitter taste of the coffee that she drank like it was the only thing sustaining her.

I wrapped my arms around her neck and scooted closer. The seat belt pulled me up short. Right. We were in a car and could be seen and...

The world faded as her hands clutched me tighter, our tongues stroking.

A loud tap came on the passenger window.

Gasping, I opened my eyes to find an airport cop peering in. I pulled my tongue back into my mouth and tried to ease away. MJ's hands slowly relaxed their grip and she turned to look at the man.

"Keep it moving."

Wearing an unrepentant grin, MJ sketched a salute. "Fuck. I needed that."

I took a minute to remember how breathing worked and then went through the process again, checking over my shoulder and this time pulling into traffic.

Once I had us out of the airport area and on the freeway, I'd composed myself enough to remember the important things.

"How's your dad?" I asked.

"The doctors are happy. They'll wait for the swelling to go down and then he starts physical therapy. Expecting a fourteen-week recovery time."

The information wasn't any different than what she said in her promised daily calls. As wary as I was of us having those calls and giving us a deeper sense of intimacy, I still made sure to take my break and be available between five and six when they happened.

"And things between you and your dad?"

"Better. We're talking." She sighed. "I don't know."

The frustration and confusion in her voice made my fingernails dig into the steering wheel. I wanted to commiserate or let her know she could talk through it with me. I understood how hard having a strained relationship with your father was. But that wasn't what we were to each other.

Stuffing the seat belt under her armpit, she drew her knee up and turned to face me. "Were you good while I was gone?"

"Of course."

"Have I taught you nothing?"

There went that slithering sensation in my stomach again. Yes, she had. So much. Which meant our deal was almost done. We were waiting for me to finish my end of our bargain, and I might have done it today.

This was never meant to be so complicated. But it was. With every day that passed it was.

I'd missed that quirk of her mouth that let me know she was amused by what I'd said, even if she didn't laugh. I'd missed the way she would hold eye contact for longer than was comfortable, and I had to push myself to keep looking. I'd missed being completely naked with her and still feeling strong.

"I started another poll while you were gone," I said.

"You couldn't be satisfied that I hired a piercer. You have to keep pushing."

"I'm sure what you meant to say is—your last survey was so helpful and astute, I can't wait to see what you've come up with this time."

"What I meant to say, huh?"

She arched her eyebrows in that challenging way she had. Now that we were getting a piercer, I wondered if she'd be open to a small hoop there. Another addition to her general badassery.

She waved her hand in front of my face. "Earth to Cassie."

I batted it away. "Driving here. No distracting the driver."

"I wasn't doing anything."

"No, but your eyebrow was."

She made a startled sound. "What?"

"Your eyebrow—it's begging for a hoop."

She stared at me like I was crazy and okay, maybe I was. But she'd been gone for four days. I hadn't had

anyone to talk to for four days beyond the general pleasantries. I still wasn't comfortable with the other artists.
Only MJ.

"I guess that's better than the clit one you were trying to get me to do before."

I so did not need to be thinking about MJ's clit right
now. Keeping my left hand in a death grip on the steering wheel, as another person squeezed in front of me
without using their turn signal, I waved my right. "Moving on. Do you want to hear my idea or not?"

"Lay it on me. What's your next crusade?"

"Getting Thorn & Thistle to partner with the painting shop down the street. She'd offer tattoo-themed
painting nights, including having some of our designs
chosen for what they put on canvas. In return we'd offer
discounts for anyone wanting to make what they painted
permanent."

Her head thunked against the headrest. "I thought
you were helping me bring in money. Now we're back
to discounts."

"Discounts matched with strategic partnering. It
could open us to a new clientele base."

"Next you're going to be telling me you've got to
spend money to make money."

"There's truth to that." I waited for MJ to finish with
her loud groan. "As long as you're being wise about
where you're spending your money. That includes research, running the numbers. If only you knew someone who was good at that."

"Ha. Ha. Why the hell didn't Jamie put the kibosh on
this? She should've had better control over you. Like I do."

"Mm. But your ways of controlling me usually involve nakedness and orgasms. I didn't know those were an option with Jamie."

MJ squeezed my thigh. "It most definitely the fuck is not."

Her pinky finger slid along the inseam of my jeans, and heat replaced the chill of loneliness that'd been there from the second she'd left.

She lifted her hand to point. "Take this exit. I want to go to the shop."

"Now?"

"Yup."

Of course she'd want to see the shop. She wouldn't trust all was in order until she saw it with her own eyes. Given her history, it made sense. It made a heck of a lot more sense than me being hurt that she wanted to go directly there instead of, say, a bedroom where we could get naked. Or even less sense that I could be jealous of a building.

Ugh. How was this me getting my head on straight and preparing for the near future?

I parked the Jeep in her spot with a lot less fanfare and squealing of brakes. Patting the dashboard, I got out. I imagined her vehicle was going to miss me and my gentle handling.

MJ unlocked the back door, flipped on the lights and went straight into the heart of the shop. She stood in the center and took a deep breath while her gaze roamed around the room. Approaching her station, she trailed her fingers over the wood divider.

Yes, I was most definitely jealous of a building. I wanted those fingers on me.

"Did you miss it?" I spoke with the quietness the moment seemed to call for.

MJ's hand stilled and she looked around the room again. When she turned to me, a small smile curled her lips. "You know what, I did." She patted the wood and then took a step back, brushing her hip against mine. "For all she aggravates me and takes up my time, she's under my skin. I missed her, couldn't wait to be back." MJ turned to face me fully. "Kind of like you."

I swallowed even as the coil in my stomach rattled. "I think I should be insulted."

"If you think you should be, then you're not. Besides you know it's a compliment."

There was no stopping my grin, caution and common sense be damned. "I like knowing I aggravate you."

"You do, huh?" MJ's hands settled on my hips and she drew me closer.

I trailed my fingers along the neckline of her tank top. "Sure do. So are you done checking in? Ready to head out?"

She reeled me in tighter. "It's almost like you missed me or something."

This was another one of the times that maybe if you didn't say something out loud you wouldn't give it too much power. If I kept it inside myself, I had a better chance of controlling it. "I missed some aspects of you."

"Mm. Like what?"

I plucked her hand off my hip and bit the tip of her index finger. "Like these. I really missed what you can do with these."

She traced her finger around the outline of my lips. Even with exhaustion deepening the lines around them, her eyes pierced me. "You don't say. Because it's your artistic fingers I'm interested in right now."

Chapter Twenty-Three

MJ

"This isn't what I thought you had in mind when you said you wanted my fingers," Cassie said, snapping on her gloves.

Goosebumps exploded on my skin. She might have a thing for when I pulled them off, but for me it was all about when she put them on. "We'll get to the other."

Her gaze dropped to my prone body. It'd be hella gratifying if I thought it was because she couldn't resist. Instead I figured it had more to do with not looking me in the eye.

On the plane I'd fantasized about our reunion, of her putting ink on me. I'd spent the return flight furiously sketching my concept for the tattoo I wanted her to put on me. It was only because of her influence that I'd been able to stop and listen to my father. To accept that my anger and defenses had played a part in our estrangement.

"You ready?"

I nodded and closed my eyes. She placed her first mark on my right side. My muscles clenched, not from pain, but because it was Cassie touching me. Gloves as a barrier or not, my body knew Cassie's touch and it reacted.

Even now with her beside me, it still felt like two states were separating us. I reached out and brushed her knee with the fingers she'd admitted to missing.

She jerked and rolled the stool back. Turning the gun off, she glared at me. "No touching. I could've made a mistake."

"You didn't."

"You don't know that. Your fairy could have a very crooked wing right now."

I shrugged. "I'd still wear it with pride."

That got her looking at me. Finally. For one breath, two, three, I could stare into those hazel eyes. Each evening while we FaceTimed I'd wonder which color was winning. Today the green was very much alive.

She searched my eyes, seeming to be doing some visual version of a lie detector test. I let her look. Whatever she laid down on me, I'd wear with pride.

She must have seen the same thing. She ditched the stiff tension she'd been carting around since she picked me up at the airport. Her face softened.

"Well, I'd prefer it if you didn't have to." She rolled the chair back up close and leaned over me, her breath brushing my face. "You know how you can help me do that?"

I could almost taste her mouth again. That kiss at the airport hadn't come even close to satisfying me. "Hm?"

"Stay still." She snapped back into position and with a warning glance turned the machine back on.

I grunted. After being around my family and trying to adjust to the knowledge that my dad loved me, had always loved me, and what that meant now, the famil-

iar drone of the gun and the feel of the needle should
be a welcome refuge. It would be if I could understand
what was up with Cassie.

Ah, Cassie.

From the second I'd gotten past security my eyes
had searched for her. Stupid. She'd told me she'd be
waiting at the curbside pickup. That's exactly where
she'd been, buckled in, engine running. That pang I
could've dealt with.

What I couldn't stand was the second of joy and excitement in her face when she spotted me, before she
censored herself and pulled it back, took it away from
me. I never wanted her to hold back with me. I wanted
it all.

I'd drilled it into her too many times that nothing
would change. I'd convinced her that sex was just some
lessons. Of course she would censor herself. Why the
hell would she fly into my arms? She didn't trust me
with anything more than her body.

The tattoo gun turned off. The chair creaked as she
leaned forward and then came the splash as she dipped
into a lighter wash. "So why a self-mutilating fairy?"
she asked.

Self-mutilation wasn't what I'd been going for when
I'd designed the fairy sitting on a tree stump sawing off
one of her wings, but the description fit. "As a reminder
I make a lot of my problems worse."

My skin tingled and I knew she was looking at me,
not the skin she was tattooing, but me. "I'd never have
pegged you as a fairy kind of woman."

That was because my obsession with fairies was new,
as in her arrival in my shop. Whereas I saw her as Tinkerbell, nothing so wholesome would work for me. My

fairy had to be dark and damaged. A black and gray tattoo with the ink washed into shaded areas around the face and wings. "It's a new direction."

Her gloved pinky swept across my hip in a few soothing strokes. I didn't know if it was in commiseration or to try to ease the pain she was inflicting with the needle. Whatever the cause, I welcomed it. I'd always welcome her touch.

While she worked, I soaked up the peace that was being around Cass, and thought of ways to show Cassie she was more than some lesson to me.

The stop of the gun and the sudden quiet brought me back to awareness.

"We're done," she said.

I shook my head. "We're just starting."

She lifted her brows. "Planning on doing a whole posse of fairies?"

"Is that what they're called? A posse?"

"I think it is when they're on you."

"Huh. The idea's kinda growing on me," I said.

"If you stick with the worst enemy theme, might I suggest flying into a rock for the next one?"

"Or should I go with your self-mutilation? I could do sewing lips shut."

She treated me to a full-fledged smile. "Well aren't we morbid tonight."

She twisted and came back with lotion. She smoothed it on my skin with a featherlight touch that continued long after my skin absorbed it.

"There. Your first fairy complete."

It'd be a good reminder to see every day. I made things harder for myself with my shitty attitude. My dad. My treatment of the girls working for me.

"Thank you."

"You're welc…"

Putting my hands on her thighs, I leaned forward and swallowed the rest of her words. God she tasted good. It was this taste I'd woken up longing for each morning. Not even my momma's Mexican coffee could take the edge off.

Easing back, I dropped a kiss on each of her closed eyelids. "Thanks for taking such good care of the shop. I felt better knowing you were here."

She was fighting letting me see, but I knew from the flush on her cheeks and the way her breath hitched that my words got to her.

I pushed off her and stood. "Let's get the hell out of here. I want your taste down my throat."

Her breath came out in a whimper and she took a step toward me. She stopped.

Turning, I followed her gaze to the tray where her machine laid. Damn it. I sat my ass back down. Respect for the machine won out over sex. Barely.

Once she'd finished cleaning up, I rose and waited while she grabbed her bag. When she stood next to me, I slung my arm around her shoulder, both of us looking out over the shop. This was mine and it looked damn good. Felt it too with Cassie up against me. Things were just better when she was near.

After shutting off the lights, I led her to the back door. "Why don't we swing by your place first and you can gather up a bag and bring some stuff over. Shop's closed tomorrow." Even though I'd missed four days of work, I'd left my schedule empty.

Cassie looked at me out of the corner of her eye. She swallowed. "A bag?"

Yes, hopefully the biggest she could find.

I nipped the tip of her ear. "We've got a lot of time to make up for. It's gonna take a while for me to get my Cassie fix."

Her eyebrow arched. I'd take that sassy look any day over the one that looked like she might be thinking of saying no. "It sounds like you're planning on keeping me locked away to do nefarious things to me. Most of them probably in bed."

Oh, my plans included keeping, but they went way beyond the bed.

Cassie

MJ was behind me. I hadn't heard her approach over the 90s pop Viv was blasting out the shop speakers, but my skin had an alarm system. Goosebumps and tingles tripped when MJ got within a three-foot radius.

"It's looking good." Her voice was right in my ear, her body so close her hair brushed mine.

I tightened my grip on my pencil. "Thank you," I said, not looking up from the sugar skull sketch I was working on.

MJ sighed. "I missed you last night."

"I had my early meeting with my support group."

"I would've driven you."

"And complained the whole time about getting up before the sun and how that's not natural and…"

"First, I sound nothing like that. Second, I'd complain a lot less than not getting to spend any time with you. My bed was all empty and boring." Her eyes went heavy lidded, like she was imagining the ways her bed wouldn't have been empty and boring if I'd been with her last night.

"Stop it." I hissed and looked around the room. Luckily no one was paying any attention to us. I didn't want the other artists aware of what went on between us. Once upon a time MJ hadn't either.

Ever since she'd come back from visiting her family she'd become a fan of PDA. She'd held my hand on multiple occasions while walking me to her car, or she'd press a kiss on my cheek while we waited for our takeout. The hardest moments were when she wanted to watch TV with me. Cook a meal together. It was so hard to say no to those.

But I had to. I longed to do those things with someone. I longed to have another person become a part of my beloved routine. But it couldn't be her. MJ was never going to be the person that I shared those boring parts of my life with. After all she'd been through with her past lovers, she deserved someone extraordinary. As extraordinary as she was.

MJ threw herself on the stool next to me, plopping her elbows down on the table. "Why don't you go to that bistro you love? We're slow and maybe you won't be so grumpy."

We were slow. Even if a walk-in came in, I'd be third in line to get the chance to work on them.

"My treat," she tacked on, bumping me with her shoulder.

I set my pencil aside. "I…"

"Your treat, huh?" Viv draped her arms over the partition. "You've never bought me my lunch. How much does a girl have to put out to get that?"

I stiffened, scrutinizing her expression for anything

accusing, sharp or even knowing. I relaxed, not seeing any. Maybe she wasn't referencing us.

MJ tilted her head back and looked from Viv's black, straight hair, down her slim frame to her thigh-high laced up boots. "You've got nothing I'm interested in." MJ's foot hooked on the bottom ring of my stool, as if she knew I was thinking of making my escape while she was distracted. "I'll still buy you lunch. I'll buy everyone's lunch. It can be a team-building thing." She looked at me. "That's the word you use, isn't it?"

Nothing like a free meal to get the attention off us. I'd suggested to my old boss that the employees would have been happier with more catered lunches throughout the year than a holiday party. He hadn't understood the morale booster of a free meal you didn't have to cook yourself.

"Hell yeah," Maya said. "I want a tuna melt with fries."

I set aside my sketch and tore off a sheet of paper to write down everyone's order.

"We're going to start doing a lot more of this," MJ said, her voice loud enough to carry.

"You buying us lunch?" Maya winked. "I'm in."

"Hell no. You mooches would bleed me dry. I'm talking team activities. Grab a drink. Bowling. Maybe a Thorn's game, things like that." MJ looked over her shoulder at Jamie. "Can you look into some things we can do?"

Jamie's eyes widened and it took her a few seconds for her to answer. "Yeah. Of course."

At least it wasn't only me that was having a hard time keeping up with this new-and possibly-improved MJ. Jamie had known her the longest and she had the same "we should check the news for reports of strange lights in the sky in case MJ had been abducted and returned different" look I'd been wearing for the last few days.

I gathered the list and stood. "I'm going to go get lunch."

"Hold up," MJ called. "You didn't ask me what I want."

"A pastrami, extra pickles and mustard on sourdough, not rye. Onion rings."

"You got it." She smiled, a full-fledged one that had her eyes crinkling at the corners.

I could tell myself that things between MJ and me were that of mentor and mentee with some instructional sex on the side. But how did I get my heart to stop racing? My mouth to stop sighing? My dreams not to include her in them?

Twenty minutes later, I was back and handing out everyone's lunches. I kept Kayla's in the bag because she was just finishing up with a client. I headed to the drafting table where a water glass with ice waited at my spot.

"Before you jump down my throat, it's no big deal. Everyone else was here, so they could get their own."

A glass of water might not be a big deal, but added with every other thing she'd been doing it felt like a very big deal. Not meeting her gaze, I unpacked the take-out bag and handed her the pastrami sandwich, ignoring her loud sigh.

"Guess who I saw today," Kayla said, coming up to the table. "I bet you'll never guess."

"Don't know." She might not have said it, but the "don't care" was in MJ's tone.

With a bravery I couldn't help but admire and hope

to one day master. Kayla continued on, undeterred. "My friend Wolf."

I took another bite of my salad. The more I chewed, the less I'd be expected to talk.

"He works at Chaos," Kayla said.

My head snapped up.

"He had so many things to tell me." Kayla looked at me, her gaze taunting and her smile anticipatory. "Shall I share?"

I almost felt sorry for her. She obviously thought this was going to be the kill shot of this battle she'd been waging against me.

"Or I can." I set my fork down and turned to face MJ straight on. "While you were…"

"Cassie had a meeting with Rusty, the owner of Chaos."

MJ

Cassie'd gone to another shop. No. I refused to believe it. There was only one reason you went to an owner of a shop.

I held her stare, willing her to do more than sit there with her mouth open. Deny it. Tell me she would never.

My arms slid down to hang between my spread legs. Holy shit. "You went and saw Rusty?"

Cassie put the lid on her lunch. "I did. While you were in…"

No. This couldn't be happening. Not again. Not with her. Not Cassie. I pushed away from the table, my chair slamming to the ground. "Wow. You're good. I can't believe I fell for the sweet, repressed girl act."

Cassie's eyes widened, her head jerking. Between

one blink and the next, she'd smoothed her expression, her eyes holding mine. So fucking calm. "What is it you think I've done?"

"It's pretty damn obvious. You've got your skills and now you're off to greener fucking pastures."

"That's what you think? That I'm out scoping jobs?"

"Yup. That backbone's coming along and I've been real useful getting you over your sexual hang-ups." As Cassie's face drained of all color, a niggle in the back of my mind warned me to shut up. To stop before I went too far. Screw that. You couldn't go too far with people that screwed you over. "Only thing holding you back is a test result."

Cassie flinched and I hated, hated, that my stomach did the same. I notched my chin up and held her gaze while I watched something die and fade out in hers.

Swallowing, she looked around the room at the audience that wasn't even pretending not to be listening. "Can we talk about this in your office?"

"I'm good right here."

Her lips pressed together and she wrapped her arms around her stomach. "I wasn't trying to hide anything. I didn't think I needed to tell you. It wasn't a big deal."

My scoff was like razorblades slashing all the way up my throat. Was that meeting the reason she'd been so restrained at the airport? Why she stiffened every time I approached her at work? Why she hadn't come over last night?

When she spoke her tone matched the emptiness of her eyes. "I went to see Rusty because I'd researched the shop and saw not that long ago it didn't have a good reputation. He let me pick his brain about what he'd done to turn things around. I was getting ideas for us, for you, to use."

She couldn't think I was that fucking gullible. Yeah, we were good in bed and yeah, I'd made no secret that I was craving her out of it too, but she wanted me to believe she'd done me some favor by talking to the owner of another shop. Sure. She'd gone to Chaos to ask questions all for me.

My breath seized in my lungs.

Cassie had gone to Chaos. One of the most hardcore shops in the city. Cassie who still jumped when Maya yelled. Did I seriously think she was going to get a job there? She'd have a nervous breakdown in ten minutes. Yet, she'd gone. She'd talked to a legendary hard-ass.

For me.

I righted the chair and sat my ass in it. All the rage drained from me, leaving behind horrible realization.

I'd fucked up.

I rubbed at the fairy on my side. I'd done it again. In front of everyone. Shit. Shit. Shit.

"So you're not planning to go work for Rusty?" I made sure my voice carried to everyone who was watching my unfolding fuck up. They needed to hear the answer. Hear the truth.

Cassie shook her head, eyes downcast.

It was damn hard to try to talk normal when my throat was so tight that it was trying to strangle me. "Good. I'm not sure your sweaters would fit in."

Several laughs floated our way, but Cassie's was not one of them. Not even a fake one. She pulled at the cuff of her sweater. "Yeah."

"I'm for one glad you're not going," Maya said.

Cassie slowly looked over her shoulder toward her.

"We'd miss you."

"Yeah, who would bring us sweets," Vivian added. She threw a nod my way like she was helping me out.

Uh, she did not see the wince Cassie gave before she covered it with a smile. There was no covering the sadness in her eyes.

I gave them all a warning glare———no more "helping"—before turning to Cassie and easing my expression. "Now that I've gone off the handle and we cleared that up, why don't we take this to my office." I held my hand out to her, palm up.

For the first time she looked at my hand as if it were something repulsive. "It's too late."

Of all the mistakes I'd made in the last ten minutes, refusing to go to my office when she'd asked was the smallest. Yet, when I'd refused, I'd known what I was doing. I'd known how much she'd hate having it out in front of everyone, how judged and embarrassed she'd feel. It'd been a chance to inflict revenge. Right now it felt like out of everything, that petty act would do me in.

No.

I wouldn't let it.

"No it's not. Come on." I took a slow step forward, watching to see if she'd follow. She did. I took another one. Step by step.

Opening the door to my office, I drew her inside.

"I'm sorry." I took a step closer and bent my knees until I was in her direct line of sight. "I'm sorry."

She shrugged. "I understand. Considering all the things you've gone through because of people who worked with you, it makes sense."

It might sound like all was good, but I knew better.

Her mouth would say a lot of polite shit that she didn't necessarily believe.

"No. It doesn't make sense. Not to anyone who knows you. You wouldn't do that. That isn't who you are."

"I don't know about that."

Not even a blip in my heart rate. I didn't need to brace myself for what was coming, because there was nothing to brace for. Why couldn't I have fucking remembered that when Kayla came in and started spouting her shit? I'd immediately gone to reliving the past.

Fuck, I had to fix this.

When I didn't jump down her throat, she continued, "If I was seeking another job, I'd make sure I had it lined up before I gave my notice."

Yeah, she would. Because she cared about eating and having a place to live. She wasn't like me, willing to say fuck it. Twice I'd walked out of jobs and imploded my life, because yeah, it took me a while to learn lessons.

Swallowing, I lifted my hand to her face, watching for any sign that my touch was unwelcome.

"That's my 'leave nothing to chance' girl." I slid my finger up and down her cool cheek.

She stood perfectly still. It should have brought relief that she wasn't jerking away. Except I knew what this was—tolerating. There was no pressing into my hand like normal. My heart kicked into "you've really gone and messed it up" speed.

"Did Rusty have any suggestions?" I asked, desperate to keep her talking, keep her in here with me.

"Many. He recommended you get your name out there in trade shows. Said it's great exposure. Also you could give a discount to the customers that review their tattoos. The words are their own, but it'd get you more honest reviews."

"I'll look into a show. See how much they are."

"I did some research into local ones. They're pricey but could be really beneficial, both in team building and name recognition."

Testing, I slid my arm around her waist. When it wasn't batted down, I nuzzled my nose into the soft hair above her ear. "Thank you."

"You're welcome."

I kissed along her ear and down to the spot behind it. That earned me a small gasp and shiver. If my knowledge of her body was the only tool I had to get back on her good side, I'd use it. I'd use the hell out of it.

"I owe you big time. Why don't we go back to my place? We could pick up some grub since neither one of us really ate, make use of the hot tub." I licked at her skin and then nibbled on the bottom of her ear.

"Not tonight," she said, untangling herself from my arms. "After I finish up I need to do some bills and get stuff done at home. Maybe some other time."

"I'm sorry." I'd say it again. However many times it took to get rid of that fake smile.

"It's okay."

The pit in my stomach turned into a crater. There it was. Cassie lied to me. Not about jobs or betraying me. We weren't okay.

Chapter Twenty-Four

Cassie

"Cassie, please. I'm sorry. So fucking sorry."

I blinked, bringing MJ into focus. "I know." I could see it in the deep lines in her face, hear it her pleading tone.

"What can I do to get you to forgive me?" She reached out and pressed on the sides of my mouth until I wasn't smiling anymore. I hadn't even realized I was still doing it. I didn't feel anything.

"Really forgive me." MJ dropped her hands back down.

I shook my head. "There's nothing for you to do."

She flinched. I didn't want to hurt her. I didn't want to inflict anything on her.

"I'm sorry," she repeated. "I didn't mean any of that shit."

That I didn't believe. In order for the words to come out, even in anger, they had to have been there in the first place. But I understood. She'd been hurt before. She thought I was doing the same. She lashed out. Completely understandable.

This was for the best. We knew it was coming to an

end. She'd already hired a piercer and just now she'd agreed to a trade show. Those were my plans to help her bring in some income. As she pointed out, I'd come along nicely as well. Our bargain was over.

I'd always thought there would be a dramatic moment where we'd acknowledge it was complete and we needed to return to colleagues only. I'd been dreading it. Now I didn't have to. Yes, it was much better this way. Better than putting a graduation cap on my vagina and sharing a toast to the special day.

I'd even learned that the other artists would miss me if I left. To be more precise they would miss the things I brought them. Well, all but Kayla.

I wasn't even hurting. Not really. I was blessedly numb. This numbness was like an old friend. It'd been with me on the day in the doctor's office when I was diagnosed. It'd been with me when I attended an event at my father's accounting firm to honor him. Most of his coworkers hadn't known of my existence, thinking he only had two children.

"Cass…"

MJ's uncharacteristically tentative voice broke through the fog surrounding my mind. "Hm?"

"Fuck, I'm sorry. I don't even know all I said. I was just spewing stuff, trying to inflict as much pain as I could." She stepped closer to me, her body helping to rid some of the cold that seemed to be spreading through me. "Will you tell me? Tell me all the shit I need to make up for."

"You don't need to make anything up."

When her pleading, tortured look didn't ease, I mentally shrugged. Doing it physically would take too much effort. Maybe this would be the closure she needed on her end.

"You said my backbone is coming along nicely."

She winced, her hands spasming at her sides. "That's bullshit. It's not 'coming along.' It's always been there. Hell, you're the only one I know who has the guts to stand up to me when I go all Tasmanian devil."

A little more warmth spread through me, cracking through the numbness.

"What else?" MJ asked, appearing to brace herself.

"That you've gotten me over my sexual hang-ups."

"Which I had to say in front of everyone." She hung her head. She put her hand through her hair, not letting the gel stop her, tugging on the dark strands. "You know that one is shit. You just needed to get your confidence back, which you did. Hell, what hang-ups? I bet you could do it all. Any position. Anywhere. Outside. In public."

I shook my head, another chunk of the ice encasing me, falling off so that my lips could lift in a natural smile. "I wouldn't go that far."

MJ hesitantly returned my smile. "We'll have to do that sometime."

But we wouldn't. From the restraint in her eyes, I think she knew it too. Our time was over. The thrill of having sex where you could be caught would be something I'd have to explore without her.

My chest pinched and I kind of wished that I still wasn't feeling anything. Or if I had to feel something that it would be the pleasure that usually came from staring into MJ's dark eyes. I didn't get my last time. My chance to know it was over.

"Wait. Not sometime. Now. Here."

MJ tilted her head, stepping closer. "What?"

"I've never had sex when other people were around." I swallowed and listened to the muffled sounds coming from the shop. "I want to now. Here. With you."

This was it. Our end. Our dramatic graduation celebration.

MJ's eyebrows were drawn in a frown. "You want to have sex with me in here? Right now?"

I nodded. At my eagerness some of the wariness left her face. "Yes. It's one of the last things I'm not comfortable with."

Her shoulders snapped straight. "I can get you comfortable."

"Yes." I looked to the metal chairs in front of her desk, then the desk itself. The numbness was fading fast, but no regrets filled its place. I needed to do this. This would be my closure. "Our full circle moment."

MJ

I reached out, keeping my fingers loose when she let me take her hand even though all I wanted to do is clap mine around her like a manacle. I didn't care for the sadness in her eyes and now at the sides of her lips, but I'd take care of it. I'd make this so good for her.

Entwining our fingers, I led her over to my desk. I kicked my chair out of the way and lifted her onto the edge of the desk. I leaned down in time to catch her gasp with my mouth.

This. This right here. I knew what to do. Our tongues wrapped around each other fast and hard as my hands made quick work of her button and zipper.

I grabbed her head in my hands and kissed her with

everything I had, wanting to imprint myself on her, to still be feeling her tongue on mine hours later. Just as quickly I released her and dropped into my chair, pulling myself as close to her and the desk as I could get.

I slid off her shoes and then started tugging at her jeans. She threw a glance over her shoulder at my office door and then she helped, lifting her hips. I made quick work of her pants, wanting to get to my prize.

With my shoulders, I spread her legs wider. I leaned forward and inhaled her deeply through the cotton of her underwear. "Fuck, your smell. I can't get enough."

She made a keening sound, her feet flexing.

I pulled her underwear down—no teasing, no drawing it out. I needed to taste her. I dove in. As her flavor filled my mouth, I groaned, licking deeper. Good, so good. Cassie moaned, spurring me on. I didn't speak. Didn't tell her how much I loved doing this for her. How fucking wet she made me. It wasn't my voice I wanted to hear. I wanted nothing but her increasing moans in my ears.

She rocked her hips, pressing up into my mouth. I centered on her clit, with long flat strokes of my tongue, knowing how much she liked it. But she was quiet. Too quiet. I eased back enough that I could look up the length of her body. She was reclining on my desk, her eyes squeezed shut, her bottom lip between her teeth.

I wrapped my arms around her waist and pulled her down on my lap. Her eyes flew open. Much better. Now there was no way she could forget who was giving her this pleasure.

I bent her legs, so she straddled me and would be comfortable. I ran my fingers along her bottom lip. "You're gonna leave a mark."

"It's the only way I can stay quiet."

"I've got you covered. No need to hurt yourself." I gave her a quick peck. "You're not into bondage, I'm not into pain."

She shifted, some of her weight easing away from me. "That's me. Plain, vanilla sex."

"There's nothing plain about you." If she was plain I wouldn't find looking into her eyes a must-have part of sex for me.

I slid my finger down until it was surrounded by her wet heat. I stroked inside of her, pressing my thumb against her clit. As she arched I kept my arm tight around her waist, making sure she didn't go anywhere. Gasping, she curled her hand around my wrist, holding me to her as I fingered her. I bucked my hips, feeling the wetness in my own pants.

I could come just from watching her. Her legs clamped around my hand. Tremors shook her. She was so fucking beautiful when she let go and the pleasure took over.

"Yes," I coaxed, pushing my fingers deeper. Right as her body tensed, I swooped up and covered her mouth with mine, swallowing her cry.

I slowly pulled my fingers from her. My head spun from the rightness. From the relief after the fear that I wouldn't be able to do this again. Bringing my hand to my mouth, I licked the taste of her off my fingers.

"Oh god. I love when you do that."

Which was my second favorite reason for doing it. The first of course being because she tasted so damn good. I ran my tongue up to the tip of my middle finger, gathering every bit of her I could. Dirty talk whispered into her ear could get me a moan, but this got her twitching and panting.

She caught my hand and shook her head. "I can't." She pushed herself up and slid from my lap. "I can't take anymore."

My heart went into a free fall. She was still pulling away. Fuck. I curled my hands around the armrests, my fingers turning white. I wanted to grab her, hold on to her, never let her go. But I couldn't. Not if she didn't want…

She hopped up on my desk, crossing her legs and giving me a glimpse of her glistening pussy.

"I want to watch you come. Make yourself come for me."

I loosened my grip and took a precious second to breathe before I fumbled at my zipper and then shoved my hand down my pants and started to finger myself.

"Mm."

The sound of Cassie finding pleasure in my pleasure was the thing of fantasies. I rubbed my fingers along my clit, spreading my legs wider. It wouldn't take me long. I was already almost there. Right there. One more…

I threw my head back, a cry climbing from my throat. Cassie placed her hand on my mouth. I opened my eyes, looked into hers. Our gazes held as I stroked myself, holding off so I could enjoy this connection for just a little longer. But it was too much. My cry erupted at the same time Cassie lifted her hand. It echoed around the room, probably down the hall. Not that I cared. Not that Cassie seemed to care. She watched me with a little smile on her lips.

My mind decided to reconnect and I fell forward, pressing my head against her thigh. Her hand landed on my head, her fingers trailing through the shaved hair at my temples, the only place that didn't have pomade in it.

"I would never want to be deprived of seeing that."

I turned my head and placed a kiss on her skin. My chest was way too small for all the feelings wanting to burst free. Wrapping myself around her leg was the only way to make the tightness bearable. "God, I love you."

Her leg went rigid. Seconds ticked by, so fucking many. Then she was scrambling off my desk. Her feet hit the floor while I was still grabbing for her.

"Cass…"

She shook her head in a negative, violent motion, grabbing her pants.

I pushed myself up from my seat, my hand out-stretched. Toward the woman I loved.

Dressed now, Cassie whirled on me. "You said it was just about sex. You promised."

It was a promise every single person I knew made. Everybody meant it until they didn't. Had she missed the part where I handed her my heart?

"Yeah, well I was stupid," I said. "When I said that I didn't know you were a woman who one night brings my cat a feather toy and the next goes and has a chat with Rusty. It can't be just about sex. Not with you. You make it impossible."

"You promised," she whispered.

I kept my hand out, suspended.

She curled her arms around her stomach. "It's not… I can't. I can't get in a relationship."

Holy fucking shit. All this time I'd focused on my issues with trust and being used and getting past them. And I was past them. Because there was no denying that Cassie made me happy. That I wanted to do things for her. That I felt I could be good for her in return, not for protection or getting her name in the business, but to show her how wonderful she was. There was nothing to stop us now except her.

Cassie. I'd never checked in with Cassie.

Cassie

I clutched myself tighter. It felt like my hands were the only thing holding me together and if I didn't keep a tight enough grip, I'd fall apart. I couldn't look at her. Not when her hurt was there to see. A huge part of me demanded I rush over and say whatever it took to erase that look.

"I can't get involved with anyone. Not right now." I wrapped my sweater closer around my middle. "Maybe not for a long time." Maybe ever. "I won't know for another three weeks."

"Sweet Cass." MJ's face softened, her hand brushing my cheek. "It doesn't matter. Whatever the results, I'll be there."

I took a step back, shaking my head. "I would never do that to you."

MJ followed. "Do what? Let me spend time with you? Let me help you?" She placed a hand on each of my shoulders and bent her head, staring directly into my eyes. "It's going to be okay. No matter what that test says, it'll be okay. We'll face it together."

I swallowed and took in her earnest face. She believed it. She believed every word she said.

But she couldn't make me believe it. I knew. I knew better.

"I know you think that, but until you're in it, you

don't understand. I'm a ghost of my normal self, which isn't exactly exciting to begin with. My life becomes nothing more than my chemo cycle. I have nothing to give someone."

MJ's head snapped back. "Don't you dare put me in the same category as your ex. I'm no Marissa."

"No, you're not. Marissa had the demands of a normal job and I hadn't been able to give her even close to enough. You're already stretched thin. What little free time you have needs to be spent on relaxing, antiquing, having fun. You need to be with someone who enhances your life, not burdens it."

The muscle below MJ's right eye twitched. "You're talking about something we don't even know is gonna happen. Down the road it could be me. You wouldn't ditch me."

No. I wouldn't. If I went deep down to all the places I spent so much time making sure no one saw, I knew I'd stay with anyone, not just her, because I'd be worried what others would think if I left someone when they needed me. It just so happened that with MJ I'd always want to be around her. God forbid, even if she got sick, she would still have so much to offer.

MJ's face hardened and she took a step away from me. "Hell, are we even talking about cancer? Maybe you're not feeling the same way."

Not feeling it? MJ occupied a permanent place in my heart. There were sections devoted to knowing what her every look meant. Parts that knew the difference between the frustrated growl when she couldn't capture just what she wanted in a sketch and her satisfied growl when she bit into a fish burrito. This wasn't about her. It was about me and what little I had to offer her.

Cancer or no, I was still an apprentice with no paycheck, living in a crappy apartment with no car, who still had to question my every action and whether I was doing it because I wanted to or because I wanted to make someone else happy. "I… I… It's not… I just can't…"

She shook her head, the gaze she swept over me an exact replica of the unimpressed one the first day I met her. "No, I get it. No need to go on."

I squeezed my fingers into my stomach. It didn't help. I was splintering.

"You can leave it open," she said, jerking her head to the door.

The fine trembling of my body progressed to full out shudders, my teeth chattering. "Wh…what happ… ens now?"

MJ sat down and threaded her fingers over her stomach. "Now you work. That's what you're here for, right? So that's what you'll be doing. All you'll be doing."

I flinched. No more outings. No more sex. No, not sex. It hadn't been that for a while. It'd been making love. Now she'd confirmed my heart wasn't the only rebellious one. I locked my knees. It hurt. The dismissive way she looked at me now hurt.

But it was better this way. This hurt was better than the devastation if we had a relationship and she made the discovery I already knew she would.

I wasn't enough. Would never be enough. Whether sick or healthy.

I'd hoped that when I stopped spending so much time pleasing people and caring what others thought that something new would emerge to take the place. Something powerful and interesting. Nothing. She'd see that too.

Chapter Twenty-Five

Cassie

I looked up from my decidedly "unhappy" sketch as Maya came up. It was pretty rare for any of the artists to hang out in the lobby. That's why it was one of my favorite spots, and this last week had been my refuge.

"Everything okay?"

"My client should've been here twenty minutes ago." She looked uncharacteristically insecure, like if her client failed to show it was a personal failing on her part. I wasn't used to this from the normally loud and energetic artist. I didn't like it.

"Traffic's always bad this time of day." I shrugged. "Or if they're anything like you, they had a little too much fun last night and are hungover."

Her mouth quirked. "I have noooo idea what you're talking about."

"Of course not. I'm sure you ditched your contacts and wore your glasses because you felt like it, not to try to hide your dark circles and bloodshot eyes."

"Damn you, nothing gets past you." She elbowed me and then sighed, returning her gaze back to the people passing by out front. "She better show up. She had me redo the sketch three times."

"She will." I turned to watch her walk back to her station. There went my gaze to MJ. The real reason I'd turned. Any excuse to look at her. Her head was bent as she worked on her client. I let myself stare. There was no danger of being caught. I could watch her for twenty minutes straight and she wouldn't glance my way. God, I wished I had her self-control. It hurt to look at her.

I blinked. Somehow in the last minutes the sketch I'd been doing had stopped being the outline of a skeleton and was instead MJ's profile.

I ran my finger over the cheekbones and chin I'd drawn. So strong and unyielding. Fingers trembling, I got to erasing.

At night when my mind was quietest was when the doubt seeped in. It wasn't like MJ didn't know about my housing and money situation or that all the adventurous bones in my body had been replaced by caution signs. Still she'd said she'd fallen in love with me anyway. Should I trust that? Trust that she saw me and had decided there was enough there to keep her satisfied?

When I woke, severing things with MJ felt right. Well, as right as it could be to no longer have the right to touch, share with, be with the person you craved. The person who'd gone from declaring her love to ignoring me completely.

"Oh hell no."

My head whipped up.

MJ pushed away from her client, jumping to her feet. "You've got to be fucking kidding me."

I ditched my sketchpad and headed toward MJ, joining the other artists who had stopped what they were doing and had circled around MJ. I wedged between Viv and Jamie, no hesitation. I belonged here.

With her face holding the same anger as MJ's, Maya explained, "I just called my client. She said she's going to Heidi's now."

MJ's ex. Not good. So not good.

"That's not the worst part," Maya said.

"Of course it isn't," MJ bit out.

"Heidi offered her a discount if she started going there. She's poaching my clients. That wasn't the only one. I got ahold of a couple other clients and they said they'd gotten calls. They didn't take her up on it because they're happy with me."

The artists exploded en masse.

"Fuck that."

"She better not be."

"I will cut her," the last one came unsurprisingly from Viv. She wasn't as reactive as Maya, but she could be fierce

While they talked over one another, I kept a wary eye on MJ. She should be throwing things, cursing, having us hold her back. Instead she continued to stand in place, body vibrating. This quiet was so much scarier.

"Hold on." Jamie stepped forward, holding up her hand. "We need to call our clients. Find out just what we're facing here."

"No what we should be doing is going over there and whooping some ass," Maya said.

Jamie shook her head. "No. We need to focus on our clients and stopping any more from leaving."

There were a few murmurs, but Kayla and Viv obeyed, pulling out their phones. All the while MJ stood there, eyes downcast at the floor.

A loud roar echoed in my head like a monster had been awoken from a long slumber. She should never look so defeated.

Damn that Heidi. The woman had already taken half of MJ's staff, shattering her trust. She'd spread rumors, bad-mouthed MJ in the industry, wrote fake reviews. Through it all MJ continued on. But this blatant stealing of customers seemed to be the blow that was finally knocking her down.

I stepped back, for once grateful for my knack for being overlooked in a crowd.

If MJ surrendered to Heidi, I knew it would be one of the greatest regrets in her life. If I didn't do something to make sure that didn't happen, it would be one of mine.

Cassie

I marched into Mutiny Rose and nodded at the woman at the front counter. My pulse slowed a fraction. This woman was nowhere near as intimidating as the bearded man at Chaos. Maybe listening to Ke$ha's "Woman" on repeat on the bus had been overkill.

"Hi, I'm looking for Heidi."

The young woman tilted her head toward the back. "She's with a client."

"Okay. I'll wait until she's free."

I took a seat, the receptionist already ignoring me. This place needed a deep cleaning stat. The dust on the window sill could be measured with a ruler. I tried to overlook the dirtiness and take in the shop. Cream walls with scuff marks, laminate wood floors also with scuff marks. Where was the passion? The color? Oh that's right, at Thorn & Thistle with MJ.

I moved on from the lobby to checking out the other artists and trying to decide which one was her. Bad idea. My ready-to-kick-ass attitude flagged. I turned my attention back to the front of the shop and the wall of sketches. Ah, that was better.

Not to go to Peter Pan-ish, but I was pretty sure I could do better blindfolded with one arm tied behind my back.

My phone vibrated and I jumped. Buoyed or not by the bad drawings, my nerves were still in the flight mode of fight or flight.

MJ: Where r u?
MJ: u should b here
MJ: u r supposed to be part of the team

Really? It'd been thirty minutes. She was just noticing I was gone now?

"Hey, Terry said you wanted to speak to me."

I hurriedly finished up my text.

Cassie: Had to take care of something really quick. I'm always on your team.

"Yes, thank you," I said, rising. So this was the woman MJ had shared so much with. Thin and a few inches taller than me, she had long brown hair. This woman carried herself in an "I'm not one to be messed with" way. She wore jeans and a tight T-shirt with the word Resist across her ample breasts. Of course she had nice breasts.

I tore my gaze away from her chest and right up to her smirk.

Great. Now she thought I'd been checking her out. Which I guess I had, but in a "she's competition" way.

"So you wanted to talk to me?"

"I'm Cassie." I held out my hand and shook hers, inwardly squirming as my damp palm hit her bone-dry one.

Heidi looked at me curiously. "Are you looking to get a tattoo?"

If I hadn't been wearing my sweater she would know the answer to that. I only let experts ink my skin. "No. Actually I'm here because I wanted to speak to you about Thorn & Thistle. MJ Flores specifically."

Her brown eyes narrowed into hard slits, any cordiality sliding off her face. "You a lawyer?"

"No." Though her thinking that I could be was a step up from the preschool teacher I usually got pegged with.

"Then what the hell do you want?"

"To talk." I pulled up the list of talking points I'd made on the bus ride over. Most of my remaining nerves eased at the sight of the little bullet points. "This path…"

"Is this a joke?" She shook her head, her long pony-tail swinging across her back. Mine used to be able to grow like that before the chemo. Now the hair broke off.

"No. No joke."

"It has to be." She gave me a dismissive once over. "Otherwise why the hell would I listen to you?"

A cocoon of calm descended on me, insulating me from her, from the stares of the other artists and patrons. I put my list away. That was for rationalizing with adults.

"You'll listen to me because I know what it's like

to not believe in yourself. I understand not feeling like you can measure up."

She stepped up to me, clipping the toes of my shoes. "You don't know what the fuck you're talking about."

"Ah, but I do. I live it every day. From the work I've seen today, you're justified in your fear."

"I'm not afraid of anything."

"No? You try to hide it behind bravado and bullying tactics, but I can see it for what it is. Soon everyone else will too."

"Now you're calling me a bully? You're lucky I don't bust your face in." She thrust her finger at me. "Get your grandma ass out of my shop."

"I will as soon as I get your agreement to stop harassing MJ because you feel insignificant."

"What has MJ done to earn this devotion, hmm?" Heidi smiled smugly. Not even her straight white teeth could make it attractive. As far as I could tell the only thing she had going for her were her large, perky breasts. "Guess she's still fucking the help. You'll wise up soon. Just like the rest of us did."

"Sorry, I don't take stock in the words of a backstabber."

Heidi snarled. "You're wasting your time. She doesn't care about you or anyone else or the shop. For her it's all about the name she can make for herself."

"You're wrong. You couldn't be more wrong." No one put in more effort than MJ. She was at the shop no less than twelve hours a day. Her house, her money, everything was on the line for MJ.

"You'll see." She gave me a pitying look that was short on the pity and heavy on the scorn. "There's a reason no one sticks around long. Not even her own family. There's something broken in her."

The cocoon incinerated. I stared at her, time seeming to slow. "What did you say?"

"You heard me. MJ is nothing but an overrated hack who deserves to be alone."

Oh hell no.

I'd been nice for too long. A lifetime too long.

I curled my fingers and launched.

Chapter Twenty-Six

MJ

I wrenched the door of Heidi's shop open. I was ready to do this. Past ready. I was done pretending Mutiny Rose and the people in it were dead to me. They'd wanted my attention, wouldn't stop until they got it. Well, now they had it. It's about time I got some answers.

My gaze swept the room. Did they even clean the place? Ah, there was Raz. So nervous when I hired her because of what showed up on the background check. She'd promised that I'd never regret hiring her, that she would prove that she was worth the risk I was taking. Ha.

Raz caught sight of me and stopped talking to her client. Something flickered in her eyes. Dare I hope regret? Nah. I didn't think she was capable of it.

I followed her shifty gaze to… Heather. Heather the social butterfly. Always arranging a party or get-together for the staff. Little did I know that they also served as bitchfests about me and planning committees to screw me over.

"Can I help you?"

"Nope," I said, walking right past the young woman

manning the front desk. I saw who I'd come here for. At one time I'd thought Heidi was a sexy woman with her curves and long hair. Not anymore. Now I knew what lay underneath.

She made my skin itch, like I needed to shed it because being near her contaminated me. Funny, considering she was the snake.

I made my way down the center aisle. My steps slowed as I went by a piercing station. Heidi would shit a brick that I'd hired Gina. She'd have an even bigger fit if she learned I'd had no trouble shooting her down every time she'd mentioned it, but had stood no chance against a sweater-wearing pixie.

Cass. I wanted to tear my useless heart out of my chest. The damn feelings could end anytime now. It wasn't like they were doing me any good since she wasn't feeling them back.

Heidi caught sight of me, her eyes widening. She stepped away from the woman she was talking to. "How nice. I'm actually not hiring right now."

"Fuck off." This is what not responding had gotten me. She thought she'd gotten the best of me, that I'd rolled over. Fuck that. She'd learn. It was all here, inside me, and I was ready to unleash. I deserved this exorcism. She'd betrayed me. We'd created the shop together. So many hours going over what we wanted. More hours sharing my body with her. All the hard work. We'd done it together and then she left me. Took half our staff and left me. No warning. No explanation.

She was going to tell me why.

"I'm done with your shit. You're trying to sabotage me like I'm the bad one. Fuck that. It ends now. If you don't…"

Heidi held up her hand and rolled her eyes. "Don't bother. Your girlfriend's already been here."

The hairs on the back of my neck shot straight out. "My girlfriend? What the hell are you talking about?"

"I must say I wouldn't have picked her for you." My ex-partner cocked her head. "She looked too sweet and innocent. Then again I'm sure it makes it easier to boss her around."

"Cassie was here?"

"Interesting. You didn't correct me on the girlfriend thing."

No, I didn't. Even though Cass and I weren't together. We weren't anything.

Bullshit.

Cass was more than a measly girlfriend. I'd had girlfriends before. I'd gone out with them, dirtied the sheets with them. I hadn't thought about them all day. I hadn't called them because I missed the sound of their voices. I hadn't offered up my sweatshirt so I could wear it later and smell them on it.

Would this ache in my chest ever go away?

Focus. I needed to focus. "Why the hell was Cassie here?"

But I knew. The text. Her having to do something. Shit. She'd come here. She'd want to make things better. She couldn't stand conflict. Damn that sweet, considerate bonehead.

Heidi shrugged. "As far as I could tell to yell and break things."

I jerked, my attention snapping back to her. That didn't sound like my Cassie. I would've expected her to come in armed with facts and maybe charts like some kind of strong-arm fairy.

"I couldn't have her doing that. It's not good for business."

Shit. I needed to get to her. She was probably freaking out.

I whirled for the door.

"If you're going after her, you might want to check the police station. That's usually where they take people when they're arrested."

MJ

My eyes darted around the police station, searching. Of course she wasn't where I could see her. She was in the back, behind bars. Oh god, I was about to puke. Swallowing hard, I went to the desk and the officer standing there watching me.

Man did that heavy stare bring me back. Back to Arizona when my pals and I had run-ins with the po-po. The cops had taken one look at us with our tattoos and brown skin and deemed us trouble. My smart mouth made sure it never ended well.

"Can I help you?" he asked.

"Yeah. I'm trying to get info on Cassie Whiteaker."

The older man, who had to be pushing retirement, bent down and clicked on the computer.

"She hasn't been released yet," a woman said to my right.

I turned, the bile returning. Marissa, Cassie's ex, was getting to her feet.

What the fuck was she doing here?

"She's seeing pretrial release services now. Once that's done we'll know if she's out on her own recognizance or needs to post money."

I nodded at the officer even though he hadn't really done anything, and I stepped away from the desk. Closer to the ex. "How'd you find out?"

"Cassie called me. Asked me to come bail her out."

Pain radiated through my body worse than any hit I'd ever received. She'd reached out to someone else and it felt wrong. Having her ex be here felt wrong.

Then again, I guess I couldn't even be considered an ex. We'd never been together.

Fuck that. No one knew me as well, no one I wanted to know me. And I knew her but still wanted more. I wanted to know everything about her, would never know enough. I wanted every piece of her.

I jerked my head in the direction of the double doors. "I'm here now so you can head out."

Marissa smiled, retaking her seat. "I'll stay. She called me."

Bitch. "She doesn't even have to call me and I show up. I'll always be there for her when she needs me."

The ex's smile grew. "Ah. Funny that she should call me then."

She could take her "funny" and shove it past her red lipstick and choke on it. "I'm still figuring out why she's kept you around."

"It's simple. I know her. I love her. She loves me. We'll always be in each other's lives."

She didn't even sound like she was trying to rub it in. It was more like she believed the shit she was saying.

"You'll be in her life unless she gets sick again, right?"

Marissa's smile fell away. "I do what she tells me. I respect her enough to listen when she speaks."

I snorted. "With Cassie it's as much about what she

doesn't say as her actual words. You can't pay attention to the first thing she says, 'cause it will always be to say everything is fine."

This woman had been all too happy to listen when Cassie told her it would too much with her cancer and they shouldn't be together.

Just like I'd only heard that Cass didn't want me. What if it was something else? What if that had only been her bullshit first response?

"It sounds like you think you know her well."

"Since it's my house Cassie will be spending the night in, yeah I guess I know her well." I searched the ex's expression and didn't see any jealousy, which allowed me to relax. A little.

I jiggled my leg and looked at the metal door leading to the back. "You know what she got charged with?"

"It sounded like trespassing and assault."

"Shit." Those were not exactly words you used when talking about Cass. They sounded dangerous and expensive.

Well, hell. Maybe it was good Cassie had called Marissa. My credit card wouldn't hold crap. My house was already second mortgaged to the max.

If she'd called me, I wouldn't have been able to get her out.

I'd have begged, borrowed, and if it came down to it, I couldn't completely rule out stealing. But that would've taken time. Time Cassie would have been stuck in jail.

That was no place for Cassie. My dad had left me in there one night as a lesson after I'd been busted for tagging. My attitude had been able to hold people off. What would save Cassie?

"Think she'll get released?"

"Yes. She has no previous record. They'll take one look in her big, scared eyes and know this is a one-time digression for her."

I hated the thought of her being scared. Hated even more that all I could do was plop my ass out here and wait. My arms ached with the need to wrap her up tight. "It's those sweaters. They're tricky. Make you think she's all shy and innocent."

Cass's ex laughed, the sound deep and throaty and drawing the attention of a few of the cops behind the counter. A totally different kind of look than any I drew from them. "That they are. I was with her two months before I figured out the trick—keep her fed if you want her to stay sweet."

"But weren't you guys friends before that?"

"Yes."

No. No, they couldn't have been. She'd been friends with the perfect, pleasing Cass. Which meant when they started dating, that's who Marissa had been attracted to. To someone who didn't exist.

Only when she'd shown me the snark and grit beneath her meek exterior did she snag me.

Marissa pulled out her phone. I did the same, typing out a message to Jamie that I wouldn't be back today and tomorrow was iffy. Next I contacted my clients that were scheduled.

What felt like forever later, the door opened and then there was Cassie. Except for her sheepish expression as she headed toward Marissa, she looked exactly the same as when she'd come to the shop this morning.

She was okay. My heart could slow the fuck down.

"Hi, thank you for coming. I'm so…" Her gaze

shifted to me, her eyes widening. "What are you doing here?"

I stepped closer, all of my instincts demanding I run my hands down every single inch of her body to make sure no one had touched her. But until we talked, until I made sure she really didn't want me, I didn't have that right. I stuffed my hands into my pockets. "I went to Heidi's. She told me."

"I see you managed not to get arrested."

"Who would've thought." Unable to resist, I freed my right hand and ran it down her warm, pink cheek. "I'm supposed to be the rebel."

She raised her chin, her nose going up in the air. "Yeah, well, I really dislike that woman." She pressed her cheek harder into my hand, her skin getting warmer. "Only you would look turned on by someone who is now going to have a record."

"It's fucking hot. I love that you went after her."

She wrinkled her nose. "Except she won."

"That round, maybe. She doesn't stand a chance against us for the long haul."

Marissa stepped closer, inserting herself into the conversation. "You doing okay?"

Cassie nodded, pulling away from me to face her ex directly. "Actually it wasn't that bad. I was speaking to one of the officers most of the time. They have a fascinating job."

That was my girl, making friends with the people that arrested her. "I'm sure it was great. Let's get you out of here anyways."

"That'd be good." She spoke to Marissa, "Thank you for coming. I know you had to take time out of work." She bit her lip. "Maybe I could pay you…"

Her ex bent and hugged her. "I know. Don't worry about it. You can pay me back by doing the tattoo we talked about. I think it's time that I join the ranks."

"I'd do that for free, you know that."

Marissa pulled back and cupped Cassie's cheek. "And you know I'll come bail you out. Let's just not make a habit of it, hm?"

"I make no promises."

"Mm hm. Now do you need a ride home?"

I grabbed Cassie's wrist, halting her before she could follow Marissa. "I'll take you."

She drew in a sharp breath. "Um…"

Jesus how had things gotten so bad between us that she couldn't even accept a ride from me?

"Come with me," I urged, trying to keep my voice cajoling instead of demanding. Surprisingly, it wasn't that hard. I didn't want to force her to come with me. I wanted her there because that's where she wanted to be.

Cass gave an almost nonexistent nod. "I'll go with MJ."

Marissa shot me a look. "Are you sure?"

No, she wasn't sure. Anyone could see that. Hell, I wouldn't be surprised if the cop Cass had made friends with didn't come out and accuse me of trying to kidnap her.

"Yes. I'll, uh, go with her."

Hell yes she would. My chest tightened, cutting off the excitement. Now I had to make sure she wanted to stay there.

Marissa nodded and then after a pat to Cass's shoulder headed toward the exit.

Finally it was Cassie and me. Now came the hard

part. My specialty was more in the wrecking of things, not putting them back together.

First step, get her the hell out of here. "Come on, let's go."

"I had no idea being a badass was so exhausting. How do you do it?"

I smiled. With all the shit that went down today, I didn't think it'd be possible, but I felt...okay. Cassie walked at my side, our shoulders occasionally brushing. My girl had walked into enemy territory and confronted the woman who had hurt me the most. She'd done it for me. Yeah, I was doing pretty damn good.

"It helps to do it in small doses, kinda build up your system." I opened the passenger door for her. "You went straight full throttle."

"Guess I can never turn off that overachiever part of me." Her tone was light but when she faced me, there were little lines around the corners of her mouth. "I'm not sure I have it in me to go back to the shop tonight."

"Good, 'cause we're going to my place." There was no way in hell I'd take her back to her place. She would not be in that loud, run-down place. Not tonight. I wanted her somewhere comfortable where I could look after her.

She started to balk. I hurried and closed the passenger side door.

As soon as I was behind the wheel, she was off. "You don't have to do that. Just drop me off at my place. I know you have tattoos on the schedule for tonight."

"They're already cancelled."

Her shock had my jaw clenching tight. It was such a surprise that I'd want to be with her and not at the shop? No wonder she hadn't fallen hard like I had. I'd done a piss poor job showing how much she meant to me. That I could fix. Whether she returned my feelings or not, she deserved to be treated like the treasure she was.

I started the Jeep. "First up is a bath. I'm going to take care of you tonight. That starts by getting you clean."

Chapter Twenty-Seven

Cassie

As soon as I walked through the door into MJ's house my pulse slowed. After the noise, so much noise, and constant state of alert of the last hours, this was a haven.

MJ closed the door and then pressed up behind me, her body warming my back as she squeezed my shoulders. "Thank you."

"I didn't do anything but get myself arrested."

"You did a lot more than that. You took action. You had my back." Her thumbs worked on the knots in my shoulders. "You made an enemy today. For me."

My insides quaked. Her acknowledgement was going to break me. I might not have accomplished anything, but she was right that it'd been a lot. I'd been arrested. I'd been in the back of a cop car. I'd been fingerprinted. I'd been in jail. For hours.

Air. I needed air.

MJ came around to my front.

Staring into her eyes, the panic receded.

I'd do it all again. For her. To be worthy of the respect I saw there. "You're welcome," I said.

She pressed her forehead against mine, rubbing it

softly back and forth. "How did it feel to go after her? Was it good?"

"I don't remember much of it. I'm pretty sure I had an out-of-body experience. We were insulting each other and then she said...something I didn't like and I snapped."

MJ pulled her forehead away and stared at me, the line between her eyebrows deepening. It only ever seemed to truly go away when she was sketching or she fell asleep. "Something, huh?"

"It doesn't matter. Everything she has to say is crap."

"Uh-huh." She pressed her lips to my forehead. "Thank you anyways."

She pulled away to stand to her full height, and I bit my lip to keep my protest to myself.

"Come on." She grabbed my hand and led me down the hall to her bedroom.

I stared down at our interlaced fingers. I should pull away. Nothing had changed. One act—an unsuccessful one—did not suddenly make me an equal. But I kept our fingers interlaced.

In the middle of her room, she stopped and faced me. She hadn't turned on any lights and the setting sun created a soft glow in the room, giving it the sensation of not being real. Her brown eyes were so warm they reminded me of pools of melted chocolate, waiting to offer comfort.

Holding my gaze, she went down to her knees at my feet. She tapped my calf until I lifted my leg. She slid my shoe off and bent, placing a kiss on my arch. She did the same to my right foot and then stood. Her hands gentle and steady, she pulled my sweater up and I bent my head so she could take it off of me. Tossing

New Ink on Life

it to the dresser, she moved on to my pants, slowly ridding me of them.

"God, you're beautiful." It wasn't arousal in her tone, but something more, deeper. If I didn't overanalyze it I would swear it was wonder. She stepped back, drawing me with her. "Time for that bath."

She kept hold of my hand as she started the bath, the rush of water echoing off the gray tile. When steam rose behind her, she twisted and ran her free hand through the water. "Come on."

"I don't need to be taken care of. I'm fine. Nothing really happened. I'm just a little tired, from all of the…excitement." Yes, that was a fine word for the terror and shock when people had to pull me off another person and I'd seen the broken glass surrounding us. Glass that I'd broken.

"No?" MJ cupped the back of my neck, drawing my head closer to hers. "I think that's exactly what you need. Even if, especially if, it's only because you're tired."

"I…that's…" That's not how things worked. I shivered.

MJ tightened her grip, no doubt feeling my tremble. "There's no reason for you to deny yourself this."

But there was. Every reason. MJ's touch on my body aroused me but I could eventually douse it. Her being solicitous to me without cause reached out to my soul. How could I ever get my soul back?

"Tonight. Give me tonight," she said.

I looked from her beseeching gaze to the beckoning water. One night. But it wouldn't be me giving it to her. It'd be me giving it to myself. It'd be nice to finally experience what I'd spent my life molding and bending myself to earn without ever managing to.

Swallowing, I put my foot on the step up to the tub.

MJ hit a switch and jets gushed water at me. The loud hum filled the room, lessening the dreamlike quality of the moment, making me believe it was real.

MJ lowered herself to the side of the tub and draped her arms over the edge. She swirled her fingers in the water but didn't touch me.

"I didn't put any bubbles in because I know you're funny about the ingredients and stuff."

I popped one eye open, not having realized I'd let them drift shut. "Do you actually own bubble bath?" Not to stereotype MJ, but she didn't seem the type. She'd never shown any inclination for anything other than three-minute showers.

Lifting her hand, she flicked water drops at me. "I could've used shampoo. You never would've noticed the difference."

I slid further into the water, the jet hitting my back just right. "This is perfect."

MJ's expression softened even more. "Good." She leaned over and kissed my forehead and then pushed to her feet. "Relax. Enjoy."

I nodded and closed my eyes.

I tried to let my brain float in the same way my body did. Instead my ears strained to catch any sounds of MJ in the house. Impossible over the jets. What was she doing out there? Was there more to her plan to pamper me? She'd cancelled appointments to be here with me. Surely she hoped to get something more out of it. Did that mean we'd end up in bed?

Did I want that? Today had changed me, like something had cracked, and I'd never be able to re-sculpt myself back into the person I used to be. Part of me was exhilarated because this is what I'd wanted, but another part, a larger part, found it terrifying. There was no going back. All because of MJ.

Before meeting her I never would have gone off on Heidi. Would I be different in bed too? Maybe I wasn't quite done with my journey with MJ. This is something I should discover with her.

I hit the drain and stood. If I was going to take this night then I wanted to spend it with her, not in here by myself listening for her. Wrapping a towel around myself, I stepped into the bedroom to find a pair of sweats and a gray T-shirt lying on the edge of the bed.

After getting dressed, I made my way into the living room and came to a stop at the fire in the fireplace. A true fire, with crackling and blasts of heat. I thrust my hands in front of it.

"That was quick." MJ stopped beside me, her body giving off nearly as much heat as the flames in front of me. I breathed in deep, her woodsy scent more calming to me than the hot bath with its fancy jets.

"You have a fireplace. Why did I never notice this before? We could have had one going every time I was here. With the way you're always cold, I can't believe we didn't."

She bumped me with her shoulder. "We didn't because I was always hella eager to get you to my bed as fast as possible."

"True." But now I wished we had taken the time. I loved the sound and watching the flames and the warmth. Even the house I'd purchased to be a symbol of my success before my diagnosis hadn't had a fireplace. If it had I would have lit a fire on the cold, rainy nights. "Wait. Aren't fireplaces a lot of upkeep? I've heard there's a chemical that builds up. It starts with a C, I think. And insurance. Don't your insurance rates go up if you have one? Are you…"

MJ wrapped an arm around my waist, cutting me off. Her laugh would have drowned out my words anyway. "And people say I don't know how to sit back and relax. You can't even enjoy a fire."

"I can enjoy it. I was just concerned about your house."

"Fear not, my house is fine."

"It really is beautiful." I leaned the slightest bit into her side. "I could watch it all night."

"Then that's what we'll do. Tonight's about…"

The doorbell rang.

MJ dropped her arm from around my waist and pulled back. "But first I need to feed you."

She returned with bags of takeout hanging from her arm. MJ snatched the throw blanket from the sofa and spread it out on the floor. She lowered herself and then patted the spot next to her.

Positioning myself so I could watch the fire, I sank down and accepted a carton from her. "I thought you didn't like Indian."

Batting the steam away from her own carton, MJ shrugged. "Some of their appetizers are okay."

"Thanks," I said, holding my fork filled with eggplant curry up. "This is exactly what I needed."

I closed my eyes and savored my bite. Next to me MJ crunched into her samosa. The fire crackled. All that was missing was a dog at our feet. Snickers still hadn't warmed up enough to me to be out here with us.

Back during chemo when I thought about what it'd be like if I was lucky enough to get a future, it had been a moment like this. Being with someone that I was completely comfortable with and enjoying a good meal. At that time I'd had zero sex drive, so sex hadn't been in the vision or maybe because—until MJ—I'd never really enjoyed sex enough to miss it. My vision had been about security and feeling at peace. Exactly what I felt now, here, with MJ.

"Done?"

I blinked, surprised to see her hand outstretched toward my empty container. I'd been so relaxed that I hadn't even noticed I'd finished eating. Nodding, I handed it to her. While she gathered the remains of our meal, I scooted so my back was propped against the sofa, taking the blanket with me.

My cell rang from where I'd left it in my purse in the entryway. Sighing, I got to my feet.

MJ turned and grabbed on to my wrist. "Leave it. You can deal with whatever it is tomorrow."

I gently extracted myself from her grip. "I won't be able to relax until I know who it is." My mind whirled with possibilities. The jail saying they'd made a mistake and I had to come back. My new lawyer. A reporter because it might be a slow news day.

None of the above. I glanced at MJ. "It's my mom."

MJ's face relaxed and the corner of her mouth quirked. "I've got to hear this. Put it on speaker."

"Hello?" I answered as I sat on the couch. MJ plopped down next to me.

"Hi, honey. How was your day?"

"Okay."

"Yeah? Did you do anything exciting today?"

MJ tucked her head into her shoulder, muffling a snort.

"You know predictable me. I went to work, tried to get the girls to like me, got arrested."

My mom's gasp could probably have set off tornado sirens back east. "Arrested?"

"Yes. I was charged with assault and trespassing."

"You're not kidding me right now, are you? You got arrested? Will have a record and everything?"

I looked down at the feel of MJ's touch. She was rubbing her thumb along my fingertips, right where they'd been scanned, the images now in a database. "Yes."

"I am so proud of you."

MJ slapped a hand over her mouth, her eyes crinkling. Rolling my eyes, I elbowed her in the side.

"I knew you had it in you," my mom continued. "I need to write this in your baby book."

"Mom, this isn't the type of thing you memorialize. It's not like I'm going to be sending out Christmas cards with my mugshot."

"Yes. Do it. Imagine Aunt Carol's face when she opens it."

MJ let out a bark of laughter, her shoulders shaking.

"Who was that?"

"My boss."

MJ's smile disappeared. Her eyes darkened and she pulled back, putting more space between them.

I looked away to the fire. "Hey, Mom. I'm going to go. I'll talk to you tomorrow."

"If I come see you, will you be in an orange jumpsuit?"

"Bye, Mom." Ending the call, I set my phone aside. I

felt MJ's stare, but kept my gaze on the flames. I wasn't ready for the magic of this night to end.

"I'm just your boss to her. I take it you never told her anything about us."

"Because that's what we agreed to."

"Did it never change for you? Along the way was I the only one falling in love?"

"MJ…" I trailed off. I'd sworn that I would tell the truth, no matter if people didn't like it, didn't like me if I said it. But would the truth hurt MJ more? If she didn't know would it be easier to get past?

MJ slid off the couch and kneeled at my feet, grabbing on to my hands. "Listen, I'm gonna say something. I'll only say it once and if I'm off base then we never talk about it again."

I braced myself as MJ took a deep breath. Her fingers trembled around mine.

"I get it if you don't want to be with me. You won't be the first."

I hated the way her mouth twisted up in a little smile. I knew firsthand how much pain was behind fake little smiles.

"I've got to say this. Maybe I imagined the connection between us. Maybe I want it so bad I'm making it up. But I don't think I did. All I can think is, what if it's not that you don't like me or that your cancer could come back? What if it's plain old fear? Fear that I'm going to reject you. That I'm going to get to know this new you, and be like, nah, still not good enough."

I sucked in a shaky breath. The fears that plagued me all my life reduced to a few sentences. How inconsequential they sounded. But they couldn't be. They influenced my every decision, most of my thoughts.

"Is it because the feelings aren't there?" MJ pressed, not letting me process her last words before throwing more heavy ones at me.

Her gaze on me was so steady and brave. She deserved the same. "They're there," I whispered.

She squeezed my hand. "Then I need you to stick up for yourself with as much fierceness as you did for me today."

Stick up for myself. Why was the concept so mindboggling? That would mean quieting that nasty internal voice who liked to point out all the ways I didn't measure up, instead of catering to it. "I don't know that I can."

"You have to. How else am I going to meet your mom as something other than your boss? She gives you just as much shit as I do. I can already tell I'm gonna love her."

"Everybody does. I'm pretty sure the few friends I had in school mostly tolerated me so they could be around her."

"Hey." MJ wrapped her hand around my knee. "You don't give yourself enough credit. There's a lot to like about you." She ducked closer to me, stopping just short of pressing her head into me. "To love about you."

"Yes, that I'm always available, and I remember everything anyone's ever told me, and I'm always the favorite because I never say no."

"Are you fucking serious?" MJ caught my chin, bringing back my gaze from the fire to her. "I don't love you because you remember returning clients by name. That just makes you a good employee. I love you because you look so sweet but your art is so dark. I love that you get excited when you try a new tea. I love that you celebrate life. I love that you make me excited about art again."

I swallowed. I could do it a hundred times and I wouldn't get rid of the thickness in my throat. MJ saw me. She saw the parts that no one ever made the effort to notice. Best of all she liked them. No, loved them.

I cupped her cheeks with shaking hands. "Thank you." I kissed her lips. "Thank you." I poured the words into my kiss.

MJ cradled my face, rising and pushing me back into the couch. She didn't stop until she was perched in front of me. "What are you saying?"

"I love you." Even though it was late in coming, the truth felt good, felt right. "I love you."

"So you're in? We're doing this?"

"I'm in." I pressed my forehead against hers. "You're right. I was scared. I was scared that I wouldn't be enough to keep your interest. I'd rather stay in and eat in front of a fire than go out. I'd rather take a walk around the neighborhood than go to a bar. I'm not successful. I'm not particularly funny. But I'm passionate about art. About your shop. About you."

"You're not the only one, you know."

I eased back so I could see her better, struck by the seriousness to her tone.

"The only one who's scared that you won't be enough," MJ said. "It's not like people stick with me."

"They're idiots." I wrapped my arms around her neck and pulled her down. We wriggled until I was prone on the couch with her on top of me. "Complete, stupid idiots. And if you ever compare me to Heidi again, I'll have to hurt you."

MJ laughed. "Ditto for Marissa." Straddling me, she

pushed herself up to sit on my hips. "I want to do this right. More dates. Meeting your mom."

I cupped her hips. "I want that too. That's all I want—to do boring, normal things with you."

Her eyebrow arched, the right side of her mouth lifting. "Not everything we do is boring."

I stretched and caressed her butt. "True." I smiled up at her, feeling contentment that I'd never known. It was like the effect the alcohol had on my brain, bringing me peace, but this time I was still in control, not along for the ride. "Maybe eventually I'll get to meet your father."

She snorted. "I wouldn't count on it, but yeah that'd be nice."

I shrugged. "It'd be his loss. I'm almost as awesome as his daughter."

MJ laughed and then leaned down. Lips hovering over mine she said, "That you are."

Chapter Twenty-Eight

Cassie

I speed walked like a pro the last block from the bus stop and then halted outside Thorn & Thistle. This place was more of a home to me than the four walls I paid entirely too much for each month. Yeah, my apartment housed my belongings, but this building held my dreams, my future.

The door pushed open and MJ stepped out, crossing her arms over her chest.

My heart soared at the sight of her. I didn't stifle it. I let myself feel the excitement, the happiness. Not even her frown put a damper on it.

I hadn't let her go with me to the doctor's. It was something I needed to do on my own. She'd disagreed with my decision. Loudly and vehemently.

Her chest rose with her deep breath. "You okay?"

"I am."

"Thank god." She snatched me into her arms, dragging me close. "Thank god." She kissed the side of my head. "I knew you would be."

"Uh-huh. That's why you're squeezing me so tight."

That earned me another smacking kiss. I squirmed out of her arms before things could get too heavy.

She frowned, but after taking a look at the busy street followed me into the shop.

For once it wasn't fear of what other people would think that had me stopping. There was something I needed to do first. Then there would be plenty of time for kissing, anyplace she fancied.

I headed toward her station, slowing at seeing all her gear put away. "Don't you have another client coming?"

"No. I'm done for the day. I wasn't sure how things would go."

Even mad, she'd kept her day free for me. In the middle of the shop or not, I couldn't resist cupping her cheek. "You're such a softie."

She nipped my finger. "No, I'm not."

"You're also cute when you're grumpy." I extracted my finger from her mouth and patted her cheek. "So I want something from you."

Her eyes narrowed, but she didn't complete her intimidating stare-down by leaning away and folding her arms over her chest. Nope, she kept her body pressed close to mine. "Yeah, what?"

"I want a tattoo to mark today."

"Oh."

"You totally thought I was going to say sex."

"Well, yeah." But the disappointment was fading fast, her eyes gleaming. This was a woman who loved tattooing and loved my skin. She motioned me toward her chair.

I took off my sweater and climbed on up.

MJ slid over with a sketch pad and pencil.

"You can put those away. I want you to freehand it."

MJ's eyebrows rose high. "You want me to free-hand on you?"

"Yes." I covered her fist with mine. "I trust you."

She ditched her pencil and turned her hand over, palm up, clasping my fingers. "Back at you." She bopped me on the end of the nose and then twisted, setting down the supplies. "So where are you wanting it?"

"Here." I held out my left arm and pointed to my outer forearm. "I want to be able to see it all the time."

Nodding, MJ ran her fingers over my skin, feeling for any abnormalities or imperfections that might mess up the ink. "Sounds good. What are you getting?"

"A pair of boxing gloves with the string in the shape of a heart."

Her hand seized around my arm, the color leeching out of her skin. "Fuck, Cass. You said you were okay."

"I am."

"So it hasn't come back?"

I placed my hand over hers in a quick comforting pat. "I don't know."

Her grip didn't ease even a fraction, nor did the fierce stare. "You don't know. What the hell does that mean?"

"I went into the office to pick up my results. I had her put them in an envelope so I could look at them. If I need to make a follow-up appointment, I'll call."

"Where is it?"

"What?"

"The envelope," she snapped. "Where's the envelope?"

I shifted and wiggled it out of my back pocket.

MJ snatched it from my hand, her fingers diving for the taped edge.

"No." I lurched forward and made a grab for it. "I need this tattoo first."

She used her shoulder to block my reach. Her fingers remained ready to tear. It was only my pleading gaze staying her hand at this point.

"Why? Why pussy out now? You've been waiting for this."

I didn't hide my wince at her pussying out comment. "That's not what I'm doing. This is me believing in myself no matter what I'm facing. I need this reminder on me before anything else."

"That doesn't make sense. You might not even have to fight it anymore."

"Maybe not that, but I'll need to fight other things. Not having cancer doesn't mean suddenly no hardships. I need to fight for what makes me happy. I need to fight to keep my voice. I need to fight for you."

"You don't have to fight for me. You have me."

Someone snorted in the background of the suspiciously quiet shop. I ignored them. "I'm going to keep you. That means constantly showing you how much you mean to me. I'll always regret that Thursday night and letting you believe that I didn't feel anything for you."

"Jesus." Her voice had a dazed quality that I quite liked. "That doesn't matter anymore."

"It does to me." I held my arm out. "This will be my daily reminder and it has to be done by you. Your caterpillar represents me in the process of breaking free. Now, I need this one to remind me to keep going."

"Okay. I'll do it. But can we...?" She held up the envelope.

"No. Tattoo first."

She frowned and initiated a stare-down. That was fine. I could look into her eyes all day.

"Ugh. You know it's not only me you're torturing. Your poor mom's probably dying to hear the results."

"Oh, low blow trying to guilt me with my mother." I walked my fingers up her shirt and tugged at the neck. "Won't work. I told her my results come in tomorrow."

She went from looking grumpy to downright outraged. "You went all by yourself?"

Now probably wasn't the time to point out how much our relationship had evolved that her angry tone didn't have me wanting to scurry, but instead to kiss her. "It was to pick up a piece of paper."

"Never again. You won't be going alone to one of those things anymore."

My smile widened in answer.

"That was not a challenge, so don't be taking it like that." Her gaze flicked to the envelope. "If you make us wait I'm doing the quickest, jankiest tattoo ever."

I presented my arm to her. "No, you won't. You don't want to look at a subpar tattoo every day."

She pushed back her chair to give me the stare-down look in all its glory. "Nothing I do is subpar."

Growling, she turned and set up her supplies, including her new organic inks. She put on her gloves and prepped me. Right before she started her gaze met mine. "I'll be with you no matter what. It won't be a hardship. It'll be an honor."

My breath hitched and my eyes started filling. Of course they did. My badass tattoo artist could be so sweet.

She shook her head and started the gun. "Enough. I know. We go forward from here. We go forward and fight. Fight for us."

Of course the tattoo MJ inked on me was far from

janky. It was bold and strong. It was the perfect symbol to look at every day and know what I needed to do. Fight. Thanks to the amazing woman who I could call mine, I had the perfect inspiration to show me how it was done.

Twenty minutes later, MJ had her own new tattoo. A tattered pink ribbon flag being raised in victory.

Epilogue

MJ

"Are we ready?" I glanced around to see if we missed anything, and then went the easiest route—Cassie. She had a checklist. Which I was totally using as inspiration for my next tattoo. A pinup Cass with a pencil in her mouth, like it was now, wearing a sweater, and of course the pearls I'd gifted her for Christmas.

Her head tilted and she threw me a suspicious look. Yup, she knew exactly where my thoughts were going. She turned to Viv. "I need your help with one last thing."

I watched them for a second but I couldn't focus on any one thing too long. I checked out the other booths. We hadn't heard anything more from Heidi, but my luck she'd be placed right across from us or something. Fuck it, then she could see how damn good we were. I had a team I was proud of and we'd show her up any day.

"Okay that does it. What do you think?"

Cassie's voice pulled me from scanning the competition. No they weren't competition, this was supposed to be fun. Or at least a healthy competition between other attendees.

I turned back and froze.

Hanging from the top of our booth was a banner with the Thorn & Thistle name and a brand spanking new logo. I stepped up closer. The rose was definitely Cassie's. I could see her handiwork in every line. The tattoo guns in the place of the thorns—those were Jamie. And the inked leaves were Maya. The closer I looked, the more details I took in. Hell there was even a piercing in the bud of the rose, no doubt from Gina. Viv had left her mark with her signature ombré background fading from gray to red.

The five of them formed a semicircle around me.

Damned if my throat didn't get choked up so much that I had to count to ten before I could speak. "You guys are the shit."

"We know," Maya said, winking at me.

Uh-huh, I saw how watery her eyes were.

"Okay, everyone gather under it." Cassie motioned for all of us to get together and I was surrounded by my team under the banner they'd created for us. She pulled out her phone, obviously intending to take a picture.

"No."

She lowered her camera.

"No picture unless you're in it."

It didn't take long to find someone willing to volunteer. Jamie made space for Cassie on my right side. I put my arm over her shoulder and tipped my head toward the camera.

As the team spread out and made sure everything was ready, I took another look at the logo. It was perfect. Like my team.

I'd fired Kayla a few months back, not wanting her work associated with mine, and none of us missed her. Yeah, we were shorthanded, but I wasn't in any hurry to replace her. Cass was full time now and Gina brought in a steady stream of revenue. Something which Cassie liked to remind me of every time I was able to pay down more debt. From now on I was only hiring people whose work I admired and was proud to have representing the shop.

Hell, if we kept like we were doing I'd have the second mortgage paid off and could maybe whisk Cassie off somewhere it was warm and with beaches. She'd be happy to slather sunscreen on me.

Cassie leaned her head against me, her arm still wrapped around my waist. I bent down and kissed her hair. "You ready?" she asked.

"Yeah."

I was. Was this costing us a fuckton of money? Yes. But was I desperate to make sure we got a return? No. We were here to have fun and to show off our kickin' talent.

"Good. Because the doors opened and people are coming in." Her eyes got wider and wider. "A lot of people."

"Isn't that the point?"

"Yes." Her chest was starting to rise and fall faster.

I snatched the pencil from the clipboard she still held. "Here, chew this."

The look she shot me told me exactly where I thought I should stuff the pencil.

Cassie'd been right, that she never was going to be an outgoing person. It just wasn't her. But now she spoke up when she had something to say and I knew to listen. The others were learning too.

"You got this," I told her, squeezing her tight.

"No, we got this."

Warmth bloomed in me. "Yeah, we do." We were a team. At work and outside of it.

She'd been living with me for three months. I'd told her it was so I didn't have to worry about her going on one of her walks alone in the neighborhood. But mostly it was because I didn't want to be apart anymore. Didn't matter that we spent all day around each other, it was never enough.

There was something about sitting on the couch and watching the same show as her. Or joining her on her walk, even if she told me to shut it so she could relax. And of course the sex was great.

"Hi." A girl in her mid-twenties or so stopped in front of the booth, staring at me. "I can't believe you're here. I looked for you last year. I'd love to get something done by you."

"I'm liking you already. Why don't we talk it over?" I kissed the side of Cassie's head and then motioned to the spot we had set up for consultations.

As I was stepping away, another woman approached, her gaze fastened on Cassie.

"You look so familiar," she said.

This woman was in her mid-thirties, androgynous, had a lot going for her and she was most definitely checking Cass out, including her chest. I stepped closer.

"I know." The woman snapped her fingers. "You were in that book. About breast cancer."

Cassie's cheeks pinkened, making her look even more fucking adorable. "Yes."

I stood down. Turning back to the potential client waiting for me, I shrugged unrepentantly.

My potential client smiled. "That's your girlfriend,

right? I thought I saw a picture of you two in a magazine."

"Yeah."

We both stared at Cassie as she spoke to the woman in front of her, who at least was looking at her face now.

"I saw that series. It was really brave of her. Did you do the artwork? It's really amazing."

"No. Not those. Our mentor did." Cassie had taken part in a breast cancer campaign with women baring their mastectomy scars. She'd decided it was time to do more than try to get past that time in her life, but to embrace it and help it define her. The same day that it came out, her calls had picked up. Before, local women had sought her out to do theirs. Now people traveled from out of state to have Cassie do theirs.

I was so damned proud of her. Of us. We'd both pushed each other to be better and we were. I couldn't wait for the next day and journey with her. My Tinkerbell.

My Cassie.

* * * * *

Acknowledgements

Thanks to the Carina Press team for giving MJ and Cassie a chance. I'm so excited to be working with such an awesome group of people. My biggest thanks go to my editor, Carrie Lofty. The day I learned that I was going to be working with her was one of the best of my life. I haven't stopped happy dancing yet.

I'd also like to thank my agent, Saritza Hernandez. Your enthusiasm for this story is so very appreciated. I feel very lucky to have you in my corner.

About the Author

Jennie Davids fell in love with romance when she was twelve and snuck her mother's books. For her it wasn't the handsome, dashing heroes that captivated her but the heroines. She is thrilled to be writing what she longed to see then: two heroines falling in love.

She lives in the Pacific Northwest with rescue animals that somehow never end up as well-behaved as their bios promise. The sound of the rain inspires her as she writes, or maybe it's the gallons of hot chocolate she consumes to stay warm in the damp climate.

When not writing Jennie is reading, watching reality TV, or bemoaning how quickly weeds grow back and keep her from reading.

You can find Jennie online at www.JennieDavids.com.